CHOOSING THEO

THE CLECANIAN SERIES: BOOK ONE

Copyright © 2020 by Victoria Aveline

First paperback edition 2023

Cover design by Stardust Book Services in collaboration with Stefanie Saw and Anastasia Johnson

ISBN 978-1-958397-05-3

www.victoriaaveline.com

CHOOSING THEO

THE CLECANIAN SERIES: BOOK ONE

USA TODAY BESTSELLING AUTHOR

VICTORIA AVELINE

∽

To my husband.

Without you I wouldn't know how to write the perfect hero.

1

"Two a.m.," Jade groaned. She had to be up for work in six hours. "Why do I do this to myself?" she muttered.

It had never been easy for Jade to sleep. She envied people who were able to lie down and drift away to dreamland in a matter of minutes. Whenever *she* tried to sleep, her fatigued body was at odds with her active mind.

As a landscape designer, Jade could get away with both sleeping and working at odd hours. Her home office was a perfectly cultivated creative area, and the majority of her designs were produced there rather than in a stifling office. It was not often that she was required to leave her home and venture into the world, and she preferred it that way.

Tomorrow she was scheduled to meet with a particularly wealthy client who wanted the yard of his lakefront home to resemble an authentic Japanese garden. Finding plants that resembled those found in the temperate climate of Japan—but could survive the humid subtropical climate of South

Carolina—would be an interesting design challenge, to say the least.

Looking at the mountain of half-finished sketches and cold mugs of coffee on her desk, she frowned.

She clicked off the TV and walked the few steps it took to get to her small kitchen. As she rinsed out her wine glass, she saw a flash of light through the window above her sink.

Odd. It wasn't raining. She waited for the thunder, but none came.

Lightning storms weren't uncommon in South Carolina. The flash she'd seen had been close though. Close enough that she should've been able to hear thunder.

She shrugged, setting her glass aside, and made her way to her bedroom.

BANG!

Jade's body tensed midstep.

BANG! BANG!

The initial panic at hearing the loud sound was replaced by annoyance. "Damn door," she grumbled.

For weeks, the latch on her screen door had been broken. If she didn't make sure to pull it closed in exactly the right way, it would end up opening and banging against its frame with the wind.

More than once this week she'd been jolted awake by the repetitive thud.

As she yanked the screen door closed, she looked toward the tree line at the edge of her property. No other flashes of light illuminated the sky, yet the night air was warm and humid. Maybe there was a storm on the way.

From the corner of her eye she saw movement in the darkness. A low rustling sounded from outside. She strained her ears. An animal of some kind, probably.

Reaching to her left, she flipped on the porch light, intending to scare away the furry intruder.

A human-sized reptilian creature stood in her yard instead.

Jade shrieked in horror and slammed the door closed. She bolted the lock and then hastily backed away. Her heel caught on the entry rug, and she toppled backward, arms windmilling.

A hideous, scaly face appeared in her porch window. The creature's blood-red eyes scanned the room before focusing on her. Jade found herself paralyzed by fear, as she watched the face vanish from the window.

Regaining control of her limbs, she bolted toward her cell phone on the living room couch. A loud crash sounded behind her just before something large and heavy collided with her back. She lay facedown on the floor, trapped under what she now realized was her own door.

Jade clawed at the floor, attempting to crawl out from beneath the door. In an instant, the weight of the door was gone and three enormous icy cold fingers were clutching at her shoulder, trying to turn her over.

Jade began kicking in the direction of the creature. Her knee connected with something hard, and she cried out in pain. The last thing she remembered before everything went black was an ear-splitting hiss and a fine mist being sprayed in her face

2

It had been about four days since Jade was abducted. All in all, she had to say, abduction was boring.

Initially she'd been terrified, shrieking in her cell until the reptilian monsters had knocked her out with the sleeping spray they kept strapped to their belts. When she'd calmed down enough to survey her surroundings, she'd deduced where she was.

Blinking lights and soft humming emanated from a silver slab near where the monsters sat. They both reclined facing a large glass screen on which strange symbols kept appearing and disappearing. Jade had watched enough sci-fi to know this had to be a spaceship. Nothing on Earth could possibly look like this unless NASA had decided to build an uber-realistic alien abduction escape room.

The moment Jade accepted she'd been abducted by aliens and not Earth monsters and was on a spaceship, not in some reptilian lair on Earth, her screaming and mindless panic had resumed.

Thinking back, Jade figured two days on this ship had been spent having a complete mental breakdown and then recovering from said breakdown. The next two days had been spent sitting in a cell and occasionally receiving food she refused to eat.

Her "cell" looked more like a sparsely furnished room with one wall missing. There was a toilet and sink in one corner and a small cot in the opposite corner. The three dark-gray metal walls were cold and bare. The last side of the room appeared empty, but Jade had learned there was actually a transparent, impenetrable force field barring her exit.

When she'd first gained consciousness, she'd tried to leave through that opening. Instead of walking into the hallway beyond, an invisible solid barrier had greeted her.

Whenever the aliens decided to give her what she assumed was food, they'd press some button on their belt and slide a tray through the seemingly empty air.

Jade had tried to get through the barrier every time they gave her food, but it seemed you could only penetrate it from the outside.

During the first few days aboard, Jade had refused to eat. At first, she'd been so petrified of what they'd do to her that, in between bouts of sobbing and hysterically muttering to herself, she'd retched bile into her small, sleek toilet.

After deciding that dissolving into a weeping mess wouldn't help her, she'd attempted to try and not think about her current situation and focus only on what she could achieve minute to minute.

Every time she felt the urge to truly take in her circumstances, she shut down her brain by bellowing any annoying repetitive song she could think of.

At present, she sat crossed-legged on the ground, staring absently at her tray of food and water that the aliens had shoved toward her earlier.

She smiled down at the pile of green slop on the tray. One of her only friends, Annie—a strict vegan—had once attempted to make her eat something that looked similar to this. She'd raved about the algae-based superfood relentlessly, but Jade, being the stubborn ass she was, had refused to try it.

Jade closed her eyes when they began to sting from unshed tears. She would never see Annie again.

Don't think about that! Don't think about that! Jade's eyes flashed open and she began singing the chorus to an annoying '80s power ballad.

One of the reptilian aliens walked in front of her cell and hissed at her aggressively. She backed into the corner of her small room and stopped singing aloud. Instead, she hummed the tune and glared at the creature.

Neither of the shiny green aliens had enjoyed her attempts to smother her feelings. Whenever she began singing, they'd rush over and hold her stare with their slitted eyes until she stopped.

She knew avoiding reality wasn't the smartest or most mature idea in the long run. She knew that facing things head on was a much healthier approach, but Jade felt sure she was one thread away from snapping. She also knew from experience that pretending to be fearless and unaffected would help to keep her sane.

The creature made another low hiss over its shoulder, and the second creature came to join the first. One of the aliens used a long, pointed claw to motion to her full tray of green goo.

The more time she spent doing nothing but observing these aliens, the more she felt she could read their moods. When they were frustrated or possibly angry, as they were now, she'd noticed that their hissing became short and spit flew off their tongues with each alien word.

Whenever they retrieved her full food tray, they'd use that harsh hiss, and their long, broad tails would flick back and forth.

It seems like they're getting frustrated with my hunger strike, she thought as she watched them hiss back and forth while gesturing to her tray.

The slightly smaller of the two walked away. When it returned to her cell a moment later and she saw what it had retrieved, she felt the blood drain from her face. The creature was pointing to her food with one claw-tipped hand and held a long clear tube in the other. It raised the tube a little higher, and she understood the creature's meaning. She could either eat on her own, or she could be force-fed.

The two lizard beings waited silently at her cell. The thought of being held down and force-fed through a tube made a jolt of fear run through her. Begrudgingly, she decided that keeping the aliens at bay was more important to her than possible food poisoning.

Tentatively she moved toward her tray and used her forefinger to scoop up a small amount of goo. Shutting her eyes, she took a bite. A cold sweat broke out over her skin, and she tried to keep her breathing even as she waited for some reaction. When her throat didn't swell, she began to relax.

She let out a relieved exhalation when she saw the two aliens had left, apparently satisfied with her small bite of food.

Her stomach gave a pained rumble, and she polished off the rest of the goo. Although awful to look at, it didn't taste too bad. It was sweet and surprisingly filling. The water, however, was stale and tasted metallic on her tongue.

Jade leaned back on her small scratchy cot and wondered for the thousandth time why she had been taken.

Apart from feeding her and occasionally walking by her cell to check on her, the aliens had left her alone.

What is the point of this? Jade thought again. Since she'd been conscious, they hadn't touched her or experimented on her but instead kept her fed and healthy. There must've been a reason for her abduction.

The possible reasons to abduct someone that kept running through her mind were terrifying. She knew one thing for sure— whatever they planned on doing to or with her would happen when they reached their destination.

How far could we have gone in a few days?

She snorted. Who was she kidding? Jade spent her life drawing gardens and shutting herself away from the world. Why the hell did she think she could logic out how far a spaceship might travel in a few days? Suddenly Jade felt exhausted and beaten. She sat back on her bed against her cell wall. Eventually, the soft humming and vibration of the ship lulled her to sleep.

***

A sharp pain deep in her ear made Jade bolt awake. Just as her vision cleared, she noticed one reptilian alien backing out through the force field. She scrambled toward it, hoping that whatever allowed it access was still working.

Bam! She ran headlong into the wall and bounced back, toppling onto her bed. Rubbing her ear, she yelled at the alien, who was still staring at her from outside the cell. "What did you do to my ear, you scaly son of a bitch?!"

Instead of answering, the alien hissed low and lumbered away.

***

Jade had been on this stupid ship for more than a week at least. Apart from the painful ear wakeup call she'd gotten a few days ago, not much had changed.

From her cell, she could study the console where the two aliens sat. *It must be where they drive this thing.*

While watching them man the controls in shifts the past few days, she'd learned some things. One, she was pretty sure she was being sold. One of the aliens, whom she'd started calling Thing 1, had come back and flashed a device at her. Later, she'd been able to make out a picture of herself being pulled up on the console screen and heard them speaking with someone not currently on the ship.

Her heart had hammered in her chest when she'd guessed at what someone buying her would do to her. Why would they want her? Was she some kind of alien delicacy? Would they display her like a lobster and then boil her alive? Jade had spent a good half hour rocking herself in the corner after that particular thought had occurred.

The second thing she'd figured out was that they were getting close to their destination. Alien number two, aka Thing 2, had thrown a large dress that resembled a sack with arm holes into her cell today.

Looking for any reason to defy her abductors, she'd refused to change into the dress. The gray fabric of the dress was thick and reminded her of wetsuit material. One glaringly obvious pro to wearing the dress was that it was clean. Taking a sniff of her unwashed clothes made her question whether this was a stupid battle to fight.

After finally accepting the water they'd provided with her food, Jade had been disappointed to learn that the small sink in the corner dispensed some kind of cleansing foam rather than water. The foam dissolved the dirt on her hands, and she'd used it to clean herself as best she could, but the pajama set she wore hadn't received the same attention, and the smell had started to get to her. Her battle to remain in her dirty clothes had been short-lived, however.

Thing 2 had hissed at her and lowered the temperature in her cell incrementally. Before long, she'd been forced to wear the dress to keep from freezing to death.

The final, and most troubling thing she'd learned, was that she was pretty sure she wasn't the only captive on this ship. She'd noticed Thing 1 holding more than one gray dress when he'd thrown hers at her. She'd also noticed they'd carry more than one food tray when delivering her food.

She'd thought the other tray was for them. *Even lizards have to eat, right?* That idea had been put to bed when she'd caught one of them walking by while swallowing a small, squealing, two-headed animal whole. After watching that, it was hard to imagine they'd also eat the green goo they'd been feeding her.

Rapid beeping sounded from the console, drawing Jade's attention. Things 1 and 2 stood up and walked to her cell. Before she could figure out what they were doing, they'd deactivated the force field and dragged her out kicking and screaming.

They each gripped one of her arms as they half escorted, half carried her down the hall. Their hands were rough and scaly but also somehow cold and moist, making Jade cringe.

At long last she was outside of her cell, and all she wanted to do at this moment was return. The air in the ship was sweltering and smelled vaguely sweet, like rotting fruit. Jade began to sweat. The heated metal of the floor made each step burn against her bare feet.

"Where are you guys from, the sun?" She panted, trying to slip out of their slimy hands.

At the end of the hallway stood a group of three large egg-shaped structures. When they neared, a rounded panel opened up on one of the eggs, revealing a small compartment with a single seat. As soon as she understood what they meant to do with her, she started to struggle frantically.

"No way are you putting me in that thing by myself. I can't fly a freaking spaceship—space pod—space egg—whatever that thing is!"

Ignoring her protests, Thing 1 lifted her over his shoulder and carried her the rest of the way to the pod, shoving her inside and knocking the wind from her. Inch by inch the door of the pod closed until it was sealed.

She watched through the small window in horror as the lizards typed something into a control panel on the wall that she hadn't noticed before.

The pod started moving backward, away from the two reptilian aliens. She could guess what that meant.

"Shit! Shit! Shit!" In desperation, she scanned every square inch of the pod for an escape, but the interior was bare, save for the solitary seat. She was about to get shot out into space and then to who knew where. "Well." She sighed, looking down into her hand at the small bottle of sleep spray she'd grabbed during the struggle. "Let's hope this spray works on everything."

3

If Jade had ever wondered whether she'd missed out on a career as an astronaut, she now had her answer. Flying through open space in an egg was terrifying. Her fear caused her to somehow experience both intense claustrophobia and agoraphobia at the same time.

When a large planet came into view, her panic attack intensified. She'd been able to breathe on the ship, and her common sense told her they wouldn't have kept her alive this long only to send her to a planet where she couldn't breathe, or one whose gravity was so strong, she'd be crushed like a pancake.

Logically she knew this. Unfortunately, at this moment, logic wasn't at the steering wheel. The closer the pod drew to the planet, the quicker her breaths became until she began hyperventilating. When the pod hit the atmosphere, her vision faded to black.

***

Insects chirped all around Jade, and a cold breeze blew, making her shiver. When her eyes cracked open, she saw she was still in her pod but the door was opened.

Eyes widening, she sucked in a sharp breath and held it. A moment passed before she chided herself. *Don't be an idiot, Jade. You would've already died if you couldn't breathe.* She released her breath and peered out of the pod.

She was in a clearing with dense forest all around her. It was night, but moonlight illuminated her surroundings. When she stepped out of the pod, she understood why it was so bright. *Two friggin' moons.*

Jade gazed around the clearing, marveling at how everything was both familiar and astonishingly foreign. The bright light of two moons, rather than one, shone down on a dark forest of trees. The forest, as a whole, was unremarkable. The tree trunks looked like wood, and the height of the trees was very tall but nothing out of the ordinary. The leaves, however, were unlike any she'd ever seen. They were very large and round like a giant lily pad. The thick, round leaves spread out and created an unnaturally dense canopy that caused almost all light to be blocked out.

The sounds of insects buzzed around her, but the noise just wasn't right. Something about the unfamiliar pattern of humming and clicking that surrounded her made fear creep through her.

At least it's a normal temperature. Jade recalled the intense heat of the spaceship.

Shaking her head in disbelief, she circled the pod and tried to take stock of her situation. *What to do now? Did I crash or something? Veer off course? Why would Thing 1 and 2 drop me in the middle of the forest?*

She heard a faint rustling to her right and froze. *The spray! Where's the spray?* The small cylinder was no longer in her hands. *Must've dropped it when I passed out.*

As the rustling grew louder, she scrambled back to the pod, feeling around for the small container. Her movements became more desperate when the rustling changed into the sound of soft footsteps against the springy ground.

There! She found the tube without a second to spare. The steps were behind her, and she could feel a presence at her back. She blindly aimed the spray over her shoulder and dashed into the woods. Before she hit the tree line, she heard the satisfying *thump* of a body hitting the ground.

Heart racing, she ran. The forest was dense and almost pitch-black. She continued to trip over fallen branches and slip in a slimy substance she couldn't identify, but she kept running.

Her instincts told her that whoever or whatever was back there had made sure she'd arrived at night, away from civilization and therefore any other people. Whatever their motivation was, Jade doubted it was noble.

Jade had no idea how long she'd been running for when she noticed the trees start to thin. Her lungs burned with exertion, but she forced them and her shaky legs to keep moving. The trees continued to thin until they cleared completely.

Jade halted. In the distance she could make out the outline of a city backlit against the large glowing moons. There weren't any skyscrapers or stark gray warehouses but rather tall, pointed towers that would not have looked out of place on a medieval castle.

To her right, the ground sloped and leveled out into a large field. On her left was a craggy path littered with bushes and boulders. Traveling in the field would definitely be easier, but she'd have no cover in case whoever was behind her caught up. The hill would take longer to traverse but had plenty of cover.

To anyone who didn't know Jade, the field would've seemed like the more attractive option. She decided to choose the more difficult terrain, feeling that if her would-be kidnapper followed her, they'd assume she chose the flat field. Keeping the city in view, she began to climb. If she kept going at this pace it might only take her a few hours to get there.

Eyes riveted to the city skyline, she came to an abrupt stop. *What if it's worse there than here?* She could be walking directly into a nightmare.

One thing was certain. The creature she'd run from had orchestrated her abduction. They'd waited for her to arrive alone. Why? She hoped it was because kidnapping was against the rules even on an alien planet.

Jade sank to her knees, hot tears running down her cheeks. *Aliens,* she thought miserably. Jade's whole universe had shifted.

This was an alien planet. Even if she could find other beings, who's to say she could make them understand what had happened to her? She was just one measly human from a world that hadn't traveled that far into space yet. Why would they even care about her?

Now that she was alone, Jade allowed the events of the past few weeks to settle over her. Her life back home had been a lonely one. She had no family, very few good friends, and tended to keep to herself.

She lowered her head in her hands and cried weakly, attempting not to make any sound. *No one will care that I'm gone. Will they even notice I was taken?*

Sure, her employer would be put out that she'd just stopped coming in. They'd probably tried to contact her when she'd missed the meeting with that client a few days ago. After not hearing from her for at least a week, she hoped they would've called the police.

Her home would show that there'd been a break-in. She chuckled humorlessly through her tears. At this moment, she was most likely considered a missing person.

Jade realized that her work ID would be the only picture of hers that her coworkers had. Oddly, imagining her sad work photo on a missing person's report made her cry harder than anything else. How could she have shut herself off to the world so completely?

Jade batted away her tears. Dammit, her life hadn't been the best, but it was hers. She had a house and a career, and if she ever got back to Earth, she swore she'd try and make more of an effort to let people in.

Somehow, she'd make these aliens understand what had happened to her. She would charade her ass off if that was what it took. Whoever abducted her wouldn't get away with this.

She started walking toward the city and let her cool anger motivate her. If what they did was illegal, she'd find someone to help her catch them and punish them.

4

"Is this city a goddamned mirage?" Jade yelled in between panted breaths.

She'd been walking in the direction of the city's spires for almost two days and was only slightly nearer. Those spires must be much more massive than she'd thought.

Jade was exhausted, dehydrated, and had discovered cuts and bruises all over her body from her adrenaline-fueled dash through the forest.

Yesterday, she'd come across a few streams of water but had refrained from drinking anything she didn't know for certain was safe. A few hours into her trek this morning, however, had made her realize that in order to keep moving toward the elusive city on the horizon, water was necessary.

At about midday, when Jade was ready to suck the moisture out of the next dirty puddle she stumbled upon, she came to a small stream running downhill. Without a second thought, she crouched down near the stream and gulped a few handfuls of water. Jade took the momentary break to study small curling plants near the stream's edge.

As a child, her aunt would take her out into the woods behind her home and teach her which plants could be eaten, which were poisonous, and which could be used for other things. In South Carolina, Jade would've been able to forage and survive in the woods for months if she had to.

The small plant she was currently examining had fuzzy curling leaves that rolled in on themselves when her hand drew near.

Jade let out a panicked squeak and snatched her hand back. She watched as the small leaves unfurled themselves once again. *This isn't home. You don't know what edible plants look like here. Don't try.*

Her aunt's voice played through her mind, chanting her favorite phrase to utter while teaching Jade to forage: *"If in doubt, leave it out."*

The phrase reminded Jade that if she didn't know for sure what a plant was, she shouldn't be putting it in her mouth. Even on Earth, the very poisonous plant hemlock was often confused with parsley.

What she wouldn't give for some green goo right about now.

A wave of sadness hit her as she thought about her aunt. *She would know what to do.*

Moving to the edge of the hillside, Jade sat on a clear flat stone that was lavender in color. With her back to the stream, she gazed down over a beautiful sprawling landscape. *Well, at least I have a killer view,* she thought as she waited for any negative side effects from the water.

The hill led down to a flat valley that stretched on for miles before disappearing into another dense forest. A shining river wove through the brightly colored grasses of the valley until it too disappeared into the forest. Jagged narrow mountains rose crookedly from the horizon, jutting into the sky at an unnatural angle.

The sun that burned brightly above her was slightly smaller and more orange than the sun back home, casting the whole landscape in warm light.

"Wow," was all Jade could manage. Up to this point, she'd been afraid and angry that she had been transported unwillingly to an alien planet.

Sitting alone and admiring the beautiful scene before her made her stop and think about how wondrous this place was. She might've been temporarily stranded on an alien planet, but she had to admit, it was painfully beautiful and surreal.

Out of the corner of her eye, she spotted movement and rolled behind a large bush.

About a hundred feet away, a round silver object slowly floated along down a narrow, cleared area of the valley. Her heart leapt. *That looks like a road!*

The large silver ball had to be twelve feet tall at least, but the gleaming silver surface was so reflective that she'd almost not seen it. If she was right and that was a road, it would make sense that the ball was a vehicle of some sort.

Fatigue threatened to overwhelm her as she gazed longingly at the floating object. If she didn't eat something or drink more, she'd never make it to the city. Hitching a ride would be her best bet at survival.

Indecision warred within her, and she bounced on her heels, trying to choose whether to chase the moving object down or stay hidden. While it was true the object could be some type of vehicle, it was also true it could be a million other things she'd never even considered.

Even if it was a vehicle, she had no idea what kind of creature she'd find inside it. What if the alien that had tried to collect her from the forest was in the vehicle now? She hadn't stuck around long enough to get a good look at her abductor, only heard their footsteps. She'd have no way of recognizing them unless they happened to be the solitary creature on this planet with two feet.

The vehicle wasn't coming from the same direction as the forest she'd escaped from, but that didn't mean much.

Glancing down at her blistered, shoeless feet, she decided she'd have to risk it. Her fear caused the small amount of water she'd consumed to sour in her stomach.

With the bottle of sleep spray clutched in her hand, she forced herself to jog briskly down the hill to intercept the flying vehicle. As she neared, it started to travel faster. *I'm not going to make it,* she thought, pleading with her legs to pick up speed. *Almost there.*

The silver ball was moving too fast for her to reach it in time on foot. Thinking quickly, she threw her tube of sleep spray as hard as she could.

Ping! The tube hit the side of the ball as it passed, but the silver object didn't slow. She sprinted, waving her arms above her head.

Just when she thought the ball was going to disappear over the crest of a hill, it stopped.

Jade fell to her knees and almost cried with relief when the large ball began to slowly move toward her. Cold sweat beaded her forehead, and spots danced in front of her eyes. She was going to faint again.

Please let these aliens be kind, she thought as she fell onto the ground.

5

Jade was getting really tired of passing out and waking up in unfamiliar places. This time when her eyes cracked open, she found herself lying on a long couch.

Mentally scanning her body, she didn't notice any sore spots. Odd. The last thing she remembered was racing after a moving silver ball. She'd been bruised, and her muscles had been strained to their limit at that time. She shouldn't have been able to move without pain, but she felt none. Why? Was she dead?

Sitting up, she examined the room more thoroughly. There was a large desk in front of a picture window across from her. The desk, combined with the couch, made the room resemble a therapist's office. She should know. She'd been in and out of enough of them.

Through the window, glimmering silver spires could be seen stretching into the sky. Crossing to the window, she examined the spires more closely. Floating round balls, like the one she'd chased, congregated near the base of the spire, and she could see very tiny figures leaving and entering the pods.

Jade stepped back a few feet and studied the wall she'd just been pressed against. She noticed a shallow curve to the wall. *I must be in one of those weird skyscrapers.*

Jade felt a momentary surge of happiness and pride that her guesses had been correct. The round ball was a vehicle, and whatever was in it had taken her where she'd wanted to go.

She jumped about three feet in the air when the door to her left opened. A tall, middle-aged woman entered, sending Jade scrambling back behind the arm of the low couch.

A woman? Jade straightened, forgetting her fear. The being in front of her looked just like a human woman.

Jade crouched back down behind the arm of the couch as she studied the woman in more detail. *Not exactly human.* This alien was taller than most human women and was drop-dead gorgeous. She moved with a supernatural grace Jade had never seen before. A cream-colored flowing jumpsuit that accentuated her waist billowed around her legs and arms elegantly as she moved.

The woman glanced over at her as she entered the small room. "Oh good, you're awake." She gave Jade a brief smile and then went to sit at the small desk.

Jade blinked, trying to force her brain to catch up. Was she having a stroke, or could this woman speak English? How was that possible?

Victoria Aveline

"Can you understand me?" she asked Jade calmly.

Still crouched behind the arm of the couch, Jade nodded. The woman had a kind face—alien, but kind. Her eyes were just slightly too big to be human, but they made her appear sweet and sympathetic. Long black hair trailed down her back, and when she tucked it behind her ear, Jade noticed the ear was pointed on both the top and bottom.

"Good!" she exclaimed, exposing elongated canines. "Would you mind speaking so I can see if I understand you?"

Jade opened her mouth to speak but couldn't for the life of her think of something to say. This was all so surreal.

"Just say 'hello' and tell me your name," the woman offered helpfully.

In a croaky voice, Jade said, "Hello, my name is Jade."

"Damn, that didn't translate." The woman frowned, clearly disappointed. "We hoped that because you had a translator installed in your ear that your language would be common."

Jade's eyes widened, and she touched her ear. So that must've been what the lizard aliens had done. Implanted a translator. If so, it was incredible. When the woman spoke, Jade heard the words instantly. Her mouth even looked like it was forming the words.

"I can see from your expression—you didn't know this had happened." She said this as more of a question than a statement.

If I have a translator, why couldn't I understand the lizard people?

27

"I'm going to ask you some questions and try to explain a few things if I can. I'd like you to nod for yes." The woman nodded to illustrate. "And shake your head for no." She shook her head.

Jade nodded briefly to show she understood. The woman seemed pleased.

"You're on another planet." She paused. "Did you know there was life on any planet but your own?"

Jade shook her head vigorously.

"I thought so." She let out a sigh. "My name is Meya. We're on a planet called Clecania in a city called Tremanta. I'm Clecanian." Looking at her seriously, she said, "I'm very sorry for what has happened to you. Your planet is most likely considered a Class Four planet, and taking you from there is against the law. Not just the law of this world but the law of most worlds in this section of the universe. Do you understand so far?"

Jade's head swam.

"You had some injuries when you were brought to us. I've given you a mild injection to help with the pain, but I cannot fully heal you or feed you until we know your species. Did you see who took you?"

Nod.

"Are they still here?"

Jade did not know how to respond. The lizards were gone, but whoever had hired them was still here. She nodded and then also shook her head.

"Yes and no?" Meya questioned. "Hmm. I need to scan the translator in your ear in order to find out which language it's translating to." She held up a small device, similar to a price scanner.

The woman hadn't done anything to Jade thus far, and if she really wanted to, Jade suspected Meya could've scanned her translator while she'd slept. Instead, the woman had waited and asked permission, which spoke volumes.

Jade nodded. The woman rose and slowly began walking over to her like Jade was a scared animal she didn't want to spook.

She could just imagine her saying, *Eeeasy, girl.* Jade frowned. She was a human, not a donkey, but to a species as advanced as this, she might as well have been.

Jade turned her head to give Meya access to her ear. The device emitted a soft hum. Meya moved to her desk, studying a small screen on the device.

"English. An Earthling language," she said, reading the display.

"Earthling?" Jade felt the hair on the back of her neck rise at the word. Only an alien would call a human that.

Looking up at Jade, Meya said, "The good news is Earthling languages have been documented in the Interplanetary Archives, so we should be able to update our translators so we can understand you. The bad news is locating the update may take a while. I've never even heard of an Earthling before." Meya glanced back down at her device. "The area of space you're from is very far from here." Meya

29

observed Jade studiously. "It's strange, how alike we are. Our species, I mean." She began studying Jade, speaking more to herself than Jade. "So amazing that a Class Four planet species could have evolved so similarly." She cocked her head and smiled.

"Hopefully you can tell us more about your kind while you're here. In the meantime, I'm going to learn what I can about humans and see how much healing I can do before a full-body scan. I'll also be sure to check which simple foods and beverages you can have.

"I'd like to call the leaders of the city together so you can tell us about what happened to you and so we can decide what to do with you."

"What do you mean what to do with me? Send me back home!" Panic and fear overwhelmed Jade, but even as she started to argue, she remembered Meya couldn't understand her. She clamped her mouth shut angrily.

"I'm sorry, I didn't get that," Meya said, concern showing on her face. "This must be frustrating, but it will be much easier after our translators have been updated." Meya rose to leave. "Are you comfortable waiting in here until I can arrange the meeting?"

Jade huffed out a frustrated breath but nodded.

Meya smiled. "Okay, I'll be back in a few minutes with something for you to eat."

Jade let her head fall back on the couch after Meya left. Not being able to communicate was more frustrating than she'd expected.

Meya hadn't said anything about taking her home. She knew what species Jade was, and it was clear she knew where Earth was too, yet she still hadn't mentioned taking her back.

I hope these aliens know what they're doing because once they can understand me, they're going to get an earful.

6

Weirdest. Meeting. Ever.

After Meya had come back, given her some beige paste to eat that had made Jade long for the green goo, and run a light-saber-type device over her body, she'd escorted her down a curving hallway to this room.

On their way, Meya informed Jade they'd located the program that contained the Earthling languages. She told her the meeting's attendees were in the process of updating their translators now and that they should be working by the time they reached the meeting room.

How could a room, lightyears away from Earth, in a building that resembled a castle spire, be like every other boring meeting room she'd ever been in? It was truly mindboggling.

A long, rectangular table occupied most of the room, dark black chairs lined either side of the table, and two chairs slightly bigger than the others were positioned at the heads of the table. When Jade entered, six people were already seated and waiting.

Meya motioned for Jade to sit at the head of the table and then moved to sit on her right.

Jade surveyed the other people in the room. There were two women seated on the left side of the table. They were both quite beautiful and both staring at her with interest.

The woman on the right was very pale and thin. Long seafoam-green hair had been intricately braided with gold thread and swept over her delicate shoulder. What stood out most about the woman were her large eyes. They tilted up more than was normal to Jade, and her irises were a bright, almost glowing red.

The woman next to her was different but no less beautiful. Her hair was cut very short and was bright blonde. Her tanned skin shimmered with gold in the light, and Jade could see geometric golden markings running along her bare arms.

Meya leaned in toward Jade and whispered, "Their names are Wiye and Treanne. They're the two who found you wandering in the hills and brought you here."

"Thank you!" Jade stammered, feeling shocked and ashamed that she hadn't attempted to ask about her rescuers until now.

The two women said nothing but smiled broadly at her.

Meya turned to glance at a holographic screen near the wall, then leaned toward Jade again. "Almost, but the translators aren't quite done yet."

Jade surveyed the others in the room while she waited. Directly to her left, a small older man waved to her cheerily. He seemed overjoyed at her presence. Jade didn't know what else to do, so she gave a nervous half smile and then looked away.

On the right side of the table, next to Meya, sat two men. They were both large and heavily muscled. The younger of the two men had sandy brown hair streaked with blond. When he grinned at her, showing even white teeth, a dimple appeared in his cheek.

If Jade had wanted to know whether or not she'd find an alien man attractive, she had her answer. He was more handsome than any man she'd ever seen in person. He looked like he should've been running shirtless on some beach in Australia, getting ready to surf.

Light golden designs ran over his arms, neck, and part of his face. They curled delicately around his strong features.

The hairs on the back of her neck stood up. She pulled her attention away from surfer boy and caught the other man staring intently at her with dark eyes. She assumed light tattoos ran over this man's body as well, but his long-sleeved shirt and shoulder-length mop of brown hair meant she could only see one curving marking winding up his cheek.

He scowled at her. His deep frown contrasted sharply with the dimpled grin of the younger man next to him. He almost appeared angry at her, and she wondered if he and surfer boy were an item.

She quickly glanced away. *He's all yours!*

The last person in the room, an ancient woman, sat directly across from Jade. She was dressed in a high-collared lavender jacket that matched the pale purple of her eyes. She sat stiffly with her chin raised, her white hair curling over her shoulders. Everything, from her regal posture to intelligent eyes, told Jade she was in charge here.

Without fail, Meya focused on her and waited until the woman gave a slow nod before speaking.

"I believe we have all been made aware of the current situation." She eyed each of them and waited for their nods of agreement. She then spoke to Jade. "Our translators have been updated now. Can you please say something so we can be sure?"

"Uh…hello. My name is Jade," she recited, not knowing what else to say.

Meya smiled. "Hello, Jade. It's nice to meet you."

All of Jade's bravado from earlier faded. She'd imagined the bitch fit this group of people would get when she finally was able to speak to them. Now, sitting in front of a group of aliens who all stared at her, she could only manage a weak smile.

Turning, Meya addressed the group. "Jade was abducted from her home world and wound up on Clecania. We need to make sure that measures are taken to right this wrong, but the main focus of our meeting today is to decide where Jade should go now." Meya paused for a moment then continued, "I'm going to let Jade explain what has happened to her, and then we'll discuss what we should do moving forward."

Meya fell silent, and all eyes focused on Jade.

Jade had known she'd have to recount what had happened, but she'd thought it would be to someone like a police officer, one on one. Public speaking had always been something she'd dreaded. "Uh…well," she began shakily. Meya gave her an encouraging nod. Taking a deep breath, she described everything that had happened.

They all stayed quiet and listened intently until she got to the part about being approached in the woods.

"Did you see this being?" one of the women asked, anger etched on her face.

"No. It was dark, and I sprayed behind me and ran. I couldn't tell you if it was a man or a woman. I don't even know if it was a Clecanian or some other species."

The pretty woman leaned back and pondered this.

"Is that the wording I should use, by the way?" Jade interjected, realizing that even on Earth, gender was more complex than *man* and *woman*. "You all look very similar to humans and I keep thinking of you and referring to you as people or men or women, but…you're not." Jade glanced around. "Is there some other vocabulary I should be using?"

The kind older man to her left leaned toward her. "Your translator uses context to translate as well as words. You may be saying a word that means a human specifically, but if your intention is to address a group, the word is translated to the word we'd use for that group."

"Wow." She peered around nervously. "You guys really are advanced here." She recalled a question she'd thought of earlier about the translator. "I couldn't understand them. The lizard people," she clarified.

"The ones who took you?" Treanne, the blonde woman asked, concern showing on her face. "I don't know who took you, but I do know your translator was only uploaded with the languages spoken on this planet. They probably didn't upload their own in order to keep you from hearing any sensitive information."

The dark-eyed man who still had a scowl on his face interrupted. "Intergalactic law says that she's to remain on Clecania for a period of one year. *Our* law says that an off-worlder needs to be put under protection and monitored by a resident for that year. If my understanding of the law is correct," he said snidely, as if he already knew it was, "we know *what* to do with her. All we need to decide today is which resident she'll be placed with."

Nope, she did not like that guy. Not at all. He was suggesting they throw her together with some stranger? "Why one year?" she interjected.

"A year will provide whichever species encounters a Class Four species enough time to teach them about the known universe," the pretty woman with pale-green hair answered in a melodic voice.

"Not everything, obviously." The woman seated next to her chuckled. "Just enough so you can function outside of the only planet you've known. We're required to help you learn how to build a new life outside of Earth."

"Before the law was enacted, displaced Class Four individuals were left on their own with no idea how to survive," Meya added sadly. "We saw many individuals taken advantage of because of this. It was barbaric."

Before Jade could once again voice her objection to not simply being returned to Earth, the green-haired woman spoke.

"Who do you suggest watch over her, Xoris?" she asked the angry man who'd suggested she be looked after like some criminal.

He frowned at her coldly. "One of us could take her, I suppose."

Putting his hand on his heart, the young man leaned toward Jade and said in a rumbling voice, "I would be honored to protect you." He shot her a wolfish grin that almost made her forget the misery of her situation in order to giggle and blush.

"You're never home, Kadion," Xoris growled. "How would you expect to protect her when you're fighting off Tagion intruders in the north? I'll take her."

"No!" Jade blurted out, drawing everyone's attention. "I mean…" She searched for a compelling argument but found none. "I don't want to go with some stranger and be 'monitored' like some criminal. I was brought here against my will by someone *from* here!"

"Yes, and you escaped them," Xoris said coolly. "That means they'll want you back. You're here now, which means we're responsible for you." Raising his eyebrows, he asked,

"Would you rather be left on your own on this alien planet, of which you know nothing? The person who took you could walk up to you on the street, knock you out, and drag you away, and you wouldn't even know to scream until it was too late."

Losing her temper, she yelled, "I would rather you send me back home!"

"Enough!" the woman at the end of the table said firmly. Everyone quieted. "Young lady," she began, addressing Jade, "we unfortunately cannot return you to your home planet. It's against not only our laws but also the intergalactic laws that keep our worlds at peace. It was decided long ago that Class Four planets should be allowed to evolve and explore the universe in their own time. We don't reveal ourselves to them, and if for some reason an individual such as yourself is taken, you may not return. It would be illegal for us to set foot on your planet or even fly near your atmosphere."

"But—" Jade fell silent at the woman's harsh expression. *Better not piss off the queen bee.*

The woman continued, "You *will* stay here for one year, and you *will* live with another, but you'll also have some say as to who that person is." She shot a stern look at both Xoris and Kadion. "I'll only require you to live alone with a Clecanian for three months. After that, you may choose where on Clecania you'd like to live. After the year is up, you may leave Clecania if you wish, but we won't break the law by returning you to Earth."

Jade's mouth fell open at the unfairness of all this.

"Luckily for you, we have a coupling ceremony tomorrow. I believe Zikas is without a female to aid this cycle." She lifted her eyebrows at the small man next to Jade.

Zikas smiled widely. "You are correct, Madam."

"Then it's settled." She rose from her seat. "Zikas, you will stay with Jade and prepare her for tomorrow. The rest of you will come with me so we can devise a plan to catch the criminals who brought her here."

Before Jade could formulate an argument, they were gone. Turning to the man named Zikas, she said, "What just happened?"

He smiled and said, "You will become a bride!"

7

"A what?" she screeched, making Zikas wince.

"The Queen has made a very good compromise on your part. You'll be allowed to choose your husband, and you'll become a bride."

"In what world is that a compromise?" *Oh yeah,* she thought. *This world.* "I don't want to be a bride!" Jade began pacing. This couldn't be happening. She was not going to become some alien's housewife.

"Our Queen is very wise," Zikas said beseechingly while trailing her around the room. "She wouldn't have decreed this unless she'd thought through all of the possibilities."

She had to get out of here. Had to get away.

Her gaze fell on the door she'd come through. She remembered there was a long hall on the other side of that door. It had to lead to a set of elevators or stairs or something. She'd just have to run again.

Jade turned and paced away, attempting to lead Zikas away from the door with her. He was shorter than her but much burlier. She still believed that even as an older man, he could physically stop her if he wanted to. She felt her whole body vibrate with apprehension.

When she reached the far wall, she pivoted and sprinted. She was through the door before Zikas had comprehended that she was running.

As she flew down the hallway, she heard him yell after her. She punched the air in success when she reached the end and found a stairway. Looking down over the railing of the large stairway, she guessed they must've been thirty stories up at least.

The stairway she ran down wasn't like any she'd seen in a large building. It was a spiral staircase. One incredibly long, wide spiral staircase.

After a while, Jade lost count of how many floors she'd passed. Circling lower and lower, she started to become dizzy. Jade paused for a moment, righting herself. She looked over the rail once more.

Only a few floors to go. She started running again. Ahead of her, a door swung open and a burly uniformed man stepped out.

She didn't slow her pace. The only way to get by a man like that was to take him by surprise.

When he spotted her, he raised his hands palms out in a gesture that said *stop*. His eyes widened when she didn't show any signs of slowing.

When she was within arm's reach, he extended his hands, hoping to catch her around the middle.

Bad idea, buddy. Always guard your face.

Balling her fist like her father had taught her when she was young, she punched him as hard as she could. Her aim was clumsy, but she managed to hit him in the eye. He let out a yelp of pain and stumbled back into the wall. She took the opening, dashing past him. She was almost there, only one revolution left.

Suddenly, the stairs beneath her moved, almost knocking her off balance. After her shock wore off, she saw that they were spiraling up. She continued to try and run down the stairs to the ground floor, but it was no use.

She was on a giant circular escalator, and there was no way for her to get off of it. Each door she tried to open on her ascent remained locked.

Turning around, she saw the now livid guard standing in a doorway with what looked like a remote in his hand. His left eye was already beginning to swell shut.

Up it is!

She began sprinting back up the steps, hoping she could dash past him once more. He was too quick for her this time, though. He grabbed her by the waist so hard that the air rushed from her lungs. Lifting her off her feet, he crushed her back to his front. His arms wrapped around her tightly, restraining her arms to her sides.

She started to struggle, but he squeezed her hard and, with a yelp of pain, she stopped. He stepped onto the escalator from hell and stilled as they rode it up.

Jade recognized the door she'd come through as they passed it. Instead of leaving through that door, they kept riding higher and higher.

Finally, the escalator stopped. The guy carrying her stepped into a hallway and set her on her feet in front of him, blocking the exit.

"Move," he grunted and pushed her forward.

She stumbled down the hallway with him at her back. *It's probably too late to sweet talk this guy. Gotta try anyway.*

Plastering a smile on her face, she faced him. "You know, you could just let me go. I would be really appreciative."

He frowned and crossed his arms over his chest. "My translator hasn't been updated."

Her shoulders fell.

"From your tone, I can guess you're asking me to release you."

She nodded at him hopefully.

Leaning down, he growled, "Maybe if you'd asked me nicely earlier instead of striking me in the face, we could've come to an arrangement." His eyes dipped to her breasts.

She let out a frustrated breath and turned to head back down the hallway. It'd be safer than staying here with him.

She heard him chuckle as he followed her. "This view is fine as well."

She shot him a glare over her shoulder.

Victoria Aveline

Zikas appeared in an open doorway. "Oh good, you're back!" His smile faltered when he took in their appearance. "Is…is everything alright, Nedas?"

"She—" Nedas motioned to Jade angrily, "—is a tiny feral guarsil."

Guarsil? There wasn't a direct translation provided to her.

"She hit me in the eye when I tried to stop her!"

"He tried to stop me," she countered.

Clearing his throat and trying to force a demanding tone, Zikas said, "Well, don't try anything like that again, Jade. Guards will be stationed around you at all times now to make sure you don't run away." With another glance at Nedas' eye, he added, "And they'll be made aware of your temper. Thank you for retrieving her," Zikas said to Nedas, ushering her through the opened door.

Nedas grunted.

After the door closed, Zikas studied Jade for a moment.

Feeling irritable, she snapped, "What? Did you expect me to just roll over and do whatever you guys told me to?"

In an even tone, Zikas said, "Tomorrow you'll participate in a coupling ceremony. There are three stages of the ceremony: The Viewing, the Choosing, and the Testing. You'll be escorted to the Viewing in the morning by a guard. There, you'll look at a group of males and choose the ones you like the most."

"Like hell," Jade hissed through clenched teeth.

"This will happen whether you want it to or not," Zikas said firmly. "I'm sorry you are not more open to the idea."

45

Zikas moved toward the door to leave. "Get some sleep. If you're unable, then I implore you to think on your situation. Even if you did escape, you'd be living your life out in the wilderness of an alien planet."

"But I'd be free," Jade countered.

"You'll be free in one year whether you run away or not. You could spend the year in the wilderness, where you'd starve, freeze, and be attacked by animals you've never seen the likes of. Or you could trust us to treat you well. You'd spend the year being fed, sheltered, and protected from whoever tried to steal you in the first place." He looked at her beseechingly. "We aren't so bad. We haven't done anything to harm you thus far, and we won't." Then he was gone.

The anger still burned deep within Jade, but Zikas' calm, logical words had reduced her ire to glowing embers rather than the raging inferno it had been.

Guarded at all times?

Curious, she opened the door to her room and found Nedas blocking her path. Her temper had earned her a constant guard. Great.

Flipping him the bird, she slammed the door in his confused face.

8

J ade stared out through a wall of glass. She'd been dragged
here and then placed, quite forcefully, on the far-right end
of the long room by her surly guard, Nedas. To her left, there
were about twenty beautiful young women looking out
through the glass as well. Some of the women were standing
in groups and talking, while others were on their own, waiting
for…something.

Jade looked around, scanning the room for a door, but
instead found two angry eyes, one of them swollen and red,
staring back at her. It was obvious from his stance and his
unwavering gaze that his job was to watch her and make sure
she didn't try to escape. She pointed at his eye and then gave
a sarcastic pout. His scowl deepened.

Zikas had been right. Last night she'd stayed up for long
hours pondering her situation. She recalled her journey to the
city after landing in the pod. It'd been grueling.

When she'd finally relaxed and inspected her room, she'd found food waiting for her. She'd been hoping for fresh ingredients she could identify—that way, if she did escape, she could pick out at least one thing she could eat without getting food poisoning. The green goo she'd been served by the reptile aliens greeted her instead.

Jade hated to admit it, but she'd have no way of fending for herself out there. She was delusional to think she could. Even the small, comfortable room in which Zikas had left her had been difficult to navigate.

The round toilet bowl had been simple enough to figure out, but the cleansing unit hadn't been as straightforward. Peering into the shining white enclosure, she hadn't spotted any knobs, buttons, or controls of any kind. After wandering around the small room and searching for any hint of a control for the unit, she'd decided maybe the controls were located on the inside of the enclosure's door.

The door had slid open automatically when she'd approached, but when she'd stepped into the unit and the door had slid closed, foam had spurted from the ceiling, covering her. Apparently, merely being inside the enclosure was enough to activate it.

She'd waited until all the fluffy cleanser had vanished and then once again donned the ugly, but very clean, sack dress. What she wouldn't give to be back in her small home in a hot bath. The cleansing foam did the job alright, but it was nowhere near as relaxing as hot water.

Her night had been altogether disappointing, and her temper had been made worse when Nedas had entered her room uninvited this morning and dragged her here.

Jade studied the women she saw milling about. All of them had human qualities, but they also had strange features that made it clear they were aliens. What Jade didn't understand was whether they were all different species or different races of the same species.

Some of the women had pale skin with thin, shining markings running all over their skin. Some had horns or tails. One hypnotizing woman in the corner had midnight-blue skin that was almost translucent and glowed from within. Her golden eyes met Jade's, and Jade quickly glanced away, feeling a flush of embarrassment that she'd been caught staring.

Jade peered down at the flowing purple jumpsuit Nedas had thrown at her that morning before ushering her here. It fit her well, but after beholding the otherworldly beauty of the alien women gathered in the room, she still felt plain. *Maybe no one will want to marry me!* she thought hopefully.

Once again, Jade glanced to the door. She felt so frustrated she could scream. This couldn't be her only option.

Just because Jade had decided not to run away didn't mean she should have to get married. Maybe she could convince them to let her stay in a room here for three months, before finding some small shack in the woods where she'd be left alone for the rest of the year. This building seemed pretty secure, and she could stay out of everyone's way.

The next time she saw Zikas, she'd try and convince him of this.

Suddenly the lights in the room dimmed and the other side of the glass was illuminated. All chatter ceased, and everyone turned to look at the plain gray hallway on the other side of the glass. Jade could now see that the hallway continued out of sight in either direction.

The other women in the room were all peering into the right side of the hallway expectantly. Curiosity burning in her, she examined the hallway as well. She'd just managed to spot a door a few feet down the hall when it opened.

A tall, handsome man walked out of the door and stood almost directly in front of her. Instinctively, she took a step back but then she noticed the man wasn't looking at her. In fact, it didn't seem like his eyes were focused on anything. Tentatively, she waved her hand in front of the glass. He didn't react. With a low chuckle, Jade realized this must've been some kind of one-way viewing room.

The Viewing, indeed.

Zikas had explained she'd be viewing a group of males, but she hadn't thought he'd meant that hunky aliens would be paraded in front of her like beauty pageant contestants. Apparently, on this planet women chose their partners by anonymously ogling them. After a second's deliberation, Jade found that she was for it.

Just because she didn't intend on becoming anyone's bride didn't mean she couldn't objectify a few fine aliens. *When in Rome!*

The man standing before her was beautiful. He was about six feet tall, lean and muscular. His pale-blond hair was short, streaked with silver, and tousled a little too perfectly. The loose, sleeveless white shirt he wore appeared almost gauzy and glittered in the dim light. Flowing white pants added to his "naturally gorgeous without trying" look. His icy-blue eyes stared fixedly in front of him, and while he seemed relaxed, Jade noticed he was clenching and unclenching his jaw.

If this guy were on Earth, he'd be a heartthrob, but she could swear he was…nervous?

Stepping closer to the glass, Jade noticed that the light, shimmering markings she'd seen on a few of the aliens were also on this man. The luminescent markings twisted and curved all along his arms, hands, and neck. It was like someone had tattooed his whole body using ink made from crushed opals. His skin was so pale that if he were standing far away and the room was dim, she doubted whether she would even be able to see the markings.

Just as she was getting lost in thought as to how much of his body these markings covered, he started moving. Jade's gaze followed him as he walked a few feet to the left and then stopped to once again stand motionless at the mirror.

When she turned back, there was another handsome man standing in front of her. This new man had decided to not bother with a shirt. Jade had no trouble understanding why. His upper body looked like it had been carved from marble. Like veins of glimmering quartz, his markings stood out beautifully against his darker complexion.

As she'd previously suspected, these strange markings ran all over his exposed chest. The design was slightly different from the first man's but close enough to make Jade believe they were a species trait rather than just personal preference.

Before long, the shirtless man walked away and was replaced by yet another beautiful specimen. Jade studied each man who came and went appreciatively but couldn't help getting bored after a while. She managed to find a chair tucked away in a corner and plopped herself down.

How many more men can there be? They all start to look the same after a while, she thought while surveying the guy in front of her.

As he stepped away, a new man came into view who made Jade sit up and take notice. Although he wasn't as traditionally handsome as the others, he was definitely attractive.

Jade assumed he realized there were tons of attractive men to compete with because he seemed to be trying to stand out in other ways. His outfit, for one, was ridiculously opulent. Thick gold rings topped with gemstones adorned every finger. An emerald-green vest, embroidered with golden thread, beads, and buttons, was crossed and belted at his narrow waist. Various precious stones and gold bands were scattered throughout his disheveled, shoulder-length black hair. On his lower half he wore tight black leather pants and tall black boots. His simple black button-down shirt would've been mundane compared to the rest of his extravagant outfit except he had unbuttoned it just enough to show off both his tanned chest and his many gold necklaces.

As she watched him grin roguishly into the glass, displaying perfect white teeth, Jade couldn't help but smile. Altogether, his ensemble made him resemble a wealthy, rowdy, womanizing, sexy pirate. Without even speaking to him, she could tell he was the kind of guy who could charm almost any woman out of her panties.

"I need to stay away from you. You look like too much fun," Jade muttered under her breath as he sauntered away.

When another beautiful but bland man stood in front of her, she almost wished for the sexy pirate to come back. Giggling from her left told her that his outfit and cheeky bravado had elicited the desired effect.

Another twenty minutes passed at an unimaginably slow pace. Jade almost considered trying to take a nap when she heard a fearful gasp from one of the women nearest to her. She looked up to see the most powerful man she'd ever laid eyes on.

Slowly, she walked up to the glass to gaze at him. With the exception of the pirate, all the other men could've been described as beautiful or handsome. Jade highly doubted if anyone had ever called *this* man beautiful, though.

Where most of the other men had been pale skinned with light, shining markings, this man had deeply tanned skin, and his markings were a dark, inky black. The black designs covered his skin in a much more severe way than the others as well. These weren't delicate vine-like tattoos. These were more like tribal designs you'd see in the South Pacific. The dark black of his markings matched the color of his hair.

He stood with his head down so his face was shadowed. Jade found herself wishing he'd lift his head so she could see his eyes.

As if he'd read her mind, he raised his head. If she didn't know any better, she would've thought he was looking at her. Dark eyelashes framed the most beautiful eyes she'd ever seen. They were an unnaturally light shade of green flecked with warm gold, a stark contrast to the rest of his rough appearance.

His lips looked like they'd be full and soft even though they were, at present, thinned in a hard, tense line.

Jade wasn't short by any means, but this man towered over her. He had to be over six and a half feet, at least. His massive biceps were tensed, and the silky fabric of his simple black shirt strained over his broad chest. She was right. *Beautiful* didn't fit. *Devastatingly sexy god of war* seemed more accurate.

Jade continued to watch him as he stalked toward the other women. For a moment, she couldn't comprehend what she was seeing. Her attention had shifted away from Tall, Dark, and Sexy to the women watching him. Half of the women appeared terrified; the other half looked…disgusted?

What am I missing here? He must be some kind of asshole. That's unfortunate.

Jade was so busy contemplating what she'd seen that she didn't notice the last man leave the hallway until Zikas appeared in front of her.

"Did you see any male you liked?" he asked with gray eyebrows raised.

Did. I. Ever. "I didn't see any human men so…no," Jade lied. "Can you take me home now, please?"

The hopeful expression Zikas had been wearing a second ago vanished. He looked at her sadly and said, "I'm sorry, but no, you cannot go home. You must choose at least one of those males."

"What happens if I don't?"

"I'll be forced to choose for you."

Her anger rising, Jade spun and glared at Zikas. "And what happens then? Huh? What happens if you choose but I refuse? Will he drag me to his house? Force himself on me? Lock me up? What kind of fucked-up planet forces abducted women to marry strange alien men?"

Yelling at Zikas didn't have the effect Jade had been hoping for. He smiled at her. "Please sit down," he said, gesturing to her chair. "Please let me try to explain."

What is it about nice old men that makes them so hard to be angry at? Jade thought as she tried to decide whether to stand her ground or sit and listen. Finally, she sat down, concluding that stalling was better than facing whatever came next.

"Your planet is a Class Four planet. That means that they don't know about life on other planets and their technology isn't advanced enough to venture outside of their own galaxy yet," Zikas explained calmly. "It's against the law for any Class One, 2, or 3 planet citizens, or their inhabitants, to contact or otherwise interfere with these planets."

"I don't know if you've noticed, bu—"

Zikas held up his hand for silence. Jade sat back in her chair, folding her arms across her chest in silent protest. "There are always those who want to break laws. So, of course, we occasionally find ourselves in situations like this. A long time ago, The Galaxy Supervision Federation and The Intergalactic Alliance signed a treaty, The Planetary Sanctuary Treaty, that outlines what we're required to do in these instances. Whichever species rescues or otherwise encounters a being from a Class Four planet is responsible for the welfare of that being for a period of one year. We're also required to report the species that exposed themselves to the planet in question, which we'll do as soon as we figure out who took you."

"The last time I checked, *welfare* does not include forced marriage," Jade said pointedly.

"Ah yes, well that is a law only on Clecania." Zikas sighed. "As you may have noticed, the Clecanian males on this planet outnumber the females twenty to one."

"You don't say," Jade commented, feigning disinterest.

"It wasn't always that way. There used to be an equal number of males and females. I believe the acts of courting and marriage were very similar to Earth—if what I read was accurate, that is."

Annoyed at her own curiosity, Jade asked, "What happened? Why did it change?"

"About three hundred years ago, there was a plague. We don't know how it started. Some think enemy species contaminated the water somehow, but we haven't found any evidence of that. Some blame their gods." Zikas shrugged. "They think we're being punished for irreparably damaging our original home planet, also called Clecania. Either way, the plague ended up killing about twenty percent of our men and seventy percent of the Clecanian females. Young and old alike."

Jade leaned forward and put her hand over her mouth. *It's a wonder this planet is functioning at all. If seventy percent of Earth women were wiped out, I can't even imagine what would happen. Wars, slavery, rape. We'd destroy ourselves in a matter of decades.* She looked up at Zikas, nodding for him to continue.

"After some time had passed and they were certain the plague was gone, people started to try and lead normal lives again. They all knew that having more children, especially girls, was a priority, so they did what they could to ensure our species had a future." Zikas' eyes grew sad as he continued, "Mating was decreasing as well as conceptions."

"Mating? People weren't having sex anymore?"

Zikas stared at her quizzically. "No, *mating.* Two beings who are drawn to one another and stay together forever. Do humans not have mates?"

"Sure, I guess. We just call it getting married."

"Marriage and matehood are two different things here. Marriage is common, matehood is not. It cannot be chosen. It's a blessing." A dreamy smile appeared on his face. "When a Clecanian meets a potential mate, someone who could possibly turn out to be their true mate, they *feel* it. They'll change, and their body will awaken in a way it doesn't for others."

His eyes traveled to the floor, the dreamy expression disappearing. "There hasn't been a record of a mating in one hundred fifty years."

Jade frowned. His tone was so wistful. She felt that although Zikas was a psychopath who was trying to pimp her out to some alien, he was also a romantic and was describing something he would always wish for and never have. "How would you know that you had a mate and weren't just really attracted to someone?"

He looked up at her. "When a Clecanian recognizes their true mate, mate markings will appear on their bodies and both the individuals will become stronger and faster in order to better protect each other and their offspring."

What he was telling her sounded more like a fairy tale. *...and then the prince broke her curse with true love's kiss.* It would be unsurprising to see tiny whistling birds perch on his shoulder.

Jade did not for one minute believe in soul mates, and the fact that the Clecanians had "stopped" finding their soul mates just proved to her this was some old wives' tale that was passed down to make their current circumstances seem more bearable.

Zikas cleared his throat hastily. He must have noticed that Jade remained unmoved by his words. "Anyway...it's always been much easier for a mated couple to conceive than an unmated one. Even so, the rate of success for an unmated couple to conceive has dropped so dramatically that we've had to adapt."

"Why can mated couples conceive more easily? You haven't been able to use artificial insemination or grow babies in test tubes?" Jade asked, thinking through other ways of having a baby.

"No one knows for sure how or why mating works, just that it does. While some races on our planet believe mated couples are spiritually bound, the more scientifically minded of us continued to study mated pairs in order to find some tangible reason. Now that mates have become so rare, it's hard for our research to continue. As for artificial insemination, we've tried, but natural conception continues to yield the most successful births. Artificial insemination can be used if the couple cannot conceive on their own, but unfortunately it's rare for couples who cannot conceive to stay together for very long."

Jade scoffed. "That's ridiculous! What if two women or two men want to be together? You're telling me they'd leave their partners and sleep with someone of the opposite sex just to become pregnant?"

Zikas looked at her sadly. "At one point that wasn't the case, but you have to understand that, in a way, we've devolved. The threat of extinction has caused our priorities to change. Females, males, and those who identify as neither are free to be with whomever they want, but most of our citizens understand that continuing our species is our top priority. I know of many Clecanian females who choose to be in marriages in order to procreate but return home to their female partners after their marriage is complete."

Jade stood and started to pace. She was beginning to feel a tug of compassion. *Housing, safety, and food in return for a wife. Forced prostitution!* That was what he was offering. She needed to remember that and not be suckered in by the sweet old man trying to pull on her heart strings.

"Infertility isn't our biggest problem, though."

"How can that not be the biggest problem?" Jade said with thinned lips.

"When females *do* become pregnant and give birth, eighty percent of the children born are males," Zikas said with a look of desperation. "Finding another species that's compatible with us would be an invaluable discovery. One we've been searching for for hundreds of years. One that might save our people from extinction." With that, he gazed earnestly into Jade's eyes.

Jade's eyes widened as she realized what this guy ultimately wanted from her. "Oh no! I see what you're getting at, and I'm truly sorry for you and your people, but I'm not going to have alien babies! If the sci-fi movies taught me anything, it's not to get pregnant with an alien. It claws its way out—"

"Jade."

"—and then it looks like a cockroach or an octopus beetle—"

"Jade."

"—and if you're *lucky*, it'll leave you alone and not eat you after it's born! But most of—"

"Jade!"

"*What?*" Rage boiled in her gut. So much had happened to her in the last week. In all her life, she'd never felt the pull to have a child. They seemed fine but not something that interested her very much. Now on this alien planet, she was being asked—no, not asked—told. She was being told to pick a guy to marry and then have his alien baby.

"I don't understand what you're talking about. Please let me finish. No one will force you to have a child."

Narrowing her eyes at Zikas, she gestured impatiently for him to explain.

"You have to understand, females are the most precious thing on this planet. Females are treasured...worshipped, even. They can create life! More than once!" Zikas added, looking exasperated, "On Earth, marriage means you stay with that person forever, correct?"

"It's supposed to," Jade said. "Doesn't mean anybody follows through with that, though."

"Well, here, a marriage only has to last three months. Matehood is forever, but marriage is more of a..." Zikas scanned the ceiling, trying to find the right words. "A trial."

"What?" Confusion now warred with her anger. Jade glared at him suspiciously. "How long in Earth days is three months?" For all Jade knew, three months could really be thirty years on this planet.

Zikas tapped his ear. "The translator uses the amount of time I intended to mean and translates it based on information from your planet. The amount of time you need to be married for is equivalent to three months in Earth time."

"Why three months?" Jade asked placing her hands on her hips.

"Clecanian females decided that three months would be a long enough amount of time to assess whether the male they've chosen is worthy of raising a child." Zikas stepped closer. "I'm not trying to deceive you, Jade. You have to understand, females on this planet can do whatever they want. Choose to marry whomever they want. They also choose whether they want to have sex with their husband during their marriage or not. When a female chooses a male to marry, she's gifting that male an opportunity, not a right. He'll do whatever he can to make his wife happy. It's a Clecanian husband's job to satisfy his wife in every way. If he does this, then she may *choose* to have sex with him. If she wants more time with the male, she can choose to extend her marriage, or she can go live somewhere else. Often, females choose to live in The Pearl Temple with other unwed females."

Jade stared open-mouthed at Zikas.

Zikas continued, "If a male ever did anything to hurt a female in any way, the female has the right to mete out his punishment."

"So—"

"And the reason we have a law that requires Class Four planet females to marry," Zikas quickly added, "is because we want all females who may have been brought here under very unpleasant circumstances to understand our customs and give them a chance. We want to show them—and you—how treasured you'd be here. The creators of that law believed, as I do, that if you experience how good life can be on Clecania, that you, and females like you, will decide not to leave after a year."

Zikas moved to stand across from Jade as she considered everything he'd told her. Finally, she looked at him and asked, "So I pick any of those guys to marry."

"As long as someone else hasn't picked them first. In which case, the male will choose who his bride will be," Zikas answered happily, sensing Jade was softening to the idea.

"Uh-huh. And whoever I do marry," she said, raising her eyebrows, "is not allowed to rape me, beat me, lock me up, etcetera?"

"Any of those behaviors will most likely result in the male's death," Zikas said, almost bouncing in his chair with joy.

"And he'll do anything I want? Happily? And get nothing in return?"

"Well, you'd live in his house in return," Zikas said, confusion etched across his face. "In a separate bedroom, of course!" he quickly added.

"I don't even have to sleep in the same bed as him?"

"That's your choice, but it would be highly irregular for a husband and wife to sleep in the same room," he said, shaking his head absently.

"Huh." Jade faltered at that. This was such a huge departure from what she was used to. She could pick any of the hunks she'd just seen, have them lavish her with adoration for a few months, get her own clean room and bed to sleep in, and then just walk away? "How do the men feel about doing all of this stuff?" Jade asked, knowing that if the roles were reversed, she'd be rebelling.

Zikas furrowed his brows at her question. "What do you mean?"

"I can't imagine most men want to dote on some needy woman endlessly. Isn't it a bit cruel to use them like that?"

Zikas still looked confused but smiled absently. "If a male is unable to be sexually interested in females, then he's exempt from marriage unless he'd like to try and have a child. I can't think of any other circumstances in which a male wouldn't be happy about being chosen for a marriage."

No matter how many times she went through it in her head, she couldn't find any downsides. The men would happily take care of her, according to Zikas. She didn't even have to have sex with them. She grinned inwardly. *But I could.* Only two weeks ago, Jade had gotten her birth control shot. That meant she had three months of protection.

Having a few fun months of sex with a gorgeous guy and then leaving? This could end up being a hell of a vacation. Just one possible catch. "Zikas, what happens in three months if I don't want to be married anymore? Do I have to get married again to someone else because I'm human?" She studied his face, searching for any signs of deception.

"No. You can either live in The Pearl Temple with other single females and do what you please, or you can get married again. We only require that you meet with someone weekly so you can learn more about the workings of our world."

"The Queen told me I could live somewhere else on the planet. Is that right?" Jade didn't like the idea of bunking with a bunch of alien women for months at a time.

"You could, but I'd advise against it until you become more familiar with our people and our planet."

She'd see about that. "And then in one year I can leave Clecania?"

Zikas looked disappointed as he said, "Yes, but as I said before, you cannot go back to Earth. Any space craft landing there or even being near there would be a breach of The Planetary Sanctuary Treaty I told you about."

"Of course. I meant just leaving this planet." *So I can find some unscrupulous group to take me back anyway.* Jade's mind rebelled against the idea that she'd never be going back to Earth. She would find a way. If there was a way to be taken from Earth, then it would be possible to return there.

Zikas nodded solemnly and inclined his head toward her.

She knew he was waiting for her decision. Would she be stubborn and be dragged every step of the way? Or was she about to make his life easier and do what he asked?

Jade reminded herself that if she didn't choose a man, Zikas would pick for her.

An image of that tattooed warrior flashed in her mind. It wasn't likely that Zikas would choose him for her. He probably would assume she'd be as scared of him as the other women were. If she wanted to go home with Mr. Sex-on-a-Stick, she'd have to pick him herself. "Okay, I'm in, then."

Zikas exhaled a breath of relief. He glanced behind him to Nedas, who was still glowering at her from near the exit. "If I can trust you not to run away again, I'll send your guard away."

Jade nodded quickly, relieved she'd no longer have to be watched by an angry linebacker.

"Wonderful! We'd better hurry," Zikas exclaimed as he sped away, motioning for Jade to follow.

When they reached the door, he said something quietly to Nedas. The sour guard glared at her for a moment before nodding stiffly and stalking away.

Turning to Jade, he continued to speak quickly. "What happens now is you'll pick three to five males you liked. I'll give you their file, and that'll tell you everything you need to know about their abilities."

Zikas ushered Jade out of the Viewing room they'd been in and down a much more lavishly decorated hall she hadn't noticed before.

Well, I had been a little angry, I guess, she thought as she now admired her surroundings. Deep magenta walls complemented the dark wood floors. Along the wall, golden lamps in the shape of large flying creatures were illuminated.

Something Zikas had said earlier finally registered. "Abilities? Am I marrying one of the X-Men?"

Zikas wasn't paying her much attention when he answered, "Yes. What? No. I don't know what that is. I can explain everything to you while you get ready." The fact that Jade had finally relented and agreed to willingly go through with this marriage seemed to overjoy him.

"I can't wait to see who you've chosen." Zikas suddenly stopped to look at her. "I'd be more than happy to make some suggestions or give you a little background about the males. I've known most of them since they were children."

"Uh. Okay, thanks. I'll probably take you up on that."

Zikas continued walking quickly down the hallway until he reached a tall, arched wooden door. He faced Jade, and with a grin, he said, "Ready?"

9

"Ready for what?"

"To choose the males, of course!" Zikas said as he guided her through the large door.

"I have to do that now?" Jade said, astonished.

Inside was a room similar to the room she'd just been in. The far wall was made entirely of glass, and the same women she'd seen earlier were milling around. Each woman, however, was now accompanied by an older man or woman. They were all talking with each other excitedly.

As she walked in the room, all eyes turned on her. Most of the people looking at her gave her a curious once over and then glanced away. Some of the women gave her small smiles or nods. Jade tried her best to smile politely back but had trouble keeping the trepidation she felt off her face.

Earlier in the day, her actions had been fueled by anger and outrage. Now that she was no longer ready to claw someone's eyes out, all the nervous energy and fear was bubbling back to the surface.

I'm in a room surrounded by aliens, Jade thought, letting that notion sink in. *I'm about to marry an alien! I'm trusting some old alien man to tell me the truth about what'll happen with this guy! What the hell am I doing here?*

Just as Jade was preparing to spin around and bolt, a very pretty woman in a pale-blue dress started gliding toward her. The woman was tall and lithe. As she walked, the fabric of her dress flowed delicately around her legs and the light danced off her iridescent markings. The effect was hypnotic. The warm smile spread over the woman's lips as she drew near, and Jade found herself relaxing.

"Hello," the woman said, peering down at Jade with beautiful periwinkle eyes. "My name is Asivva. What is yours?"

"My name is Jade," she answered, feeling like a veritable minion compared to the woman.

"It's nice to meet you, Jade."

"It's nice to…" Jade's eyes widened in shock. "Wait, you understood me! How are you doing that?"

Asivva laughed. "I'm a member of The Intergalactic Alliance, and when I heard that a Class Four species female had been found, I made sure I had my translator updated so I could speak with you. I assume you must be very confused and nervous. I wanted to make sure you were all right. And I thought you may be more comfortable talking with another female." Asivva looked pointedly at Zikas.

Zikas gave Asivva and Jade a quick bow and then ambled over to another older man by the window.

"Wow. That's really nice of you. Yes, I didn't realize how nervous I was until I walked in here," Jade said as she scanned the room again.

"Your first marriage is always nerve-wracking, but you will get used to it. After a while you may even look forward to them," Asivva said nonchalantly.

"Are you getting married tonight too?"

"Oh, no. I'm just here for you. I'm currently in month four of my marriage. I decided to prolong my marriage by three more months." Asivva smiled. "You're very beautiful, Jade. I haven't met many females with your coloring before. Your hair looks like it's made of fire."

"Oh, thanks, but I'm nothing compared to you." Jade eyed the statuesque woman, marveling at how her markings glistened as she moved. Unable to stop herself, Jade blurted, "Do all Clecanians have those markings?"

Asivva glanced at her hand as if she'd forgotten about them. "No. Those of us with Lignas ancestry have them."

Jade gazed at her, hoping she'd continue. *These are aliens! How have I not been asking questions nonstop?*

The corner of Asivva's mouth quirked. "Most Lignas Clecanians live in the city you're currently in, Tremanta. That's why you may have seen markings on so many of us."

So, the hunky possible jerk Jade was still fantasizing about was not Lignas. "What do Clecanians from other places look like?"

"There are so many variations it's hard to name them all." Asivva blew out a long breath. "The Mastana have sharp fangs and darker coloring. Those in the mountains, called Pesque, are much smaller in stature but have loud voices meant to carry for miles. Beautiful winged Clecanians live in structures built high up in cliffs above the sea. There are many races of Clecanian, all with different ancestry and rituals. The marriage ceremony is very different in other parts of Clecania, for example."

Asivva leaned in conspiratorially and whispered, "Be glad you aren't marrying a Rotun male. They choose their wives by wrestling them. Potential wives of the Tuvasta males are chased, and whichever male catches the female becomes her husband. They have horns."

Jade was in awe. Maybe she should stay for longer than a year just so she could learn about all of these different races.

Asivva chuckled at Jade's dumbstruck expression. "I take it most humans are more similar to one another?"

Nodding in agreement was all Jade could manage. Across the planet, humans had very different cultures, but the media and access to technology were ensuring that cultural and social globalization occurred at a faster pace every year.

Jade was astounded and confused about how an advanced civilization could not only contain so many races that were so physically different but also retained their own identities to such an extreme.

"Yes, our old planet was vast. Races from all over prided themselves on their evolutionary gifts and their cultures.

When our ancestors moved to this planet, they sought to separate themselves again rather than come together. Maybe they wanted to preserve some semblance of their old lives by staying separate and keeping their own cultural traditions alive." Shrugging weakly, Asivva looked in Jade's eyes. "We came to a new world but clung to our old prejudices. Try to be better than us."

Jade's brows drew together, she didn't have anything against any race. "What do you mean?"

"I've read what I could about your species, and I see problems that may arise if you don't have an open mind. Our ways may seem strange to you, but it doesn't mean they're wrong. Try to remember that."

Was Jade one of those people who looked down on other cultures? There was a term for that. She'd learned it in an anthropology class a long time ago. *Ethnocentrism.* Judging other cultures based on your own culture.

"Did you enjoy the Viewing?" Asivva asked, interrupting Jade's thoughts.

"Uh. Yes. Well, sort of," Jade said, taken aback by the sudden question. "Maybe not as much as some of the other women." She thought back to the smiling women who'd giggled while watching the sexy pirate.

Asivva continued to peer at her for a moment. Jade could almost feel her analytical stare running over Jade's body, assessing her. Jade shifted nervously. Then, as if Asivva had come to a conclusion, she said, "If you'll excuse me, I have to go and speak with someone about getting you some extra clothing. Your husband may have clothes waiting, but just to be on the safe side I'll provide you with a few things in your size until you can pick out your own."

"Wow. Thank you so much."

"My pleasure." Asivva nodded regally at her and then sauntered toward the door.

As Jade stared after Asivva, she was startled by a voice in her ear. "Isn't she wonderful?"

Jade turned to find that Zikas had returned. Jade chuckled as she said, "She is something."

The lights in the room dimmed.

"The Choosing is about to start," Zikas said, his excitement palpable. "Come to the window. Take this as well." He handed Jade a small pad of paper and a ruby-encrusted pen. "The males will be holding up numbers. When you see the males you want to choose, just draw their numbers here. I realize you can't read these numbers, so just do your best to copy the symbols, alright?"

"Alright."

"I'll be standing back by the wall if you need me." Zikas gave her a quick squeeze on her shoulder and then walked away.

One by one, the men came just as they had before, except this time they were holding symbols on small white cards. After they stopped in front of the one-way mirror long enough for the women to write their numbers down, they backed against the wall and waited.

Before long, the last man had presented his number and joined the waiting group of men. Altogether, the men gave a low bow and departed. Jade had done her best to copy her three choices, but Clecanian numerals were much more detailed than the numerals she was used to. Hopefully Zikas would be able to figure out what she'd meant to draw.

Jade closed the pad and walked toward Zikas.

"Now we'll go to your room and talk about your choices!" Zikas said happily.

"Zikas, do you have any alcohol by chance? I could really use a drink right about now," Jade asked.

"Oh, we do, but I'm sorry, you can't have any yet."

"What? Why not?" she said, just stopping herself from whining. *Nobody likes a whiner!*

Zikas gently grabbed her elbow and guided her out of the room and down the hall once again. "Because you haven't received your off-worlder health clearance yet."

"What's—"

Guessing her question before she had finished asking it, Zikas explained, "Right after we talk about your choices and I tell the men you chose that they'll be moving on to the Testing phase, I'm going to take you to the doctor. They'll give you various scans and heal any injuries or health-related issues they're capable of healing. Since you're an off-worlder, they also need to run a cross-check of all ingredients and materials you may come in contact with, to make sure their chemical composition won't cause you to have any reactions.

It wouldn't be good if on your first night as a Clecanian wife you died from a food you didn't know was poisonous to you."

Jade gulped as she realized she hadn't considered any of that. "Suddenly I'm no longer thirsty."

"We're here!" Zikas said, motioning to a dark-burgundy door.

The room behind the door looked like it was modeled after a spa from an ancient Indian palace. In every direction Jade looked, she saw vibrant gem-toned fabrics and pillows. The couch in front of her was overstuffed and plush. She wondered whether it'd be out of the question to ask her new husband, whoever he was, to bring it home with them.

To her right, Jade saw an enormous sunken stone bathing pool. Steam rose off the water in curls, and beautiful purple flowers similar to water lilies floated on the surface. Jade gazed longingly at the tub. "Is that for bathing? I didn't think you guys used water baths to bathe, only that weird foam."

"Our planet is considered a Class Two planet because we still live a little archaically compared to Class One planets. The cleansing unit is useful if you want to get clean in a hurry, but bathing in warm water is a luxury we don't see the need to replace."

Jade had noticed that many things she would've assumed would be automated on an alien planet were not. Many of the doors she'd used, for example, were normal doors you pushed to open. Clothing, while not tailored in a way she was used to, was surprisingly similar to clothing on Earth. She'd even been provided with thick underwear but unfortunately no bra.

The style of the city and the buildings also didn't match her preconceived notions about what alien furnishings should look like. In her mind, the decorations of an advanced culture would be minimalist and geometric. Taking in the decorated, colorful room, she realized she'd been wrong.

A part of her relaxed. This might be an alien planet, but this room was close enough to home that she felt comfortable in it.

In the far-left corner of the room, Jade spotted Asivva. She was rifling through a rack of clothing and was so absorbed by her task that she didn't hear them come in.

"Asivva. Is everything in order?" called Zikas as he walked quickly toward her.

Asivva glanced up and smiled. "Everything is wonderful. I'm excited to hear who she's picked." Asivva moved toward the couch and motioned for Jade to join her.

As Jade sat next to Asivva, Zikas retrieved an enormous cerulean blue box from a cabinet near the entrance. He then sat down in a large chair across from Jade and clapped his hands together. "I can't wait any longer! Who have you picked?"

Jade flipped her notebook open and handed it to Zikas. He grabbed it eagerly.

If she remembered correctly, this was the number the sexy pirate had held up. She didn't intend on choosing him in the end, but he looked like such an interesting guy. She couldn't resist the opportunity to learn more about him.

"Ooh, Fejo. Good choice. He's very charming and funny." Asivva nodded approvingly.

Zikas pulled out a large folder from the blue box and handed it to Jade.

"It also appears he's never been married. He'll be very eager to please you," Zikas said with a wink.

"Who's next?" Asivva urged.

Zikas flipped to the next page and shrugged. "Athnu. He's a favorite among the females this year, I think. If you really want him, I would have no doubt he'd choose you, but I don't like him for you."

"Why not?" Jade frowned as she pictured the gorgeous man who'd walked into the hallway first.

"Well, he's very good looking, so all the females like him." Zikas paused here, thinking about his next words. "I'll just say he spends a great deal of time making sure he looks attractive, and if all you want is to look at him, you'll have a very happy marriage."

Jade and Asivva exchanged amused glances and then started laughing.

Zikas' face reddened. He sheepishly added, "You strike me as the kind of female who prefers to be engaged in conversation from time to time."

"That is very true, and I appreciate your honesty. Let's take him out of the running," Jade said, crumpling Athnu's number.

"I think that would be best." Asivva smirked.

Jade chuckled and felt some of her tension lifting. These aliens weren't so bad. If she was honest with herself, she could even admit that this was the most human contact she'd experienced in a long time, even if they were non-human. She couldn't remember the last time she'd relaxed with a group of people and laughed.

"Alright, last on your list is…" As Zikas studied the last page, his face fell and he peered up at Jade, his confusion clear. "Are you sure you copied this number correctly?"

"Why, who is it?" Asivva chimed in.

Zikas silently handed her the paper, and the grin on her face also faded.

"What? What's wrong with him?" Jade said as she glanced between the two of them. Damn. She knew the hunky man with the black tattoos was too good to be true. He must be an awful guy. That's why the women acted like that around him. *Well, sexy pirate it is!*

"Nothing, nothing. His name is Theo. Asivva and I have both known him all his life. He's a very good male," Zikas muttered while sharing a knowing look with Asivva.

"One of the best I know," Asivva agreed.

"Then what's the problem?" Jade said, baffled.

As she sat there staring at the bewildered faces of her two new friends, she remembered the odd reaction this man had received at the Viewing. Theo, also known as "devastatingly sexy god of war" man, seemed to frighten and disgust the women in the room. The reaction her choice was getting from Asivva and Zikas was different but no less bizarre.

"Some women acted weird when they saw him at the Viewing too, but I didn't understand why. What am I missing? Is he cruel or something? Will he hurt me? Some of the girls seemed scared of him."

A flash of anger crossed Asivva's face as she said, "He'd never do anything to hurt any female."

"Then as I said before, what's the problem? What aren't you telling me?"

Zikas and Asivva both looked at Jade quizzically. Asivva started to mouth something but then thought better of it.

Zikas was the first to speak when he said, "You're a very beautiful female. You could have any male you wanted. We're just confused as to why you picked Theo."

"I'm not sure I follow you," Jade said in a puzzled tone. "I know he's a little rough around the edges, but I thought he was the most attractive guy there. I really only chose the other two as backups in case he didn't want me."

Asivva snorted and then immediately clapped her hands over her mouth.

"Most females find his scars unappealing," Zikas explained. "He's never been chosen, and I don't think he ever expected to be chosen. He won't be prepared for a wife."

Asivva jerked her head toward Zikas. "You're right, he never expects anyone to choose him. He only comes to these because he's required. Normally he leaves immediately after the Choosing."

Zikas stood abruptly and addressed Jade. "Are you sure you want to marry Theo?"

"Well, I thought so, but now I'm having second thoughts!"

"We were both just shocked that you'd choose him." Zikas regarded Jade seriously. "If you're patient, Jade, you'll see that there are very few better males than Theo."

"Before giving Zikas your final choices," Asivva quickly added, "you should know that Theo hasn't needed or wanted to try and impress a female in a long time. It's very likely he'll not have the faintest idea how to behave with you," she warned. "That being said, I think you should take a chance on him."

"Okay, I'll trust you both, but it's on your heads if this goes wrong." Jade said, nibbling her bottom lip.

Zikas nervously rifled through the box of files. He handed a slim folder to Asivva and backed away toward the door. "I'll go and give Theo and Fejo the good news. Asivva, while I'm gone, can you please explain the information in those folders to Jade? After she's had a chance to examine their scores, escort her to the physician and then help her to get ready for the Testing."

"Good luck talking to Theo." Asivva glanced at Jade briefly. "He enjoys having a drink or two after the ceremonies are over."

As Zikas exited the room, Jade heard him let out a long groan.

10

Ugh, another ceremony day over with, Theo thought as he fell onto his couch. *How many more of those must I be subjected to? It's humiliating, standing there being judged.*

"It's pointless," he growled into his empty living room.

Once per year, every male eligible for marriage in Tremanta was required by law to participate in a ceremony. As he took another swig of his preferred after-ceremony beverage, mott, he surveyed his surroundings, allowing the comfort of his home to soothe him.

Theo had meticulously handpicked each and every item within his house. Visitors, not that he had many, were always surprised when they saw the interior for the first time.

He supposed they imagined his furnishings would reflect what they saw when they looked at him. They expected to find rooms full of uncomfortable, monochromatic, sharp-edged furniture accompanied by cold stone floors and bare black walls.

In fact, Theo preferred the exact opposite. All of his seating was overstuffed and soft. His floors were coated with large, dark-green Saquen leaves and then lacquered. Plush rugs were layered over the natural floor, adding softness to each room. Almost every room in his house contained a fireplace and dim lighting. The combination of light from the fire and soft lighting from above cast each room in a warm glow.

Whenever Theo lost his temper, which happened often, the warmth and comfort of his home calmed him.

Since his graduation from school at age twenty, Theo had spent his life, like many Clecanian males from Tremanta, working for his planet's government as a kind of mercenary. Over the years, his skill had earned him the reputation of being one of the best in the business. Government officials, celebrities, royals, and dignitaries would request Theo specifically and offer him extravagant amounts of money for both his expertise as well as his discretion. Before long, Theo had amassed a sizable fortune.

He used his money to build a grand house facing the Northern Sea, as well as a large parcel of densely forested land. Since Theo no longer needed to make money, he spent most of his time at home and only chose jobs that were interesting to him.

Theo treasured his solitude and despised visits to the city. He especially loathed the ceremony. Taking a big gulp from his bottle, Theo closed his eyes and tried to focus on the quiet crackle of the fire.

He didn't have much time to relax before he felt an enormous forked tongue slide across his face.

"Ugh!" he yelled as he sat up and wiped the drool off his cheek with his shirt. Sitting before him, looking very pleased with himself, was Cebo, Theo's giant hound. Theo smiled down at Cebo and patted him on the head.

A rumbling noise emanated from Theo's stomach, and he realized he hadn't eaten much today. Cebo cocked his head at the sound.

Resolved to eat something while continuing to drink, he rose and padded to the kitchen. As he searched for food, a wave of fatigue passed over him. Theo grabbed two more bottles of mott instead and flopped back down on the couch, where Cebo was now lying.

Theo drank in silence as he watched the flames dancing in the fireplace and absently stroked Cebo's head, now heavy in his lap. He'd just finished his second bottle of mott and was halfway through with his third when he heard a knock at the door.

Cebo let out a loud bark and leapt down, dashing to the entryway door. Theo's head fell back as he groaned. *Who the hell would be coming to my house this late?! Maybe if I don't answer, they'll go away. Or maybe if I go out there and punch them squarely in the jaw, they'll go away.*

"Theeeooo! I know you're home. I can hear Cebo growling at me through the door!" shouted a familiar voice.

Theo had known Zikas since childhood. The old male had always been very kind to him and had even helped him through some hard times he'd had while growing up. Theo had too much respect for the male to turn him away.

Slowly he stood and made his way to the door. "What do you want?" he yelled.

"It would be nice if you opened the door for a start. It's cold out here, and I have some news for you."

With a grunt, Theo opened the door. Immediately he turned and walked back toward the couch. Cebo, now recognizing the visitor, started jumping up and trying to lick the old male. Normally Theo would help keep Cebo at bay, but he was annoyed tonight and just drunk enough to enjoy watching the male struggle to sidestep the massive beast.

"Yes, Cebo, it's nice to see you too. Get down! No! Stop it! Theo, control your animal!"

"Enough, Cebo!" shouted Theo.

Reluctantly, Cebo padded toward the fireplace and laid down at Theo's feet.

"I don't understand why you chose that creature as a pet. Wazzies are very loving and quiet and don't attack visitors upon entry." Zikas shuffled toward the couch while trying to remove copious amounts of drool from his clothes with a small cloth.

"They're boring. Cebo is unique and loyal." Theo scratched behind Cebo's ears, feeling a kinship toward the large, misunderstood creature.

When Zikas reached Theo, he inspected him, then with a glint in his eye, said, "I have some news."

"What news could be important enough for you to come all the way up here on a ceremony night? Aren't you supposed to be with a bride right now?" Theo sneered as he took another swig.

Zikas reached out with a speed impressive for someone his age and snatched the bottle from Theo's hand.

"Hey! You can't—" started Theo.

"You have been chosen," Zikas said, looking at Theo excitedly.

Theo glared at Zikas for a few moments and then said, "I'm not in the mood for this shit today."

"A bride chose you! That's a good thing!" Zikas said earnestly.

"We both know why this bride chose me. The same reason I was chosen last time. She wants to see the beast in the flesh. Get up close and personal because she knows I can't do anything about it and that I won't know who she is." Theo yanked the mott out of Zikas' hand and finished the bottle.

"No, it's not like that this time. She—"

"I don't care why she picked me. I'm not going. Now, go away and leave me alone."

Stiffening, Zikas scowled at Theo. "Fine, don't believe me, but you will go. It's against the law to refuse, as you well know."

"Lock me up, then." Theo shrugged.

"They won't lock you up. They'll drag you to the Testing, tie you up, and leave you there. You can go willingly, with dignity, or you can be dragged. Your choice," Zikas finished, crossing his arms.

"Are you threatening me?" Theo barked as he rose to his full height. Any other male would have cowered in the face of an enraged Theo.

Zikas, however, leaned in close, looked Theo directly in the eyes, and said, "Yes. I am."

11

Jade looked at the contents of Theo's folder blankly. It seemed the translator in her ear did not also translate written words.

"Can you help me out here?" she asked, handing the folder to Asivva.

"Mm-hmm." She nodded. "Before I read this to you, I need to explain a few things."

Jade sat back on the couch and waited. *This oughta be good.*

"In many cultures on this planet but especially here in Tremanta, Clecanian children start going to school when they are about seven years old. The subjects at that time are what you would consider normal. Reading, writing, history, arithmetic, technology, science, and so on. When Clecanian *boys* turn seventeen, their education is split in half. Half of the time, the boys take classes that coincide with whatever job it is they've chosen. The other half of the time is spent in husbandry school."

A grin spread across Jade's face. "Are you messing with me? This must be a joke. They go to school to learn how to be husbands?" An image of teenage boys wearing dad jeans and mowing the lawn popped into her mind.

"As you know, there are many more males than females here. The way our society decides who's deserving of a wife and child is based, in part, on their grades in husbandry school."

"I guess that makes sense." Jade shrugged, too tired to be surprised by any more absurdity today. "What else is it based on?"

"Many things. They have to make enough money to care for a wife and child, they have to have a clean bill of health, be of a certain age…things like that. Females mostly care about their grades, though."

"What are they graded on?" Jade asked, curious.

"There are a few classes every male has to take, and then there are some they can choose. Cooking and childcare, for example, are mandatory. A husband must know how to make a good meal for his wife and, with any luck, his children. A class about pairing beverages with food, however, is optional. The males train in both schools until they're about twenty, then they take their final exams and earn their grades." She held up the folder Jade had handed her. "Everything you need to know about them is in here."

"And you're sure they're okay with this?" Jade said, feeling guilty about what the men had been put through in order to have the chance at a family. "Being forced to learn how to do all of these things for women? Don't any of them feel used?"

"I don't believe so." Asivva frowned as she thought about Jade's question. "If they were resentful, all they'd have to do is not dote on their female. They wouldn't be picked for marriage again and could go on living how they choose. Many males here will never have the opportunity to prove themselves to a wife, so when they're given the opportunity, most are grateful, not angry." Asivva grasped one of Jade's hands. "I can answer as many questions as you want about the dynamics here, but it's unlikely you'll truly understand our culture unless you've lived in it. Our culture isn't perfect. It's been molded by our needs, not our wants. For now, try to accept what we tell you as truth and make your assumptions about the way we do things after a few months have passed."

On some level, Jade agreed with Asivva. There was no way for her to truly understand what the people of this world felt about this system. Not until she lived in it for longer than a few days. So far, she'd only spoken to a few men, but none of them had seemed oppressed.

"Well, let's hear it, then. What kind of scores did these boys get?" Jade asked, clapping her hands together.

"I'll start with their backgrounds. Fejo specializes in retrieving lost goods. Clients hire him to find stolen and or lost items," Asivva said with pursed lips.

"And…?" Jade asked, sensing the woman did not approve of Fejo.

"Well...there's a rumor that not all of his jobs are completely legal." She glanced around the room uncomfortably. "In addition to retrieving stolen goods, he may also, on occasion, do the stealing."

He actually is a pirate! Am I ready for a life of crime?

"On to Theo," Asivva continued. "I know he's a mercenary hired through the government, but there isn't too much information available about any specific job. I do know that most of his work is done undercover and alone. He's very good at what he does and is often hired by powerful individuals. That is probably why no details are available."

"That sounds ominous." Jade wondered if it was better to choose someone who did bad things out in the open or in secret.

"Both Fejo and Theo are wealthy. Theo is slightly more so." Asivva continued, "They're also both in excellent shape. Fejo tends to travel for work, which may be why he hasn't been married yet. Females generally want their males to be close by at all times. A child wouldn't do well if their parent was always gone. Theo lives about an hour from the city and rarely accepts jobs anymore."

"Maybe we should focus on Theo," Jade suggested. "I don't know if I'd feel safe being alone all of the time." *Lie!* Being alone was something Jade enjoyed immensely. She was inventing excuses in order to make sure she ended up with Theo, and Asivva knew it. Jade noticed the side of Asivva's mouth quirk at her suggestion.

"As you wish," Asivva said nonchalantly. "Shall I list Theo's required class scores first?"

"Please do," Jade mumbled, flushing with embarrassment.

"Alright. A perfect score is ten. Males need to average a score of seven to qualify as a potential husband," Asivva explained. "Cooking: ten."

Mmm, I love a man who can cook.

"Massage: ten. Childcare: eight." Asivva paused and glanced at Jade warily before reading the next scores. "Conversation: three. Appearance: one."

"One? I don't understand why no one except for me seems to find him attractive. I feel like I'm in *The Twilight Zone*," Jade said, throwing up her hands in exasperation.

Asivva let out a relieved breath. Quirking a brow, she asked, "What's *The Twilight Zone?*"

"A TV show where odd things happen. In one episode, a man is stuck all alone in a world full of books but he doesn't have any reading glasses. In another, a beautiful woman is called ugly because all the people around her look like pigs and she's normal." Asivva wrinkled her forehead as if she'd understood only a few of the words Jade had used. "It's hard to explain, I guess. Why do you think he got such a bad conversation score?" Jade asked, changing the subject.

"Theo isn't the most patient male, and he has always had a hard time talking with females. Conversation classes teach males to use charm and compliments while conversing with females, but Theo never felt natural speaking in that way. I'm guessing he became frustrated during his exam and forgot his lessons. I warned you that acting the part of a gentleman isn't something Theo has an easy time doing. It'll likely be frustrating for him."

As Jade listened to Asivva talk about Theo, she realized Asivva was very familiar with his mannerisms. "How do you know so much about him? Were you two together at one point?"

"Me and Theo?" Asivva asked with a surprised look on her face. "No! I've known him my whole life. He's family."

"Oh, okay, good. It would be awkward if I were getting your leftovers."

"Leftovers?" Asivva wrinkled her nose. "That's an odd expression, but I suppose it makes sense. Anyway," Asivva continued, "preferences: nine. In their preferences classes, males learn about the different types of things females prefer to have on hand. That way they can get a rough idea of what to stock their homes with in case they end up being chosen by a female. Preferences covers things like clothing fabric, jewelry, household furnishings, and beauty products. Females buy most of those things themselves when they arrive in a new house, but it's good for the males to understand what the items are, what they're used for, and why some may be better than others. Anatomy: ten."

"Anatomy? As in female anatomy?" Jade interrupted.

"Yes. If they want to please their wives, they need to know where everything is, don't they?" Asivva's tone made it clear she thought Jade's question was idiotic.

Jade had to admit, understanding the opposite sex's anatomy seemed like a brilliant idea. So many guys on Earth spent their whole lives searching for the elusive clitoris. Jade then had a disturbing thought. *What if I'm different? They are aliens! Our anatomy is probably very different. Oh my God! He probably has a tentacle or some other crazy shit instead of a dick!*

Sensing Jade's sudden unease, Asivva asked, "Is something wrong, Jade?"

"I just realized our anatomy is probably very different, and I doubt they covered humans in that anatomy class."

"Our doctors did a little research when you arrived, and they believe you're very similar to us. We'll know for sure when we go to the doctor in a few minutes."

Although still on edge, Jade felt a little better knowing the Clecanian doctors had already thought through the possibility of her anatomy being different and had ruled it out.

"Theo's last grade is for sexual proficiency, and he received a score of ten."

Jade stared at Asivva for a long time before she said, "How would they even know that unless they…" She gasped. "Did they test him by having sex with him or watching him have sex?"

"Yes. How else would they know whether he would make a suitable sexual partner? Sex education classes are a very large part of their training during the last year of school," Asivva said matter-of-factly.

"Who trains them?" Jade croaked.

"Volunteers. Older females who can no longer have children, mostly. There are some younger females who volunteer between marriages as well." Asivva rifled through Theo's folder as she added, "During the exam, the tester is blindfolded so the encounter isn't affected by the male's appearance. They try and make sure each test is judged without any bias."

"How admirable," Jade muttered with a roll of her eyes.

Clearly annoyed, Asivva said, "Would you prefer your future husband be a virgin when you marry him? Or would you prefer he be experienced and know how to please you properly?"

"I—"

"You should criticize customs only after you've experienced them," she chastised. "The males can opt out if they want, but very few do. The low female population doesn't allow males the luxury of experiencing sex organically."

Remember, alien planet. Vastly different. Jade had to remind herself not to judge, no matter how odd their customs were. "You're right. I'm sorry. I shouldn't be judging based on what we do on my planet. My world isn't exactly a stable place most of the time."

Asivva still looked annoyed but relaxed. "It may seem selfish that these classes are all centered on how to make a wife happy, but there's a strong correlation between a happy female and fertility. Females who aren't sexually satisfied by their partner and don't orgasm, for example, rarely get pregnant."

Asivva sighed and gave a small smile. "It's getting late. We need to get to the doctor. I can tell you about Theo's remaining scores later."

12

Don't let there be probes. Don't let there be probes, Jade chanted in her head as she stared up at the ceiling through a curved piece of glass.

A large portion of the exam room Jade and Asivva had entered was dominated by a bulky glass tube placed horizontally in the center of the room. Mounted on the front of the tube were thin glass screens. The doctor, a beautiful raven-haired woman, had skipped introductions and instead asked Jade to lie down on a gurney. She'd explained that Jade would be pushed into the tube and her body would then be scanned and repaired.

After both Asivva and the doctor convinced Jade she'd be safe, she agreed to enter the tube. Now that she was inside, she started berating herself. *How could you allow yourself to be locked in this glass cylinder of death?*

The doctor pressed a few things on the glass screens, and a blue light illuminated all around Jade. She stiffened, expecting to feel pain. "This device," the doctor explained, "scans your body and diagnoses any current, past, and, occasionally, future illnesses. It'll also identify any damage or deterioration. After it's done scanning you, I'll relay the findings and then get your permission to program the device to cure or fix anything that needs fixing."

After a few minutes, the scan was complete. Examining her screen, the doctor began, "First off, our database has concluded that the only items which are poisonous to you are things made from the Ripsli tree. Make sure to stay away from any fabrics, foods, or products that contain any part of that tree."

"Your husband will be notified of this. Don't worry. Products from Ripsli trees are not too common," Asivva said reassuringly.

Clearing her throat, the doctor said, "The cartilage in your right knee is slightly damaged. Also, your thyroid gland is producing less hormone than optimal. Do I have your permission to repair your knee and thyroid gland?"

Jade looked at her nervously and said, "I guess so. Will I need surgery? Will it hurt?"

"No. The machine will fix it in a matter of minutes. I'll send a small amount of gas into the tube so you don't feel any pain. You will be conscious, though."

Jade paled.

Not noticing Jade's unease, the doctor continued, "Now on to cosmetic procedures. There are many scars and other types of skin damage all over your body. I recommend repairing them all."

Before Jade could respond, the doctor said, "I don't know what the grooming customs are on your planet, but females from Tremanta usually only have hair on their head, eyebrows, and eyelashes. I can go ahead and remove all the remaining hair permanently if you want."

"You can remove the hair," Jade agreed before the doctor could speak again. "I have a question about the skin-damage thing, though. Do you consider tattoos a form of skin damage?" she asked, pointing to a small star tattoo behind her left ear.

"Yes," the doctor said, confused. "Was that done on purpose?"

"It's common on Earth."

"Well, I can program the machine to leave that area of your body alone if you're sure you want to keep it."

"I do. Can you please also program it to keep these two scars?" Jade pointed to a small scar on her knee and her arm.

The doctor grimaced but nodded.

Gee, they really don't like imperfection here.

She typed a few things onto the pad and then said, "The last treatment you should receive is the elixir. The elixir repairs your body at a cellular level. You're young, so you won't need much, but if you continue to get elixirs throughout your life, you'll age much more slowly. We estimate that our citizens will live to be about three hundred on average. Because you're the first human to receive an elixir, that number could be much higher or much lower. Time will tell." She paused. "Does all of that sound acceptable to you?"

Three hundred years? Jade was dazed. If she stayed here rather than returning to Earth, she could live for hundreds of years.

"Jade?" Asivva interrupted her thoughts.

Jade was overwhelmed and couldn't remember everything the doctor said she'd be doing but nodded anyway. *Anything to get out of this tube.*

"I'm sending the gas in now."

Red gas floated up from somewhere underneath her head, and a feeling of euphoria swept over her. As she laid there, feeling more relaxed than she had in years, her mind wandered to an image of Theo. "Mmm," Jade murmured.

Somewhere in the back of her mind, she noted her body was tingling all over. It also felt like someone was softly tapping her knee and throat. *Curiouser and curiouser,* she thought and giggled. All at once, the tingling stopped and her mind started to clear. "Did something go wrong? Why did it stop?" Jade asked, worried.

She found Asivva smiling at her through the glass. "No, the machine is done. You're all healed."

Jade couldn't remember the last time she'd felt this good. There were no aches or pains anywhere, and all vestiges of fatigue had vanished.

"Wow," was all she could think to say as Asivva guided her back toward the door. "Oh, wait!" Jade said, stopping. She turned and saw the doctor typing notes into the pad. "Is there anything different about me? My anatomy, I mean."

"A few small things are different," the doctor said absently as she continued to type.

Jade came up short. "How is that possible? We're completely different species from different galaxies. How can we be so similar?"

The doctor tilted her head thoughtfully. "It's true that you're very similar to us, but it isn't something I haven't seen before. Have you ever heard of convergent evolution?" Jade wanted to smile at the woman's excited tone. This was obviously a topic she had great interest in, and for a moment, the proper doctor was letting her nerd show.

"No," Jade said.

"Convergent evolution is a phenomenon that occurs when completely different organisms evolve with similar traits, independently. If both of our planets' landscapes were close enough, it isn't impossible we would've evolved in similar ways." The pretty doctor crossed her arms as though she'd just made her point. "To be fair, there are many races of Clecanians that you have less in common with. There are no humans with wings, correct?"

"Not that I'm aware of, but hey, I only learned that aliens exist a few days ago, so I'm not one to talk." The past week had been an eye-opening and humbling experience to say the least. When Jade thought about the vastness of the universe and how many things were happening in it that humans had no idea about, she couldn't help but feel like she had to relearn everything she thought she knew. Who was she to say paranormal creatures didn't exist on Earth?

Still curious about how reproductive anatomy might be different here, Jade asked, "Doctor, you're sure there isn't anything significantly different about my *female* anatomy?"

The woman shot her a perplexed and slightly annoyed look. "I already told you there isn't. Is there something else you need from me?"

"Um. Is there… I mean, will there be…uh…" Jade was unsure how to phrase her question in the least embarrassing way.

"She wants to know whether anything unexpected will happen during intercourse. Is her anatomy the same as ours in that way?" Asivva asked bluntly.

Jade felt heat rising on her cheeks but waited for an answer.

The doctor laughed as she returned her attention to Jade. "There are a few differences, but I believe they'll all cause sex to be more pleasurable, not less."

"Oh?" *You have my attention now, Doctor.*

"Clecanian females have one main center for pleasure located deep within our core and then a great many other nerve endings on both the inside and outside of our sex. You're different to us in that you have two pleasure centers. One is deep within like ours, but you also have a secondary, very sensitive pleasure center outside your body. I believe it's called a clitoris?"

Jade nodded absently.

"Overall, you should be much more sensitive than we are." Smiling, the doctor continued, "Whoever you marry will be very lucky. You'll be much easier to please because of this. As for the males, they are, on average, a little larger than Earth males, but you should be able to accommodate their size. Everything else is the same." She chuckled. "I think the way in which you have sex may be different, but sexual predilections aren't something I can scan for."

Thoroughly embarrassed, Jade muttered a quick "Thanks," then retreated through the door.

***

After leaving the doctor's office, Jade marveled at how advanced Clecanian science was. Asivva had explained that after the plague had hit, Clecanians had made medical research a priority. Today, Clecanian medical technology was superior to many others in a lot of ways but hadn't yet advanced enough to save their people.

"We've made some incredible discoveries out of necessity, but we still haven't discovered why we're not always fertile and why we continue to have a greater number of male babies than female," Asivva said with a forced smile.

"How did that doctor know so much about my anatomy?" Jade asked, wondering how an alien doctor could possibly know what a clitoris was called.

Asivva shrugged. "The same records that contained your language program had information about your anatomy as well. One or more species that are members of The Intergalactic Alliance must've come in contact with humans at some point and documented their findings."

Jade felt a chill run through her as she thought of how the human might've been observed in order to learn about their anatomy.

Seeing Jade's distress, Asivva added, "It wouldn't have been against their will. For example, we've already updated the records on humankind based on what we learned from speaking with you, along with your medical scans."

This made Jade feel a bit better, but she knew there'd be no way for Asivva to know for certain that the human had given their consent to be studied.

"I haven't known you very long, but I'm surprised to learn you are so uncomfortable talking about sex," teased Asivva on their way back to her room.

Jade just grumbled in response. Jade wasn't a shy woman when it came to sex. On Earth she'd even be considered very free with her sexuality. Jade had realized in college that sex didn't always have to be tied to feelings. As long as both parties were consenting and of age, there was no wrong way or time to have sex.

Talking about sex on this planet made her uncomfortable, though. If she talked openly about sex, she was afraid the Clecanians would assume she was comfortable with interspecies sex. While her lady parts liked the look of these men a lot, her brain hadn't given her the all-clear to jump on board the alien-sex train just yet.

"So, what's next?" Jade asked, trying to change the subject.

Asivva smirked and then said, "Bath. We also need to run a scan to see what your scent and food tastes are."

"Another scan? What does this one do?" Jade sighed, her mental exhaustion returning. She'd only been on this planet for a few days, but it seemed like weeks. Everything she learned was new and terrifying and exciting, but her brain was too overwhelmed to take in any more new experiences.

"Not every bride has to do it, but I think it's especially important for you to do it." They reached the room, and Asivva continued to talk while retrieving something bulky from the far wall.

Three kind-looking women were now milling around the room, tidying and gathering objects from small trunks.

Asivva propped the clunky object on her hip and gestured to the women. "This is Rena, Cefy, and Shey. They'll be helping you get ready after your bath. They haven't updated their translators yet, so they won't be able to speak with you."

The women nodded politely at Jade before returning to their work.

Asivva lifted the large, round metal object for Jade to see. It resembled an early space helmet. "You put this on and then put this mouth piece in." Asivva showed her something similar to an overlarge mouth guard. "Then one by one, images will appear on a screen inside. As each image is displayed, the part of the helmet that's touching your head will scan your brain activity to see how you respond to that image, and the mouth piece will detect whether your salivary glands react or not. After you've viewed all of the pictures, the front of the scanner will spray different smells into the air to see how you react to those. It takes all the information it collected and supplies you with a list of foods, drinks, and scents you'll probably prefer. The list goes into your file and is supposed to be given to your husband so he knows what your preferences are.

"I think the list will be very helpful to you, as well as your husband, though. Not every suggestion will end up being correct, but since you're not from here, it'll be very hard for you to know what you like and don't like. This helps you figure that out."

"Clever," Jade admitted.

"Why don't you go bathe? When you're done, you can get scanned while you get your nails shaped."

"Bathe. In front of all of you?" Jade said, eyeing the three women, who were now sitting on the low couch.

"Is there a problem?"

"Most people on Earth aren't that comfortable being naked in front of others."

"Ugh! Shy about this too?" Asivva said, shooing Jade toward the pool. "We don't have time to waste being timid. Get in."

Jade stood by the pool but didn't move to take her clothes off. Asivva let out an annoyed huff and walked over to Jade, clearly intending on removing her clothes herself.

"Okay, okay!" Jade cried. "Calm down. I'm going."

She removed her clothing and ducked into the sunken tub. Once Jade was in the water, Asivva sauntered toward the other women and started talking. Jade turned her back on the women and began allowing the warm water to relax her.

Looking down at her arms, Jade noticed they were smooth and her skin was buttery soft. All of the small wrinkles from her hands were gone as well. *These people really know what they're doing.* Glancing over her shoulder to make sure the women weren't watching her, Jade rose out of the water a few inches to inspect her body.

Women would kill for a boob lift like this! Her breasts, which were a full B cup, had started to sag slightly over the past few years. Now it looked like all the elasticity they'd lost had come back. Jade shook her head, amazed as she ran her hands over her skin. *I have the skin of a baby and the boobs of a college freshman. I may have to figure out how to steal that magic tube before I leave.*

"Yes! They're very nice breasts!" Asivva called from the couch. Jade immediately ducked under the water and shot her an angry look. Asivva laughed and said, "Can you please finish washing them so we can do your scan?"

"You haven't given me any soap to wash myself with," Jade said, annoyed at her lack of privacy.

"The water contains everything you need. It's been mixed with our cleansing foam as well as hydrating oils. Just submerge any part of you that you wish to be cleaned."

Jade finished bathing and then quickly wrapped herself in a towel Asivva held out to her. Suddenly the parts of her body that touched the towel felt dry, she peeked under the fabric and saw the skin there was, in fact, dry.

Jade realized this towel must be one of those archaic but modernized items still used here. As she ran the soft fabric over her wet skin and hair, the towel warmed and seemed to suck the moisture from the surface of her body. In a matter of minutes, she was completely dry, as was the alien towel.

Not addressing anyone in particular, Jade examined the fibers of the towel closely and said, "How does this work? It feels dry."

"It was evaporated within the cloth." Asivva handed her a loose-flowing dress and motioned for her to sit on the couch.

"That's really cool," Jade said, dutifully setting the towel aside and donning the soft dress as she sat down.

"After we get ready, you'll go to the Testing, and then whoever you choose will be notified. You'll be taken to the entry hall, where he'll see you for the first time."

"Then I just...leave with him?" The momentary wonder she'd felt when examining the towel turned to apprehension. She was just starting to become comfortable in this new environment with these people. The thought that she'd have to start adjusting all over again made anxiety spear through her.

"What? The ceremony isn't long enough? You want to do more?" Asivva asked with fake exasperation in her voice.

The ceremony had taken almost an entire day already. She did not want or need to do more of this, but the time now seemed to be moving much more quickly. Soon she'd be alone with a stranger. A handsome, deadly-looking stranger.

Instead of voicing her concerns, Jade decided that being preoccupied was the best course of action. "What happens in the Testing? Do we watch them do husband-esque things?"

"Not quite." Asivva chuckled ominously.

13

Jade trudged down the hallway. She'd never been so uncomfortable in her whole life. Asivva had explained "testing."

Moans emanated from the many rooms along the hallway. Products of the men being "tested." Apparently at this point in the ceremony, the women were allowed to do whatever they wanted with and or to the male they'd chosen.

Jade was lost for words. Even after Asivva had assured her she didn't have to do anything if she didn't want to.

Shyness was not something Jade often felt. Picking a man by leering at him through glass made him seem like an abstract idea. Standing in front of said man and interacting with him in such an intimate way made him very, very real. She wasn't ready for real.

Luckily, if you could call anything that had happened to her thus far "lucky," the men were supposed to wear blindfolds. At least they wouldn't see her looking mortified. Yet.

A very loud female cry of pleasure came from the room next to her, making her jump.

"Nervous, are we?" said Zikas from behind her.

He had returned a short while ago to escort her to the Testing. He'd been very irritable, though he'd tried to hide it with a contrived smile. Whatever Zikas had been out doing hadn't gone as smoothly as he would've liked.

This only added to Jade's anxiety.

Zikas moved toward the door that the scream had come from and said, "We'll be visiting Fejo first."

Feeling more than a little manic, Jade let out a short, high-pitched laugh. "He seems preoccupied."

"He was chosen by two other females. We can wait until they leave, or you can go in and watch while you wait."

"I am not comfortable watching him get it on with other women." Especially not when she could hear what she'd be competing with. "Next!"

"I'm not sure I understood all of that, but I believe you're saying you'd like me to eliminate him?"

"Yes. Wait." She faltered; this might not have been an isolated problem. "Did Theo have any other offers?"

Zikas answered loudly to drown out the sound of ecstasy coming from Fejo's room. "No."

"Then he's the winner!" Jade said, giving Zikas an awkward thumbs-up, which he eyed.

"Okay!" he said grinning and grabbing her thumb in his palm and shaking it. "Let's go to his room." He led Jade to a door at the end of the hall. "I'll be out here if you need anything. Just come out when you're done."

"You're not coming in?"

Perplexed, Zikas gradually asked, "Do you want me to come in?"

It dawned on her that if he did, he'd be watching whatever she did with this guy. Awkward. "Oh. Uh, no. That *would* be weird."

A small, relieved breath escaped Zikas. He nodded and moved to a chair on the far wall.

Facing the door, Jade rocked back and forth on the balls of her feet.

"Do you need assistance?" he asked, leaning forward in his seat.

"No. I'm fine!" she snapped. With an apologetic glance she added, "Nervous."

"Okay. Just remember, he hasn't updated his translator yet. If he doesn't respond to you, that's why."

She lifted her hand to the door, nodding absently. The handle was slick under her sweaty palm. Taking a calming breath, she opened it.

About ten feet away, sitting on a couch, was a blindfolded Theo. His head snapped in her direction as she closed the door.

Jade didn't know how long she stood motionless at the entrance, staring at him. Two minutes? Two hours? Maybe if she didn't move or breathe, he'd think she'd disappeared. She'd no sooner had this thought than he began to move.

With a scowl on his face, he rose from the couch to his full height. His towering, massive frame and dark energy made the large room feel cramped. All she could do was stare at him. Then, to Jade's astonishment, he started to remove his clothing.

A quick intake of breath was all Jade could manage as she surveyed his naked chest. She started walking toward him, hypnotized. Nearing, she saw that what she'd assumed to be a blindfold instead resembled hard black tar. There was no way he could see through that.

Theo angled his head in her direction. His tightly corded muscles tensed, and he balled his fists. Jade began her retreat when she saw his knuckles turn white. Sick curiosity made her freeze when he bent down to remove his remaining clothing.

Squaring his shoulders and raising his chin in what looked like defiance, he positioned his body so he was facing her. Jade's eyes widened as she caught a glimpse of his shaft. He was big all over.

He cleared his throat, and Jade's face heated. Logically she knew he couldn't see her staring, and yet she couldn't shake the feeling that he could sense her movements.

He hadn't lunged at her or made any aggressive moves toward her as of yet, so she inched closer to him, wanting to see more. His dark black markings ran around his shoulders and down his pecs. They continued to travel across his abs and lower until they stopped just above his shaft. Blushing, she quickly glanced away.

Only a foot separated them now. His head had followed her movements as she'd closed in and now was tipped down at her. His imposing height put her head in line with his chest. As close as she was, she could see that he had faint scars all over his body. *Are these the famous scars Zikas said women hated?*

One near his chest looked particularly bad. She winced as she pictured what kind of weapon must've done that sort of damage.

Without realizing what she was doing, she lifted her hand to touch the scar.

A low growl was the only warning she had before his hand shot out at lightning speed and gripped her wrist, now an inch from his scar.

The blood drained from Jade's face, and she was too frozen with fear to speak.

His large hand encircled her wrist firmly but not painfully. Gaining her wits, Jade attempted to tug her hand away. It was no use.

Tightening his grip, he told her without words that she wasn't going anywhere. Slowly, he placed his other hand on the small of her back and then leaned toward her face. She jerked away, but the hand on her back ensured she couldn't move far.

As his lips neared hers, he paused. Dipping his head to the column of her neck, he inhaled deeply and exhaled with a groan. His hot breath on her sensitive flesh made her shiver.

He pressed her closer to him, and she felt his erection prodding her stomach. Then he gave the sensitive spot on her neck a slow, hot lick, making her toes curl. Heat flooded her, and she whimpered.

His whole body tensed at the sound. He released her and stepped back abruptly, looking...ashamed? Jade wobbled on her feet as she watched his chest rise and fall rapidly. A muscle in his jaw ticked, and he turned his back to her.

Jade backed toward the exit, feeling dazed as she left the room.

Zikas hurried towards her, a worried expression on his face. "Are you okay? What happened?"

Not knowing what else to say she explained, "He...um...he smelled me." *And it was the most erotic thing I've ever experienced.* The memory of his tongue on her made her core clench.

"Smelled you?" Zikas said blankly.

14

After he heard the door close, Theo angrily reached for his clothing. How could he lose control like that? When he'd grabbed her, he'd been angry. He'd merely meant to stop her from touching him, but then he'd gotten a whiff of her scent. He'd grown dizzy and had felt the desire to be closer to her so strongly that all reason had left him.

Her smell had been intoxicating, to say nothing of her body. Soft skin and soft curves. He hadn't felt much of her body and he couldn't be sure what she looked like, but if the curve of her back was any indication… The thought had him groaning.

Pure lust had surged through him when he'd tasted her. His shaft ached just thinking about it.

The scent of her fear had been intoxicating as well. Usually fear smelled sharp and sour, but hers? Delicious. Sanity had returned to him when she'd whimpered in fright.

He wrenched his pants on roughly, forgetting his hard erection. Running his hands through his hair, he cursed himself for scaring her.

Fully dressed now, he sat on the couch, head in his hands, and attempted to calm himself down. Through his inner turmoil, he heard the door open, and he sniffed the air. "Hello, Zikas."

"Ready to get that blindfold off?"

Theo sat up and nodded solemnly.

Warmth spread over his eyes, and he felt the covering soften. Theo tried to focus his vision when Zikas peeled the material from his eyes.

"What happened?" Zikas asked with knitted brows.

Theo heated with embarrassment and paced the room. "Nothing. I lost control for a moment. That's all."

Zikas said nothing but watched Theo pacing.

His silence only enraged Theo, however. "Can I leave now? I've fulfilled my obligation."

Nodding, Zikas agreed. "You may." Theo had crossed the entirety of the room before the man murmured, "You'll need to get your wife first, though."

Impossible.

"What did you say?" Theo asked over his shoulder.

"She chose you to be her husband." The grin on Zikas' face was radiant.

"No."

"No?"

"No. There's something wrong." Theo faced Zikas. Taking into account all he knew, he concluded there was no way in hell any sane female would've chosen him. Not after he'd grabbed her like that. Something else had to be going on. "She must want something."

A moment ago, Theo had felt ashamed and angry, his male pride hurt from her fearful rejection. Now, his devious mercenary mind took over. There was no scenario he could think of that didn't include this female trying to get something out of him.

Most likely she'd been sent as a spy. *Look through my records, no doubt, and gain valuable information about my clients.*

Could she be some kind of assassin? Sent by one of the many disgruntled would-be clients?

He'd turned down a handful of dangerous people recently. People who didn't like to hear no.

It was a smart plan, he had to say. It was well known that any attempt to rob or kill Theo was met with violent retaliation. A female, though? A curvy female who'd mysteriously agreed to be his wife. His enemies might have thought he'd be too overjoyed at having a willing female that he wouldn't sense their scheme until it was too late.

Theo held up a hand when Zikas began to speak again. Pacing the room once more, he devised a plan. If he were to deny this female, he'd likely be arrested. Any real or perceived slight to a female was met with punishment, no doubt about that. If, however, he brought her home as his wife, he could keep an eye on her and discover what her plan was and who'd sent her.

A ruthless grin spread across his face as he wondered how far she was willing to take this act. He might be able to have some fun with her before he inevitably rid himself of her. Making up his mind, he turned to Zikas and said, "Very well. Take me to her."

Another smile spread over Zikas' face. It looked like he was relieved by Theo's change of heart. *Too bad he has no idea what my real motives are.*

***

Waiting for his new bride, whom he'd learned was named Jade, Theo considered his situation. She wasn't Clecanian, so it was unlikely someone here had hired her. *If she's very beautiful then she must be getting paid very well, and I can narrow down the suspects to the wealthier individuals I know.*

She wasn't a very good actress. He remembered the frightened sound that had come out of her when he'd touched her. A good spy would be willing to use sex as a tool. If she couldn't fake it for five minutes, how did she expect to get through a whole three months?

Light footsteps sounded from down the hall. *Okay, let's see what we're dealing with...* When she came into view, his mind blanked. All he could do was gaze at her, enraptured.

Fire-red hair curled gently around her face and fell over her shoulders. A thin, flowing emerald-green gown accentuated her ample curves and complemented her green eyes. Theo had never seen a more beautiful creature in his whole life.

He barely stifled a moan when she caught his eye. When her face pinkened and she looked away, as though shy, he remembered what he suspected she was. An actress. He needed to control his reactions around her. *Stay alert!*

Unable to help himself, he watched her as she gave Zikas a hug and said goodbye. A sudden urge to pummel his old friend came over him when he saw Zikas touch her.

He crossed to her and offered his arm so he could lead her away. His scowl deepened when she hesitated. Seeing the look on his face must have added to her concern, for her eyes widened and she walked toward the door ahead of him.

The anger he felt at her refusal to touch him faded when he caught a glimpse of her pert ass as she sauntered away. Feeling himself growing hard again, he concluded this would be much more difficult than he'd thought.

15

When you're young, you're told that staring is impolite. Most, if not all, people will grow uncomfortable if stared at for too long. Theo had evidently never learned this. For the last twenty minutes, he'd stared at her with unblinking intensity.

His gaze had roamed over her body hungrily. The way he looked into her eyes now, like he wanted to bore a hole in her mind, was very unnerving. She'd much rather he gawked at her breasts.

It didn't help that he was sitting opposite her.

The machine they were seated in was one of the round silver balls she'd chased a few days ago.

After leaving the ceremony building, she'd seen the vehicle hovering nearby. As she'd drawn close, a curved panel had opened onto the ground, creating a ramp and revealing a small but comfortable seating area. Two plush couches faced each other, and in between them was a metal table.

Choosing Theo

When they'd both been seated, Theo had started typing something on the top of the table. Leaning forward, Jade had noticed a small screen that was almost imperceptible against the metal. Without any warning, the ramp lifted, sealing them in, and the pod had started to move. The ride was so smooth that if Jade hadn't felt the initial soft jerk, she wouldn't have known they were moving at all.

Jade's initial curiosity and joy at experiencing something so new was tempered when she noticed Theo's attention was on her. It was stupid for her to complain about a gorgeous man staring at her, but she couldn't figure out what his look meant. It was as though he couldn't decide whether he wanted to fuck her or kill her.

Once again, she tried to look away, but there was nothing to focus on. For all of its pros, this vehicle's one big con was that it had no windows.

Spotting movement out of the corner of her eye, she turned to see Theo pulling something cylindrical from a compartment under his seat.

Never taking his eyes off her, he slowly unscrewed the top of the cylinder then held it to his mouth and took a swig. Then another.

No normal drink comes in a container like that. It has to be alcohol.

Holding out her hand, she glanced at the container and then back to Theo. A silent request. Confusion showed on his face, but after a moment he handed the cylinder to her.

A quick sniff confirmed it was indeed alcohol. Strong stuff too. Jade took a small swig and waited for the burn. The drink was smooth, however, and it slid down her throat easily. She took another long drink and then handed the container back to a stunned-looking Theo.

"Do women not drink here?" she questioned.

His eyebrows drew together, and she remembered he couldn't understand her yet.

In spite of her fearfulness of the man across from her, she started to relax. "That's strong stuff," she said, motioning at the container. "Works fast."

Theo put the cap back on and resumed his unblinking glower.

Liquid courage and the fact that he couldn't understand anything she said emboldened her. "Can you please stop staring?"

His chin lifted, but he continued to frown.

"It's making me nervous. Aren't the men here supposed to be happy about having a wife? Shouldn't you at least stare with a smile on your face?"

Crossing his arms over his massive chest, he leaned back in the seat, looking extremely frustrated.

"Ah. Upset because you can't understand me?" she said, pointing an accusing finger at him. "Well, I have a lot more to be upset about than you."

Jade started picking at her nails. A nervous habit. "Zikas really oversold this marriage thing, huh?" She continued without waiting for him to answer "I bet that when you finally get your translator updated, you still won't talk."

Yep. She was definitely buzzed now.

Choosing Theo

"You're more the strong, silent type, right?" Eyeing his muscled arms, she sighed. "Mmm. Very strong." She giggled at that.

Evidently, her tone and the fixed direction of her eyes had given him enough information to guess the meaning of her words because his stare became heated. He leaned toward her and flexed his hands, as though wanting to touch her.

Jade shifted in her seat nervously until the vehicle door slid open, telling her the pod had arrived at their destination. Theo glanced outside, and she took the distraction to sidle by him and jump out of the car. A dense forest came into view as she rushed out of the vehicle.

The air outside was cold and crisp with a slight tang. Jade inhaled deeply, smiling when the wind rustled her hair. She imagined the air on a Scottish island might smell like this.

A warm hand on the small of her back sent a jolt through her body, reminding her of their earlier exchange during the Testing. When she turned to face him, she noticed the vehicle had silently floated away. In its place stood a magnificent house. The word *house* didn't quite fit, however.

The large building was situated in a clearing within the thick forest. Imposing trees with the same large round leaves she'd seen on her first night towered all around her. Although the woods were beautiful, they were eerily impenetrable. There would be nowhere to run even if she somehow got an opportunity to do so.

The walls of the gently curving building looked as if they were made out of translucent glass. The warm orange of the setting sun, which was now behind them, illuminated the shining exterior. Rather than reflecting off the building as she'd expected, the light seemed to be trapped within its walls, giving Jade the impression that she was staring at a giant luminescent animal.

Beautiful flowering plants, whose petals were unnaturally larger than the leaves, grew all along the base of the glowing building, seeming to bathe in the sunlight.

Feeling Theo's eyes on her, she peered up at him and saw he was studying her reactions. Did he want her to like his home? Gesturing toward the house, she said, "Beautiful."

His shoulders relaxed, and he started walking away from her toward an enormous wooden door tucked between two rows of crawling, flowering vines. Theo's hand paused a moment on the large handle, and she heard a heavy bolt sliding out of place.

Panic crept through the awe she felt after admiring the building. The door could only be unlocked by him? Did that mean she'd be trapped inside?

Theo glanced over his shoulder at her and lifted his open palm. Jade looked pointedly from his palm, then back to his eyes and gave an exaggerated shrug. "I don't know what you want."

His jaw clenched. Slowly he reached toward her and let his hand hover above her own. He held her gaze and waited.

She chuckled, still feeling a little buzzed. "Well, since you asked so nicely."

She lifted her hand and placed it in his. Warmth spread through her at the small contact.

Gently he circled her wrist with his large palm and tugged her forward until she stood in front of him facing the heavy wooden door. With one large hand still holding her wrist, he brought his other arm around the side of her face to touch something on the center of the door. She eyed his large bicep appreciatively.

He was so close to her back that she could feel his heat radiating off him and enveloping her in warmth. Her breathing hitched when she felt his breath brush against her hair.

Snap out of it Jade! she chided herself. *He's just standing behind you. No reason to get worked up.*

She turned her head to peer at him, craning her neck since he towered over her. He glanced down at her briefly then guided her hand to lie flat against the center of the door.

A light pressure against her palm startled her, causing her to jump back against his hard chest.

Theo groaned softly behind her and then pressed her hand more firmly to the door.

She felt the soft pressure run over her palm once more and fought the urge to pull her hand back.

A small ding chimed from somewhere near the handle of the door, and Theo guided her hand to wrap around the curving metal of the handle. A second ding sounded just before she heard the noise of a heavy bolt moving into place.

Theo released her hand and stepped away from her.

A light breeze chilled her now-exposed back, and she felt sorry for the loss of the warmth he provided.

He motioned for her to touch the door handle once again. When she did, the handle recognized her touch and unlocked.

Relief washed over her. *He gave me access to the door!*

When Jade just held the handle and beamed at Theo, he seemed to grow uncomfortable, glancing all around her until finally he reached past her and pushed the heavy door inward.

"Oh, right. Sorry," Jade said sheepishly, feeling like an idiot for not attempting to open the door.

As Theo ushered her into the dimly lit interior, she studied the thickness of the door, and a sense of foreboding crept over her. She might have been able to unlock it, but she doubted whether she'd be able to move it.

Initially, she thought the door had been crafted from what she'd assumed was wood. Looking at a cross section of it, however, she could see that the wood-like material was just a veneer. The middle of the door was dark gray metal. Rather than one bolt near the handle, many latches and bolts ran the length of the door and frame. Once locked, it would be impenetrable.

It unlocks for me. It unlocks for me, she chanted, trying to remind herself she wouldn't be locked inside.

As they moved farther into the house, soft lighting began to illuminate the interior. Jade's steps faltered when the room before her came into view. The inside of his home was as glorious as the outside had been.

The large open room in front of her contained a sunken living room with a large roaring fireplace, an open kitchen, and a small dining area. What was most breathtaking, however, was the fact that the walls and ceiling formed a large glass dome, providing sweeping views of the scenery and sky. The front exterior of the building must've been the only side you couldn't see through.

The house overlooked a crescent-shaped beach comprised of glittering black sand. The rising moons hung gently over the sparkling water.

Glowing glass bubbles of various sizes floated softly around the inside of the home, providing warm lighting. Some congregated around large potted plants, and Jade wondered whether the lights were able to drift wherever they were needed. Glancing above her, she found that a few glass bubbles were, in fact, hovering a few feet above them, providing light.

Theo urged her forward with a soft hand on her back. Jade craned her neck to take in as much as she could while allowing herself to be guided through the many rooms of the house.

As he led her through one exceptional room after another, she had to admit that Theo had good taste. They'd been walking through his home for a while now, and she had yet to see something she didn't like. Theo pointed to a door at the end of the hall and gestured to himself.

"That's your room." She nodded. She wondered why he didn't want her to see the interior. Was he messy? The state of the rest of the house made her think not.

Pointing to a door across from his own, he gestured to her.

Her door and his couldn't have been more than ten feet apart. "So we're neighbors," she said awkwardly, motioning between their two rooms.

Theo glanced in the direction of his door before leaning past her and opening her door. This room, like all the others, was beautiful.

The glass dome that extended into this side of the house gave her a full view of the dark forest beyond. A dozen feet or so of land had been cleared between the house and the tree line of the forest, allowing a large beam of fading sunlight to highlight the mossy ground.

Jade had to stop herself from mentally planning the perfect garden to go in that sunny spot. *I won't be staying for very long.*

A comfortable-looking bed large enough to fit five of her was situated across from another glowing fireplace. Sighing, she thought of lying in the plush bed and sleeping. The loveliness of Theo's home had temporarily distracted her from her exhaustion as well as her hunger. To punctuate her thought, her stomach gave a loud rumble.

He was already glancing at her stomach when she turned to ask, "Do you have any food?" She clutched at her stomach and then pointed at her mouth, attempting to mime her needs.

He nodded and waved her ahead of him toward the door but halted when she didn't move.

When Jade had seen herself in the mirror earlier after donning the green dress, she'd had to admit, she was hot.

Back on Earth she was considered overweight, and although she was pretty, men didn't notice her often enough for her to think of herself as hot.

Seeing Theo's expression when he'd glimpsed her for the first time, she'd realized he definitely thought she was hot. If the bulge in his pants was any indicator of attraction toward her, then he must've thought she was downright gorgeous.

"The sad truth about looking this good is that it can be uncomfortable," she said, gesturing to her dress. "Clecanians have the most advanced medical technology in the universe, but pretty shoes hurt on every planet, big guy."

Jade wanted to change and be comfortable. Something about Theo's house made her feel like she could find a soft place somewhere by a fire, cuddle up with a blanket, and sleep.

How to make him understand what I want? Noticing a dresser along the wall, she crossed to it and pulled a drawer open. As she'd assumed, the drawer was empty. She motioned to the empty drawer and then her dress. Plucking at the fabric, she theatrically mimed being uncomfortable.

His dark glare told her he was offended by what she did. Maybe he thought she was admonishing him for not providing her with clothing. Slowly she approached him and reached out to tug the bottom of his soft shirt. She then pointed to herself.

Wrenching the shirt out of her hand, he turned on his heel and left the room. "Great!" she said, throwing her hands in the air. "I've pissed him off again."

Not knowing what else to do, she started exploring her room more fully. A door stood on either side of the fireplace. An empty walk in closet was located behind one. Behind the other, she found a small but elegant bathroom containing a tall, sleek bowl she gathered was a toilet, as well as a large rounded corner. Hundreds of small holes lined the ceiling and walls of the alcove, and she guessed it was a high-end cleansing area.

Jade groaned, wondering if her bath this afternoon would be the last she'd have for a while. Even a lukewarm shower sounded better than the unsatisfying dissolving foam she'd grown used to.

Asivva had been right about the disappointments of some technological advances. The foam was marvelous and could be used for everything from cleaning dirt off your body to cleaning your mouth and teeth. Zikas had looked at her strangely when she'd asked for a toothbrush her first night. But foam could never compare to the luxury of slipping into hot water.

By the time she'd finished her business in the bathroom and used a tall pillar with a spout to foam-wash her hands, Theo had returned. He was standing in her room, holding some clothing. She took the clothes from his outstretched hand and waited for him to leave the room. When he didn't move, she shooed him with her hands.

He tilted his head at the gesture but eventually did leave with a scowl still securely placed on his face.

She closed the door behind him and attempted to unfasten the tight laces lining the back of her dress. By the time she'd detangled herself from the dress, she was sweating.

Theo had left her a dark-red silky shirt and soft black pants. The shirt fell to her mid-thigh and the neckline hung so loosely that she had to remind herself not to bend over for any reason or she'd be in danger of flashing her bare breasts.

The underwear she'd been provided was made out of an oddly thick fabric, and although she was grateful for the coverage, she wondered why women here only wore underwear but no bra.

Jade did everything she could think of to prevent the soft pants from falling off of her body, but no matter how many times she rolled them, they kept sliding down her legs.

Maybe he has a belt I can borrow. Poking her head out of the door, she glanced around, hoping to ask him for something to hold the pants up. He was nowhere in sight.

A delicious smell greeted her, and her stomach rumbled more insistently. "Well, he is my husband. I guess he can see my legs."

She padded down the hall, toward the kitchen. She saw Theo hunched away from her over the corner of a polished purple stone island she hadn't noticed before. As she drew closer, he straightened and picked up a thick glass filled with amber liquid. When she was within arm's reach, she stopped. He downed the glass, then turned to face her.

His eyes widened when he saw her exposed legs. The glass he was holding shattered.

Shards fell all around her bare feet. Without moving from his spot, Theo threw his thick arm around Jade's waist and lifted her until she was crushed against his chest. He spun on the spot and deposited her onto the island. Jade's hands shot forward, trying to pull her shirt down over her thighs.

Why did he just do that? For a moment she thought his motives in picking her up had been more passionate in nature.

Now, as she watched him examine her feet, she felt he was merely trying to make sure she didn't get hurt by the glass. A small part of her had been thrilled by his sudden show of attraction, but now as she watched him carefully lift and turn her feet in his big hand, a warm, fuzzy feeling overwhelmed her.

He might look like a hulking angry tattoo enthusiast most of the time, but he was showing a caring side she hadn't expected.

Why had he broken the glass in the first place? Was he angry at seeing her in his shirt? Unlikely, since he'd tried to protect her from the shards almost as soon as they'd fallen. It may be that he was too strong for his own good. For all she knew, he could go through hundreds of glasses a month.

Seeming satisfied that her feet weren't hurt, he dug in his back pocket for a slim black rectangle. Silently, he pressed a few silver buttons and then put it back in his pocket.

A low humming sounded from behind her. Peering over her shoulder, she saw a small vacuum-like appliance had appeared out of nowhere and was working its way toward them.

"That's really handy. You know, I..." Jade trailed off as she twisted back toward Theo and found his eyes riveted to her legs.

He was very close to her now. A balled fist rested on the counter on either side of her. Sitting at this height, with him bent as he was, put her nearly at eye level with him.

Jade cleared her throat. Theo lifted his eyes to hers slowly, unapologetically. He tried to scrub his hand over his face and winced. Tracks of red blood ran down his wrist from his palm.

Jade gasped as she reached for his hand to examine it. Jagged shards of glass jutted out of his palm. Blood had pooled on the counter where he'd rested his fist.

"Why didn't you tend to this? It must hurt like hell," she said, picking a small piece of glass out of his finger and dropping it on the ground for the small machine to clean up.

Theo watched while she attempted to remove the glass from his hand without causing too much pain. She winced in sympathy as she pulled a deeply embedded shard from his palm.

Theo didn't wince or flinch once. In fact, she thought he looked...calm. His eyes had lowered to half mast, his shoulders relaxed, and his breathing was slow and even.

She shot him a puzzled look. "Do you enjoy pain or something? Are you a masochist?" When he didn't answer, she continued, "Because I do not. I'd be crying like a baby if I were you.

Victoria Aveline

"Why did you break that glass, huh? Don't know your own strength?" Knowing he couldn't understand her, Jade had started speaking more to herself than him.

"How did I get myself into this?" she said absently. "One day I'm at home watching movies, and the next I'm sitting, half-naked, on a countertop within inches of the sexiest man I've ever seen."

The last piece of glass was out, so Jade grabbed a cloth from nearby and started wiping away the blood. "I don't understand why everyone is so scared of you," she babbled. "I mean, sure, you glare at everyone like you'd like to rip their heads off, but you've been looking at me like that for hours now and you haven't done anything cruel."

Jade set the towel away and examined one of the black marks curving around his wrist. "Those markings..." She sighed, tracing the mark with her finger. "I'd like to lick every one of them," she said with a wicked smile.

Theo leaned in close and said in a low, rumbling voice, "Is that so?"

16

Jade's eyes widened in shock, and color flooded her cheeks. "W-what— Y-you—"

"I'm curious to know what a 'ma-so-kist' is. That word didn't translate."

"You can understand me?" she squeaked.

"I updated my translator while you were changing." Theo eyed her long, pale legs again.

The whole ride to his house had been torturous. Her scent had overwhelmed his senses in the small space. In order to keep himself from pouncing on her and burying himself deep within her soft body, he'd had to concentrate on his anger.

She had to be a spy. Sent to him for some nefarious reason. He wasn't going to let this female get the best of him. But then…she'd given him a heated look.

He hadn't understood anything she'd said, and yet she'd kept talking, taunting him. Her voice had become sultry when she'd stared at him. If the cruiser hadn't arrived at his home and if she hadn't dashed out of the cab so quickly…Well he wasn't sure what he would've done.

He vowed that as soon as he had a moment alone, he'd update his translator, without her knowledge, and learn everything he could from her.

Theo didn't enjoy failing, and yet he'd failed himself. Not even ten minutes after updating his translator had he revealed himself. He'd found it odd when she'd requested his clothing, but hadn't seen the harm in placating her.

Glancing down at his bloodied hand, he noted he needed to remember not to underestimate her again. The minute she'd walked out wearing his shirt, his mind had reeled. Her intoxicating scent had mixed with his own, made him wonder if she would smell that way after a good fucking.

When he'd seen her bare legs and thought about how easy it would be to slip his hand under his loose shirt, he'd completely lost it and shattered his glass.

Whoever had hired her had chosen well. Her mannerisms and reactions looked genuine.

"Why didn't you speak before?" she snapped, regaining her composure.

"You did enough talking for the both of us," he lied. "And I was intrigued by what you were saying." He grabbed her backside and scooted her forward on the counter so quickly that her legs were forced apart. Swiftly, he positioned himself between them.

She sputtered and tried to move away. He pulled her closer, grinding his hips against her. He was sad to say that she wasn't completely nude under his shirt.

"What's the matter, pet?" he crooned in her ear. "Isn't this what you wanted?"

Her voiced faltered when she said, "I, uh, didn't say I... Um, no, I don't."

His shaft was aching now as he rubbed against her more fervently. A divine smell was coming from her, but he couldn't identify the cause. Was this the smell of her fear again?

She squirmed harder, trying to get away. He shot her a wicked grin. "If you wiggle any harder, I'm going to come right here."

She froze at that. "You can't do this. Not if I say no."

He told himself he was continuing to hold her in order to rattle her and hear her confession of guilt. He didn't want to admit this weakness to himself but, in truth, moving away from her after feeling her this way wasn't something he felt entirely sure he *could* do.

"A minute ago, you were wishing you could lick my scars," he said, scowling at her. "What's changed?"

"Your scars? You mean your tattoos?" Again, she tried to pull away, and this time he allowed it. "I didn't know you could understand me!" she squeaked. She hopped off the counter and moved away from him. "I was just blabbering. I do that when I'm nervous."

"I think," he began as he stalked toward her, "that you knew I could understand you and wanted me to think you were attracted to me."

"What? Why would I do that?" Jade continued to back away.

"Part of whatever game you're playing, I'm sure." Rage boiled in him, knowing that this persona she'd donned worked on him like a charm. "Who sent you?" he barked, making her jump. A bittersweet scent radiated from her, confusing him further. Was *this* what her fear smelled like?

"Sent me?" she asked, reaching her hand in front of her protectively.

"What are you trying to do here? Kill me? Steal something from me?"

Jade was backing herself into a corner without realizing it. "No one sent me. I was abducted from my planet, you psycho!"

"Lie!" he roared as he lunged at her.

She tried to sidestep him, but he boxed her in. She attempted to scratch his face with those little nails, but he easily caught her hands and placed them above her head. Holding her wrists steady with one palm, he pressed her into the wall.

"Whoever sent you must be stupid, and you along with them." She glared at him as he spoke. "I'd never, for one instant, believe you just happened to pick me because you thought I was *sexy*." He said the word with a snarl.

She let out an exasperated breath, her eyes growing glassy. Was she going to cry? His gut clenched, and he had to squash the urge to release her and console her. "Well, I did! I regret my decision now. I should've trusted the other women. They all looked terrified of you, and now I know why!"

"Just tell me who you're working for, and I'll let you go."

"No one sent me!" Her voice broke, and she wrenched her wrists downward forcefully. If she didn't stop, she'd hurt herself.

Theo released a frustrated bellow, then threw Jade over his shoulder and bounded down the hall to her room. Once inside, he flung her on the bed.

She scrambled away.

In a tone dripping with venom, he said, "Fine. I'll play your game. Treat you like a wife. We'll see how long you last." He stalked toward the door and before leaving, added, "I own miles of land in every direction. If you run, I'll chase you. I like a good hunt, but you won't like what happens if I catch you."

He slammed the door as he left.

17

*W*hat. The. Fuck!

Who the hell did he think he was? Now that he'd left, Jade had time to replay their conversation in her mind. She'd been so taken aback and confused when he'd accused her of being a spy that she hadn't defended herself. Now that she had her wits about her, she was livid.

She scoffed, recalling Zikas' earlier comment. *"There are very few better males than Theo," my ass! He's a paranoid psychopath!*

When he'd grabbed her and pulled her close on the counter, the logical part of her mind had rebelled. He was an alien, and she didn't know him at all. She'd also been incredibly embarrassed that he'd understood what she'd said.

Jade's body, however, had responded to him in a way she'd never responded to a man before. At first, he'd been seductive. Aggressive, but seductive. Calling her pet and whispering in her ear. When he'd rubbed himself against her like he had, she'd grown wet and had almost given up fighting him.

Then he'd changed. She'd seen it in his eyes. Whatever she'd said had made him drop his act and lash out.

In what world could I ever be a spy? she thought, fuming. Jade had always been a terrible liar. Hotheaded too. Many times, she'd said things in the heat of the moment that she'd later regretted.

She couldn't even fake an orgasm properly. One boyfriend she'd had on Earth had dumped her because of her lack of "enthusiasm" in the bedroom.

The idea of her as some femme fatale, plotting against the fire-breathing giant next door was laughable.

There was no lock on her bedroom door, so Jade angled a chair under the knob and flopped down on the bed. She thought back through their fight in the kitchen. *The markings... Those are the scars everyone was talking about? Everyone hates them? Why?*

Jade recalled the doctor's odd look when Jade had asked to keep her tattoo.

How could they be scars? The designs were so intricate and deliberate. Many of the other aliens she'd met had markings, but theirs were white or light gold. Was the color of Theo's what made them unappealing to others?

"Stupid sexy asshole alien!" she muttered angrily. This was going to be a difficult three months.

And what had he meant when he'd said he would play along?

18

A loud knocking sounded from somewhere. "Just leave it on the porch!" she yelled groggily.

A deep, gravelly voice said, "Leave what?"

Jade shot upright in bed and took in her surroundings. It hadn't been a bad dream. This was really happening.

A loud crack sounded, making her jump and pull the covers up to her chin.

Theo stepped through the door and glanced at the remnants of a wooden chair. *Shit, this guy is strong.* His jaw clenched as he looked back toward Jade. "Did you sleep well?"

"What do you care?" Jade glowered.

With thinned lips, he replied, "I'm your husband and thus required to care."

"Some husband," she mumbled.

"Breakfast is ready."

"Did you poison it?" she said in a sardonic tone.

"No," he grated through clenched teeth. "I realized you never ate dinner last night after…"

"You accused me of being a spy and using my feminine wiles to seduce you and lure you into a false state of security?" she finished for him.

"Discussion," he corrected. "After our discussion."

Jade snorted. "I would love to see you *discuss* your problems with Zikas."

A muscle ticked in his jaw, indicating his rising anger. "I came to tell you breakfast is ready. You can come down on your own, or I can carry you there. Your choice."

"You can't—" She started to argue but stopped when he took a step toward her. "Fine! Fine! I'll be down in a minute."

Theo exited the room without a word.

Jade used the bathroom and washed the sleep out of her eyes, grumbling about Theo all the while. *"I made you breakfast."* What did he want? Why suddenly be civil?

Mornings did not agree with Jade. She was a night owl through and through and was often grumpy in the morning. This morning was particularly vexing since she hadn't gotten much sleep the night before.

After arguments, Jade had the bad habit of stewing. She replayed the scene over and over in her head to figure out what she *should* have said or done.

When she'd finally fallen asleep last night, her treacherous subconscious had made her dream about steamy encounters in kitchens with one infuriating alien. More than once she'd woken up hovering on the verge of an orgasm.

She was sexually frustrated, tired, hungry, and more than a little pissed. Theo had better watch himself around her today.

When she entered the living room, she spotted him through the windows and groaned. He was stretching shirtless on the patio. Soft, early morning sunlight highlighted every muscle as he flexed.

"Why did you have to be crazy?" Jade sighed, watching him appreciatively. "We could've had so much fun."

Theo turned as if he sensed her watching him. She glanced away and started walking casually toward the kitchen. Spinning in place, she stared at the ground.

She was currently standing in exactly the same spot the stone island had been, except now the area was empty. Her stomach gave a hollow rumble, and she decided she'd solve the case of the missing island later.

When she reached the small dining table positioned in front of the windows, she found plates and plates of odd-looking food and a steaming beverage that smelled slightly sweet.

She hadn't heard him come in when she sensed him standing behind her. Clenching her teeth, she prayed he'd put a shirt on.

"I didn't know exactly what you liked so I put out a few different things," he said softly behind her.

"Why are you being nice all of a sudden?" she asked wearily.

"I told you. I'll play along. You're my wife. I'm your husband. This is what husbands do."

Jade turned to look at him suspiciously. *Thank God he put a shirt on.* She was so aroused and frustrated from her sleepless night that she might have been provoked to jump his bones if he'd come in sweaty and naked.

"What, so you're just going to treat me well from here on out? After the way you terrorized me last night? Do you expect me to just forget about it?"

Crossing his arms over his chest, he said, "I didn't say that. I'll treat you like a wife, but I'll be watching you closely. If you are a spy, you won't get what you came for. If you're not a spy, then you'll spend three uneventful months with me." He shifted his shoulders and added, "Yesterday was…unexpected. I behaved badly, and I apologize."

Jade was unconvinced. "What evidence do you have that makes you think I could be a spy?"

"The fact that you're standing in my house as my wife is evidence enough for now. If there's more, I'll find it."

Jade rolled her eyes, "So in other words, none. You have nothing. Which means you're just one paranoid alien and I'll have the pleasure of being the subject of your paranoia for the next few months. Great."

Apparently done with their conversation, he declared, "I'm going for a run. I'll be back soon."

"Aren't you worried I'll rifle through your things while you're gone? Report back to my contacts using my nonexistent communication device?" Jade quipped.

All Theo said before leaving was, "I'll know if you do."

***

Cebo bounded around Theo's legs excitedly when he entered the small domed guesthouse.

Squatting down, he said, "Sorry you have to be locked up in here." He scratched behind his ears. "Females don't like animals in their home. Want to go for a run with me? I need to clear my head."

Cebo barked in response and then tore out of the house, Theo on his heels.

Theo dodged trees and hurdled fallen limbs as he sped through the forest. Running helped him clear his mind, and boy did he need a clear mind at this moment.

His last plan, allowing Jade to incriminate herself, hadn't worked well at all. He found he was unable to control his reactions around her, which was highly concerning.

No, he'd have to approach this problem differently. She didn't scare easily, that was for sure. In spite of himself, he admired her courage.

The way he'd spoken to her last night would've caused many males to cower in fear and tell him whatever he wanted to know. In fact, a handful of unlucky males had done just that when faced with his rage.

Pain would probably get her talking. He waved that thought away. *I couldn't hurt a female. Would never want to.*

Starve her?

No.

Lock her up?

No.

He couldn't use any of the methods of information extraction he was used to using. Frustration caused him to pick up speed. Cebo fell behind.

What she'd said this morning was right. He had no real evidence that she was a spy. He needed to remember that and not let his erratic emotions punish her more than she might deserve.

Recalling her responses to his accusations last night got him thinking. She claimed to have been abducted from Earth and brought here directly. From what he could gather, she also acted as though everything she experienced here was foreign to her.

The look of wonder on her face as she'd walked through his home would've been difficult to fabricate. She'd stared incredulously at basic items he'd never given much thought.

He needed to make sure she was put into situations that surprised her and forced her to drop her act, if one existed.

Coming to a stop, he grinned as an idea formed.

In order to keep up this ruse, she'd have to pretend to have little knowledge of how a husband and wife behaved. If he told her, for example, that a husband was required to massage his wife nightly, she wouldn't be able to contradict him without giving herself away.

She claimed she liked his scars. His cock gave an involuntary twitch when he recalled her saying that she wanted to lick them.

If he came in close contact with her enough, her disgust would surely come through, and she'd have to admit that she was lying about finding him attractive.

He needed more, though. He had to make sure she wanted to leave badly enough to come clean.

Ecstatic at having finally caught up, Cebo licked every part of Theo he could reach.

Glancing down at Cebo and grinning widely, he said, "I think I'll start with you."

19

Jade had spent the morning exploring the house. In addition to the rooms Theo had shown her yesterday, she'd found a gym that looked like it received little use. Jade had wondered what Theo did to stay in such great shape if not lift weights in a gym.

She'd also found a few more guestrooms on the other side of the house. For a moment, she had felt pleased to know that Theo had chosen the guestroom closest to his to be her room rather than on the other side of the house.

Her happiness had been smothered when she'd realized he'd probably done this to keep an eye on her rather than because he wanted to be close to her.

Jade wandered the rest of the house, puzzled at her own reactions to Theo. On Earth, her current therapist had made her understand she tended to shut people out as soon as they made one wrong move. She'd called it "door slamming." Jade had comprehended, after agonizing weeks of painful self-reflection, that she'd "slammed the door" on many people, often for small, stupid reasons.

Annie, who'd been her best friend since college, had bailed on a trip to Florida that they'd planned, and Jade had overreacted to the extreme. She'd accused her poor friend of prioritizing her boyfriend over their friendship and cut off communication with her.

Keeping herself at a distance from people and never allowing herself to be emotionally connected was Jade's default. So why wasn't she acting that way with Theo? He'd given her a multitude of valid reasons to shut him out, but she hadn't. On the contrary, the smallest show of kindness on his part made her feel weak in the knees.

Jade reached the last room she had left to explore, and her worried thoughts melted away. The room contained only a massive bath. A literal bathroom. It reminded her of what an ancient bathing house must have been like, except smaller. The floor and walls of the room were covered in dark blue stone veined with gold.

The ceiling was elaborately tiled to resemble the night sky. Sparkling gold stones scattered across the ceiling, glowed in the dim light, and very tiny glowing bubble lights floated near the ceiling, giving the impression that stars were hovering in the room. Steam rose from the inky black tub, making the whole room appear hazy and dreamlike.

Jade decided then and there that she'd be spending an exorbitant amount of time in this room. It was her favorite by far.

"Lovely, isn't it?" came a rough voice from behind her.

Jade jerked and then spun around. "You need to wear a bell," she said, clutching her heart.

"I need to speak with you about something. Can you come with me?"

He was still wearing a shirt, but now the material was soaked with sweat and clung to his impressive physique. She ogled his wide upper body, wondering if this sight was better or worse than shirtless Theo. It was certainly more tantalizing.

"Well?" he said impatiently.

Jade tore her eyes away from his chest. "Yeah. Sure."

He turned and walked toward the large open room in the front of the house.

"So," he began when they were both seated in the sunken living room. "I thought it would be a good time for you to meet Cebo."

"What's a Cebo?" Jade said nervously.

"Cebo is my…our pet." His eyes twinkled, and the corner of his mouth twitched. Something was wrong.

"Okay," she said slowly.

"It's customary for the female of the house to bond with the pet. You should make sure to keep him with you for at least twenty-four hours."

"What kind of animal is he?" she asked apprehensively. He was relishing this exchange, which made Jade assume that "Cebo" was some kind of disgusting, giant, two-headed possum.

"Maybe it's best if you just meet him." Before Jade could protest, he'd started walking toward the door.

***

I can't wait to see her face. Theo snickered inwardly.

Taking a last look at the distressed expression she wore, he opened the door. Cebo shot past him, detecting a new person in the room.

Theo watched Jade with barely contained excitement.

"A dog!" she exclaimed, and her face broke into a wide grin.

As Cebo charged for her at a pace that would make any female cry out, Jade fell to her knees arms wide.

Theo stood with his mouth agape. Cebo was licking her face! Drooling everywhere! Any other woman would be appalled. They would've demanded the animal be removed from the house.

Jade, however, was now on the floor with Cebo. She hugged him around the neck and when he rolled over, she rubbed his belly, all the while smiling and speaking to him in a loving voice. "What a handsome boy you are! Good dog." Jade sat up and glanced at him, perplexed. "How do you have a dog? There are dogs on this planet?"

"This animal isn't native to this planet. I bought him from an exotic breeder." The one animal that had stood out to Theo on that trader's ship resembled an Earth animal! What were the odds?

"Well, he looks mostly like a dog," she said, tilting her head to study Cebo. "I've never seen any dog with a tongue like this. His eyes are a little funny too. He's also much bigger than normal dogs are, but he's close enough."

"So, you like him?" Theo croaked.

"Oh, I love dogs," she said, never taking her eyes from Cebo. "When I was growing up, we always had at least one dog in the house. I was planning on going to the pound to rescue one in a few weeks actually."

"Rescue?" She likes animals *and* she protects them from harm too?

Her smile faded. "Yeah. On Earth there are *so* many dogs without homes. People don't want them roaming free on the street, so they catch them and put them in pounds. If nobody adopts them after a certain amount of time, many places will put them down."

"Put them down? Down where?"

She placed a hand by the side of her mouth and whispered as if she didn't want Cebo to hear. "Kill them."

"That's barbaric," Theo hissed.

"I agree, but sadly, many of the things that happen on my planet are pretty barbaric."

Theo gave his head a little shake, trying to get back on topic. "You don't mind keeping him with you? All the time?"

"Now that I know he's here, I don't want him going anywhere. Can he sleep in my room?" she pleaded.

Theo released a defeated breath. "I suppose."

She stood and ran towards the stairs. "Let's go see my room, Cebo!"

Cebo chased after her happily.

When she was out of sight, Theo dropped onto the couch. He was disconcerted. Introducing her to Cebo was supposed to infuriate her. Annoy her at least. It was supposed to be the first step toward making her time here intolerable.

She liked him. No, she loved him. Theo scratched his head.

He needed to do more research on Earth. Thinking back, he did buy Cebo from a vendor who claimed he sold "exotic" animals. If Cebo was similar to…what did she call them? Dogs? It stood to reason that Cebo could be part dog. If the vendor were selling things collected from Class Four planets, it was unlikely he'd make that information known. It was highly illegal.

Tomorrow he'd request more information about Earth from some of his work contacts. Once he knew more, he'd adjust his plan accordingly. Until then, he'd continue to try and shake her resolve. Seeing her in the bathing room had given him another idea.

Before he put that plan into motion, he first needed to address another, more pressing, issue. He couldn't let her walk around the house wearing only his shirt. Staying focused was crucial right now. Seeing teases of her cleavage whenever she bent over made him want to rip the shirt off her body.

She needed clothing.

20

"I believe your dad thought I wouldn't like you." Cebo laid on the bed next to Jade. While she pet his head, she talked to him softly. "Who wouldn't like you, though? Huh?" Cebo's tail hit the bed with a *thwap, thwap, thwap.*

"I still can't believe you're here," she muttered, shaking her head in astonishment.

Already feeling an unnaturally strong attachment that she reserved for dogs rather than people, Jade wondered if there'd be any way to continue to visit Cebo after her marriage was over.

Theo entered the room without warning. He was carrying a smooth black cube in one hand and a thin, black, rectangular object in the other.

"Do you knock?" Jade said, pulling her shirt down over her thighs.

Eyeing her movements, he said, "Not in my house."

"*Our* house, darling," Jade said in a sickly sweet tone.

A frown was his only response. He set the cube down in the middle of the room then moved to Jade.

Feeling it was best not to be lying on a bed while he was in her room, she stood.

"You need clothes," he said simply.

No shit, Sherlock. Annoyed, Jade cocked her hip and gestured to the small cube. "Have you stuffed them in that box?"

He shoved a thin rectangle into her hands. "You can pick out whatever you want with this." He slid his hand over the top of the device, and it illuminated. Pictures of different types of clothing were displayed on the screen. She touched the picture that resembled a dress, and pictures of a variety of dresses appeared.

"So, it's like a tablet. And you want me to do some online shopping." Jade scrolled through the dresses and tapped on a short, flowy dress that looked comfortable.

Suddenly, a woman's body appeared in the center of the room.

Jade leapt back, and the tablet tumbled out of her hands.

Theo's hand shot out faster than lightning and caught it before it hit the floor. "Careful."

"Sorry. I was surprised by the headless body of a woman appearing in the room. Can you blame me?"

As Jade looked closer, she saw that the black box on the floor was projecting an *image* of a woman. She also saw that the projection was wearing the dress she'd selected. "Oh, cool. So, it shows you what the clothing will be like on a person. That's clever."

"It shows what it'll look like on you," Theo corrected. "I entered your measurements into the program."

"You know my measurements?" Jade asked, appalled.

Theo seemed unconcerned. "They were in your file."

Jade didn't have a problem with her body. She may be a little curvier than the beauty ideal back home, but *she* thought she was very well proportioned. For some reason it rankled to know that Theo knew how much she weighed.

Why should she care? He was a lunatic, anyway. Hot one minute and cold the next. It shouldn't matter to her what he thought about her body.

"On Earth, it isn't polite to ask people about their weight or measurements. We're sensitive about that kind of thing," she explained awkwardly.

"Why?" he asked, unperturbed.

"What do you mean, 'why'?" She eyed him and clicked her tongue. "You wouldn't understand. I haven't seen one overweight person since I've gotten here. You all have perfect bodies."

Theo silently ran his gaze over her body. The intensity in his expression made her stomach flutter.

She didn't know what else to say so she continued trying to explain. "Everybody looks different on Earth. Some people are fat, some are thin. Some are muscular," she added, glancing at his arms. "The type of body most people want is thin and fit."

She pressed her lips together and frowned. "I thought the beauty standards back home were unrealistic, but every person on this planet is perfect, so I guess I was just being lazy." Giving him a sidelong glance, she admitted, "It just makes me a little uncomfortable knowing that *you* know how much I weigh and how much weight I need to lose, okay?" she finished with a huff.

Tilting his head, he studied her body. "You shouldn't lose any weight," he said matter-of-factly.

"Yeah, right."

He swung his smoldering gaze on her. Voice gone low, he rumbled, "I've only felt the soft curves of your body twice, but it's been the highlight of my year, and I haven't even seen all of you yet." No sooner had he said this than a look of anger crossed his face.

Silence hung between them as they stared at each other.

Did he regret telling her that? Even if he did, she didn't care. She liked hearing it. The way he'd said it with such conviction. Her breasts had grown heavy and sensitive. She felt heat flood her core.

Theo inhaled deeply, his eyes widening. "You understand how to work that device?" he said hastily.

Before hearing her answer, he started toward the door. "In addition to clothes, you may buy whatever else you desire. Don't worry about the cost. I don't have anything for you here." He turned, not looking her in the eyes. "Come down to the kitchen when you're finished. Dinner should be ready by then."

Jade stared at the doorway he'd vanished through long after he left. Speaking to Cebo, she said, "If he keeps that behavior up, I may have to like him."

* * *

So instead of making sure she felt uncomfortable here, he'd plied her with compliments and gave her leave to buy whatever she wanted? Great.

Theo sat in his room and fumed. *Vexing female!*

When she'd started talking about herself negatively, he couldn't keep silent. The way she'd described how the people of Earth judge beauty was ridiculous. Theo couldn't imagine a male not salivating over her. He certainly had.

In the end, what had caused him to speak up was the look she had in her eyes when she'd talked about herself and compared herself to the Clecanians. For a moment, he'd been sure she actually believed she was substandard in some way. His instincts screamed at him to comfort her and convince her she was mistaken.

Replaying the interaction in his mind, he recognized how preposterous it was for someone who looked like her to think she had to alter part of her appearance. It was obviously an act. An act aimed at appealing to his own insecurities.

There was one other piece of information Theo had learned. The sweet scent that made him lose all reason was her arousal, not her fear.

Last night when he'd truly scared her, he'd identified the smell of her fear. It had been bittersweet, more similar to what he would've expected. More troubling than the fact that he'd scared her was the idea that she'd been aroused not only in the kitchen, but also during the Testing.

Just now in her room he'd smelled it again and had needed to leave as quickly as possible. The damn underwear worn by Clecanian females was meant to mask scents so males could control themselves around females who were aroused for whatever reason, but it hadn't concealed the scent of Jade's arousal enough for Theo's liking.

Theo allowed himself to ponder what could've aroused her. *Me?* he thought momentarily. Could she have been attracted to *him?* Chosen him for that reason?

Theo shook his head miserably. His male ego had been injured one too many times for him to believe that. It still made the most sense to him that she was using him for something and happened to be a phenomenal actress.

What he had planned for tonight would surely rattle her.

21

"Whew. Done," Jade said, tossing the tablet onto the bed. Glancing through the glass, she saw that it was now dark outside. Cebo was snoring loudly on the bed next to her. "I'd better go down to dinner," she whispered.

She had spent the last few hours buying a year's worth of clothing. That was how long she was supposed to stay on this planet, after all. *Three months here, nine months looking for someone to take me back to Earth.*

She'd also browsed through the wide selection of toiletries and beauty products listed but ended up not purchasing anything. It was easy to recognize the clothing, especially since she could see them on the projection in her room. All of the other products were a mystery.

She couldn't learn what they were either, because the descriptions of the products were written in Clecanian. Jade had decided it was better to wait to buy those items until she knew more about their function and their ingredients. For all she knew, they could be made from that plant she was allergic to.

Side note. Remember to ask what the name of that plant is again.

Tonight, at dinner, she planned to ask Theo if she could invite Asivva to come and visit. It would be nice to see her again. Heck, it would be nice to talk with anyone who didn't look like they were angry with her seventy-five percent of the time. Also, Asivva could explain what the items she'd scrolled through earlier were and help her pick out the things she needed most.

Jade tiptoed out of her room so she didn't wake Cebo and headed toward the kitchen. As she neared, she spotted Theo sitting at the table and gazing out the window contemplatively. Plates of delicious-smelling food were already piled on the table in front of him.

Passing the stone island on her way to the table, she asked, "How is this here sometimes and not here others?"

"It retracts into the floor when not in use," Theo said blandly, as though retracting 1,000-pound islands was mundane.

Jade gazed at the floor for a moment, wondering what the underside of Theo's house looked like. Was there a whole selection of furniture just waiting to be called to the surface?

Moving to the table, she sat across from him and waited for him to acknowledge her.

Without glancing up, he filled her glass, then his own, with fizzy red liquid. "Did you buy everything you needed?"

"I bought clothes and shoes, but I wanted to wait to talk to you before buying the rest. I don't read Clecanian, so I didn't know what most of the products were."

A muscle ticked in his jaw, and he motioned to the food and drink on the table. "I used the recommendations from your file to prepare this. Hopefully the suggestions were accurate and you like these things. Please let me know if you don't." Lifting the glass he'd just filled and taking a sip, he added, "The scan estimates you'll like this beverage."

Lifting her glass, she asked, "What is it?"

Raising his eyes to meet hers, he answered, "It's an alcoholic drink made from Wanget, a type of fruit."

Jade hesitantly took a sip. A sweet yet slightly tart flavor exploded over tongue. "Mmm." She took a larger sip this time. It reminded her of an experimental sparkling wine. "It tastes similar to one of my favorite drinks from Earth."

"Good." Theo leaned forward and swept away the small glowing bubble lights that were keeping the food warm. "Let's eat."

Although his face didn't show it, she sensed he was pleased that she enjoyed something he'd provided. After all, it did look like he went to a lot of effort to choose specific things she'd enjoy.

Jade examined her glass and noticed it was already half empty. "Wait. How strong is this?" she asked uncertainly.

He quirked his brow at her.

"The drink I had in the car on the way over here tasted really good, but was very strong."

The corner of Theo's mouth quirked in a smile. "You're the first female I've met who thinks mott tastes good." He downed the rest of his drink in one gulp and then refilled his glass. "This is not nearly as strong. Mott is three times as strong as this."

Upside: he'd finally cracked a smile. Downside: her appreciation of hard liquors made her seem like an alcoholic.

All of the food she ate during dinner was both confusing and delicious. Nothing on the plate was familiar to her and every time she ate something new, she'd been entirely disconcerted.

She decided to try some small, round blue items first, since they reminded her of blueberries, but when she tasted them, she found the texture to be more crunchy than soft and the flavor spicy rather than sweet. After each bite of food, Jade needed to take a moment to work through her confused senses and decide whether she liked what she was eating.

After some trial and error, Jade was able to work out which foods she enjoyed the most. With her preconceived notions about what the foods should taste like out the window, she decided the items she enjoyed were delicious.

Whoever graded him on cooking had gotten it right. He could've been a successful chef back on Earth.

"You're enjoying the meal?" he asked quietly. He was sitting back in his chair watching her, having finished his own meal a while ago.

Between bites, she replied, "It's incredible but strange. I can't tell what anything is, but it all tastes wonderful. Do you always eat this well?"

As he'd done many times throughout the meal, he refilled their drinks before answering.

Is he trying to get me drunk?

He leaned forward and placed his elbows on the table. "Not always. Clecanians mostly just use the food synthesizer."

Jade finished swallowing a mouthful of red mush that tasted like cheese and garlic, then asked, "A what?"

Theo lifted his hand pointing into the corner of the kitchen at a small panel. "A synthesizer makes food for you. Type the dish you'd like, and it'll appear."

"Wow, that's amazing! Why do you even cook at all? If I had that back home, I'd use it every day." A machine that could cook for you sounded like a dream come true. "I'm a terrible cook. My aunt always said I could burn boiling water."

Jade averted her gaze, taking another bite. The sudden mention of her aunt had sent a jolt of sadness through her.

Theo rested his elbow on the table, lifting his glass for another sip. "The food tends to be a bit bland when made in the synthesizer. Cooking the food by hand always yields better results for special occasions like tonight."

Jade's chewing slowed at his cool tone. Her mouth was still full, so she raised her eyebrows, implying a question.

"Tonight, we'll bathe together as husband and wife for the first time."

Trying to swallow too quickly, Jade choked and coughed. After a moment, she managed to wheeze, "Come again?"

Handing her the glass she had been clutching for, he calmly repeated, "Tonight, we'll bathe together as husband and wife for the first time."

Eyes still watering, Jade set her palms on the table and took a couple of deep breaths. "I understood the words, but I don't know what you're talking about. I'm not taking a bath with you."

Theo sat back in his chair and stretched his long legs out in front of him. Irked, she realized he was enjoying this.

"Traditionally, a newly married wife and husband bathe together the second night of their marriage and then again once a week thereafter."

Her eyes widened further. "I don't care about your tradition! I'm not getting in a bath with you. I didn't know about this, and I'm certainly not doing it."

"Ignorance won't get you out of this. It's not my fault you didn't learn enough about our culture before you married into it," he said coolly.

Jade saw red. She opened and closed her mouth wordlessly before screeching, "How dare you! I didn't *choose* to get married! I—"

"It doesn't matter how you got here," he waved a hand dismissively, "You'll be in that tub by the end of the night whether you want to be or not."

"You can't force me to go in there with you! I know that much."

"Who's going to stop me? You?" He chuckled.

"I'll tell Zikas!"

"How?" He flashed her a wicked grin like he'd been waiting for her to make this threat. "Do you know where the communicator is? Do you know how to use it? Can you even read the numbers?"

How would she call him? She hadn't realized it until now, but there was no way for her to get in contact with anyone unless he showed her how. He was right. He could do what he wanted, and she couldn't stop him.

He smirked. "That's what I thought."

A plan. She needed an escape plan. She could take her chances in the woods. The front door looked too heavy to open quickly, so she'd have to run through the glass leading to the beach. She'd learned while exploring this morning that all she had to do to get outside was walk close to the glass.

"You wouldn't make it to the door," he chided, reading her mind. "It's time. Let's go."

Gotta try! she thought as she sprang out of her seat. Hefting the chair above her head, she threw it at him.

Before seeing whether he was hit, she bolted to the glass wall. A pane of glass formed from the solid wall and slid out of her way silently. She dashed through the new opening and ran toward a trail on the opposite side of the beach.

Chancing a glance behind her, she saw Theo stepping onto the patio. He didn't bother to run at first. He stalked toward her, like a predator. Then he bared his teeth in a terrifying grin and began to sprint.

Her legs ached as she tried to pick up speed while running through the sand. The night air was cold, but the sand felt warm against her feet as though the dark color of the sand had trapped the sun's heat from the day before.

She could see the small trail drawing closer. *Only a few feet away.*

Strong arms wrapped around her waist and threw her forward. Before they hit the ground, he turned their bodies so she landed on top of him.

Once on the ground, he rolled and pinned her underneath him. Her wrists were secured above her head in one of his large palms. He wedged his hips against hers and forced her legs apart with his own legs, ensuring she couldn't kick him.

Jade writhed and hissed underneath him like a feral cat. "Get off of me!"

"Calm down!" he bellowed.

His hold on her wrists tightened painfully. Jade whimpered but stilled.

Theo rested his forearm in the sand by her head. "That's better," he said, loosening his grip again.

The moons above backlit Theo so she couldn't see his face. She could tell he was turned on, though, from the feel of his hardened cock as he absently rocked his hips against her. "You shouldn't have run," he grated out, his whole body tense.

He started to grind his hips more vigorously, and so help her, it felt wonderful. Jade had to stifle a moan as his shaft pressed against her clit.

This couldn't happen. He'd just chased her like an animal.

"Theo," she said, her voice shaky.

It seemed to take all of his control to stop, because he shook violently.

"Theo?" she called softly.

Growling, his left hand shot out to cover her mouth. He leaned down and pressed his forehead to hers. It took him a few moments to regain control of himself but when he finally did, he jumped off her.

Shaken, she got to her feet, but before she could rise all the way, he threw her over his shoulder and headed toward the house.

22

I could kill him!

After all that, she'd still ended up in the bathing room. He'd roughly dropped her here after coming in, then left, locking her inside.

Her treacherous body was still feeling the effects of their beach scuffle. How could someone she despised turn her on that much? If he hadn't stopped, she would've come right there in the sand. No question.

Jade shivered. *It felt like it would've been a really good orgasm too.*

Was he going to come back? What was she going to do if he did come back?

The fear of getting naked and wet with a complete stranger wasn't the only reason she fought so hard to get away. The sexual attraction she felt toward Theo was undeniable. She didn't trust herself to be naked in a tub with him.

They'd been together less than two days, yet she was already so sexually frustrated that being in a bath with him might send her over the edge.

She rifled through the contents of a nearby cupboard but only found towels and a large bottle with thick, shimmering liquid. As she closed the drawer to the cupboard, she noticed something shiny on the wall.

She concluded it was some sort of control panel. The screen illuminated when she waved her hand in front of it. Four small squares appeared on the panel.

What's the worst that could happen? The tub drains, and I get to leave?

The first button she pressed caused a blinding light to fill the room. Shielding her eyes, she pressed the button again to turn the light back down. The next two buttons she pressed caused the steam in the room to intensify and abate.

A loud whirring sound filled the room when she pressed the last button. She turned to see that jets in the bathing pool had been activated. Her shoulders slumped. *Well, that doesn't help.*

Maybe I'll leave them on anyway. When she was young, her father had owned a jacuzzi for a while, and she'd always liked to run the jets on and float on the softly bubbling water. When she was about seven, they'd had to get rid of it because...

An idea came to her in a flash. She dashed to the cupboard and pulled open the drawer containing the bottle of thick liquid. She ran to the edge of the pool and dumped the contents into the water, all while chanting, "Please let this be soap. Please let this be soap."

Frothy bubbles started to form, covering the surface of the water like a blanket.

Ha! She smiled triumphantly.

The reason her father had to get rid of the jacuzzi when she was a kid was because she'd broken it. She'd poured bubble bath into the water, thinking it'd be fun to use the jacuzzi instead of the bathtub, not knowing that soap clogged up the jets.

Suddenly the door opened and Theo strode through, carrying two large bottles of that red drink. He looked slack-jawed at the mountain of bubbles now forming in the pool.

Shooting her a lethal glare, he stalked toward the panel to turn off the jets. "Here," he said, holding out the bottle to her.

She eyed it warily but made no move to take it.

He clenched his jaw then started walking toward her, at which point, she quickly backed away. Setting the bottle on the floor, he returned to stand near the front of the room.

He stared at her menacingly as she retrieved the bottle and sipped. "Strip and get in."

"No," she said firmly.

"If I have to come over there and do it for you, I will, but I doubt you want me near you right now."

She crossed her arms and narrowed her eyes.

It only took one step in her direction before she cried, "Okay! At least turn around."

"So you can throw that bottle at my head? No thanks," he snapped.

"I'm not stripping in front of you," she argued, shooting him a lethal glare.

Gradually he turned away. "You have ten seconds to get in that tub!" he barked.

She stripped quickly then slid into the tub from the ledge. Once in the water, she made sure the bubbles shielded her body from view.

Theo turned back around and stared at the bubbles as though trying to see through them.

After taking a swig from his bottle, he set it on the ground and started to undress. Jade tried to look away, but it was like her eyes were magnetically drawn to him.

He pulled his shirt over his head and revealed his broad shoulders, rock-hard chest, and chiseled abs. She barely contained an appreciative sigh. As he started unbuttoning his pants, Jade forced herself to look away and focus on retrieving her booze.

Bottle in hand, she chanced a glance over her shoulder and saw that Theo was now sitting on an underwater ledge, staring at her.

"What was that on the beach?" she snapped. "Does tackling people turn you on or something?"

Theo scrubbed a palm over his chin. "Chasing does. Not tackling."

Jade arched her eyebrow. She hadn't been expecting that answer and she couldn't for the life of her understand why the thought excited her.

Not knowing what else to say, she asked, "How long do we have to stay in here?"

"We can leave when we're both done bathing." Theo made a show of stretching his arms over the ledge of the pool.

Pursing her lips, Jade said, "And I suppose you've decided to take your time."

"What's the rush?" he replied casually.

Locating another submerged ledge, Jade got comfortable. His stubborn ass would probably make her stay in here all night.

"What was your life like on Earth?"

The only conversations she'd had with Theo were either fraught with sexual tension or anger. Jade was surprised to hear a genuine question about her life from him. Not knowing how to traverse this new terrain, she decided an honest answer would be best. What was the harm in him knowing about her life?

"Well, I live in a house alone and I work as a landscape designer." At his confused expression, she added, "I help people make their yards and gardens beautiful."

"Do you enjoy that work?"

Was landscape design her passion? No. Jade had chosen her career because her aunt, who'd raised her for the most part, had been a landscape designer. Although very good at her job, Jade had never enjoyed it.

"I was good at it and it paid the bills. Do you like your job?"

Theo tensed and ignored her question. "Why did you live alone?"

She didn't know exactly how to answer that question. "Why does anybody live alone? I hadn't found anybody I wanted to live with, I suppose."

"No husband or family?"

His tone was very casual, almost too casual. Jade rolled her eyes. "You don't care about any of that. You're just trying to interrogate me again. Aren't you?" Why else would he care about her life outside of here?

"Why can't it be both?" If he was bothered by the fact that she'd just caught him trying to suss out information about her, he didn't show it.

"How about this...I'll answer your questions as long as you answer mine. If you don't answer my questions, though, I can leave." Jade reasoned that asking him about himself would help to distract from the fact that they were in a tub together naked. And that was the only reason. It definitely wasn't because she was curious about the hot, mysterious, brooding man sitting across from her.

In answer to her proposition, Theo gave a small nod.

The only downside to this agreement was that she now had to answer his earlier question about her family. Jade had always hated talking about her family or lack thereof. Her heart ached whenever she talked about her parents and her aunt. The pity she saw in people's eyes only made it worse.

Better get it out fast, Jade thought, taking a long swig from her bottle. "My parents died when I was young. I was raised by my aunt." She spoke quickly, fearing that her already frayed emotions would snap. "After my aunt died, I decided to stay in our house. I live there alone now. I don't have any other family."

When she met his eyes, she expected to see the usual pity. Like she was an animal with a broken leg that everybody "awwwed" over but couldn't help.

Instead, she saw…compassion? "How did your parents die?" he asked solemnly.

More curious about Theo than before, she chose not to answer his question and instead said, "It's my turn. Do you have any family?"

He shifted his shoulders then replied, "Yes. Four brothers and one sister. My parents have both passed on."

"Do you see them often? Do they live near here?"

He looked as though he weighed his answer carefully before responding. "They live close by, but I don't get to see them as often as I'd like. Out of all of them, I see my sister the most.

"You owe me two answers now. What happened to your parents and aunt?" he asked firmly.

Her protective shield of humor firmly in place, she answered, "They refused to get me the pony I wanted for Christmas, so I killed them all. That's how my life as an assassin began."

The corner of Theo's mouth quirked, but otherwise he stayed silent and waited for a real explanation.

"Tough crowd," Jade quipped under her breath, then with a deep sigh, her gazed fixed on the bubbles in front of her, she answered honestly. "My mother died during childbirth…while having me," she added feeling a familiar tightness in her throat.

"My father raised me for a while but then he got sick. I don't want to go into a lot of detail, so I'll just say he was very sick for a long time and then, when I was ten, he died and I went to live with my aunt."

Feelings of sadness and loneliness always tore through her when she talked about her father and aunt. When she talked about her mother, however, she felt guilt.

When Jade had gotten old enough to understand what had happened to her mother, she'd felt such a weight of responsibility that her birth had caused her mother to die.

Her sweet father had always tried to reassure her it wasn't her fault. He told her he loved her more than anything in the world and her mother never would have blamed her, but a small part of Jade had never believed him.

Maybe if he'd remarried, she might've believed him, but he never had, and he'd always teared up whenever he'd spoken about the great love of his life, her mom.

"I'm sorry you never knew your mother and that your father died when you were a child," Theo said frankly. "My mother died when I was young as well."

Jade glanced up into Theo's eyes and recognized the ache she saw in them.

"Jade I…I'm sorry you had to experience all that pain and death." Sincerity shone through his eyes when he said this, and she found herself feeling a little better. It was strange how his acknowledgement—not of her "loss," as so many liked to call it, but of her pain—soothed her.

Not wanting to talk about her parents anymore, Jade rushed to finish answering his question. "Anyway, I was raised by my aunt, and five years ago she became sick the same way my father had. After she died, I started shutting everyone out." Jade took a long drink from her bottle. "You can't feel the pain of losing someone if you don't have anyone to lose."

Emotion suffocating her chest, she attempted to change the subject. "Are there any more surprise mandatory rituals I'm unaware of?"

Instead of pressing her for more information about her family, he allowed the conversation to shift. "A few. I don't want to ruin the surprise, though."

The annoyance she experienced at his smug tone was a welcome relief from the sadness she'd felt a moment ago. Jade couldn't help but wonder whether his tone had been purposefully used to change her mood. She smiled inwardly at the thought and then scolded herself.

Stop crushing on the alien who just manhandled you! She was leaving in one year, and even if she weren't, he hated her. Sure, he definitely wanted to have sex with her, but they could never have a real relationship.

Jade needed a reminder of his temper, so she decided to ask him about the one thing that would rile him up and get him to storm out. "What's the story with your marks? They're different than everyone else's. Why?"

As if on cue, he tensed. "I don't want to talk about my birth marks," he replied in a low growl.

"No answer? Is bath time over then?" Jade asked hopefully. Theo would have to pick which battle he lost now.

As Jade waited for his answer, she could almost see the gears turning in his head. "We'll stay," he said finally.

Both disappointment and excitement washed over her. At last, she'd find out what the deal was with these marks.

"My mother was an off-worlder too," he began.

Jade couldn't see how this related to his scars but she didn't want to interrupt.

"She was a leader of her clan, from a planet called Traxia, a Class Three planet. Everything is much harsher there. The whole planet is very hot and dry. Covered in desert. The people of Traxia live in different clans, and they're all constantly at war with one another."

It was no wonder his mother wanted to stay here instead. But how did this relate to his scars?

"One of the more ruthless clans from a neighboring city was planning an attack against my mother's people. My mother knew they wouldn't win if attacked, so she sought help. She made a deal with the Clecanians. She'd stay on

Clecania and try to produce offspring, if they provided her with soldiers."

"What happened?" Jade asked, enthralled.

"She stayed and had many children, and Clecanian mercenaries fought against the invading clan until they were defeated." Theo's eyes became unfocused. "Everything was good for a while. She chose to stay married to one male, and they were happy together. I was their first born."

Theo paused here to take a long pull from his bottle, obviously dreading the next part of his story. "When I was a young male, she decided it was time for me to visit Traxia and meet the rest of my family. My siblings were still too young to go, so they stayed behind with my father. A day after we arrived, the city was attacked. They stole everything of value then burned everything else." Theo's eyes grew unfocused as he continued. "I remember fires raging all around me while my mother and I ran. Then an explosion went off right next to us, and I was knocked out. When I woke up, everyone was dead. The intruders were gone, and I was alone. I wandered that planet for weeks, surviving off of bugs and small animals. There was no shelter from the sun anywhere since all the buildings had been destroyed and most of my clothing charred. By the time my father finally found me, I was so badly burned that I was unrecognizable."

"And your mother?" Jade questioned breathlessly.

"My mother had been crushed by debris saving me. My father never recovered from her loss. He was a hired soldier and died in a battle off-world a few years ago." Theo gulped and took another swig of his mott.

Turning his attention to her, he stared. "My mother died because of me as well. Guilt…can be a hard thing to overcome."

He knew how she felt about her mother without her explaining those emotions. She would never have to justify the irrational guilt that plagued her. He understood.

Jade marveled at the thought that two people from different worlds, galaxies apart, could share such similar emotions. She nodded, silently agreeing. "How old were you?"

Theo stared into the water before him stoically. "Thirteen."

Thirteen? What kind of emotional damage had been done to him? Had people always treated him with fear and disgust? Even as a young man starting husbandry school? It was no wonder he had a hard time believing she found him attractive. He'd probably been rejected relentlessly.

Had he ever been looked at or touched by a woman with affection? *No,* Jade concluded.

She found herself softening toward him as she recalled the way his body had relaxed, lids going heavy when she'd tended to his injured hand the night before. "Couldn't those machines heal you?"

Theo's eyes snapped back to Jade as though he'd just remembered she was there. "For most of my body, yes. But our birth marks are different. The skin is more sensitive and doesn't respond to our healing machines as well as the rest of our bodies. If they'd found me early enough, they might've been able to fix them, but after weeks in the sun, they were damaged beyond repair," Theo finished.

Without thinking, Jade blurted, "I can see why you hate them. The marks, I mean."

Theo narrowed his eyes and clenched his fists. "So, you finally admit—"

"Wait! No, I didn't mean it the way you think," she interrupted. "I just meant it must be hard to constantly see those marks and be reminded of what happened."

Unconvinced, Theo continued to glare at her. How could she make him understand that she didn't see what others did?

"I don't think they look like burns. When I first saw you, I thought they were tattoos."

"Tattoos?" Theo grated.

"They're very common on Earth. They are like permanent drawings on your body. Most people nowadays have one. The design chosen usually has some special meaning to the person getting the tattoo."

He still didn't seem convinced. "These," he said, motioning to the markings running along his arm, "are not intentional designs. They're burn scars. *Here,* on Clecania, they're ugly and they represent imperfection and weakness."

"Not to me," she said, eyeing him seriously. "Not every girl wants a knight in shining armor."

"A what?"

"It's an expression. A long time ago on my planet, some soldiers, called knights, used to wear heavy pieces of silver metal all over their bodies to protect them against weapons. The image of a knight in shining armor became something women referenced when they were wishing for a good man to come into their lives."

Theo continued to scrutinize her.

"So today instead of saying, 'I wish a strong, handsome man would show up and take care of me,' they say, 'Where's my knight in shining armor?'" Jade was starting to get heated thinking about the way Theo had gotten his scars and about how everyone had treated him like some kind of pariah for it.

"The problem with that expression is that no woman should wish for a knight in shining armor. A knight with shining armor has probably never been to war. They've never fought or been hurt. If you want a strong man who can protect you, then you should hope for a knight in dented, scratched, rusted armor. *That* knight has fought and survived."

She motioned toward Theo and said, "You earned those scars. You survived. The marks that cover your body are an outward representation of your inner strength. Those marks represent the opposite of weakness, and anyone who thinks differently is an idiot."

He was staring at her now with his head cocked to one side.

"Also, perfect people are boring," she snapped. "Every imperfection tells a story. I'd be very upset if I didn't have some of my scars. That's why I told that doctor not to heal them."

That caught his attention. "You chose to keep your scars?"

"Some of them. My tattoo…" she pulled her ear forward, exposing the small star tattoo behind it, "…and a few others that remind me of different things."

He scanned the exposed parts of her body.

"They aren't in a place you can see right now."

Theo's eyes lowered to the thin sheet of bubbles shielding the view of her body and growled low in his throat.

She shivered and felt the inexplicable urge to jump out of the water and give him a better view. *Cool your jets, girl! He's the enemy, remember?*

As she learned more about him, Jade started to wonder if that was still true. Sure, he had a temper and was a little heavy handed with her, but he hadn't actually done anything to hurt her. Physically or verbally. All his bluster was meant to scare her off because he believed she was there to betray him in some way.

If what Asivva had said about his job was true, then she could understand how a deeply insecure man might come to that conclusion.

Jade wanted time to think through her feelings. For now, she couldn't trust herself around him. She'd have to make sure and choose her words more carefully.

Even after what everyone had told her, Jade still didn't understand why women didn't want him. She'd assumed the inexplicable draw of the "bad boy" was universal. Did he ever interact with women?

Jade was feeling bold, so she decided to voice her question. "Do you have sex often?"

He wasn't expecting her to ask him that, that's for sure. It took him only a moment to recover. "Every few weeks. Why?"

"I think you're exaggerating about your scars. You said women don't like you, but they like you enough to have sex with you occasionally."

With a deep scowl, he said, "There are some females from around here who like to visit me every so often, it's true. They chose to marry soft, pretty males and have pretty babies. They come to see me when they want to be fucked."

Yep. Jade was right. The draw of the "bad boy" factor was universal.

"When these females visit, I bend them over the closest surface. They don't spend much time admiring my looks." He sneered. "How many males have you been with?"

Jade guessed it was only fair that he ask her about this as well. "Been with in what way? Dated? Had sex with? Kissed?"

Theo looked puzzled. "Kissed?"

"You know...kissed. With your mouth." Jade didn't know what to say. Kissing was kissing. Did they not kiss here?

"Do you mean oral stimulation? Do females do that for males on Earth?" he questioned.

Jade's face heated as she deduced what he might mean by "oral stimulation." "Yes, women from Earth do...that, but that's not what I'm talking about. Kissing is when you press your mouths together." Explaining how to kiss wasn't easy, Jade realized. She couldn't think of a way to describe it that made it sound pleasurable.

The expression on Theo's face made it clear that kissing wasn't common on Clecania. "That doesn't sound pleasant."

Jade's eyes locked on his lips when she imagined kissing him for the first time. Although he'd never kissed before, something told her he'd be a fast learner. "Kissing is wonderful. I guess it may sound gross at first, but trust me, it can be wonderful. If you kiss the right person, anyway."

He looked at her mouth, brows drawn, trying to imagine it.

Uh-oh. Have to change the subject before I decide to teach the alien more about kissing. "Theo, I was wondering if I could ask a favor?" His eyes focused on hers.

"I wanted to invite a woman named Asivva over to help me finish picking out the things I'll need. She was very nice to me at the ceremony, and she said that she knew you." Jade noticed a muscle twitch in Theo's jaw at the mention of Asivva's name and again she had the sense that there was a long history between them.

Still raptly gazing at her, he said, "I'll let her visit, but I want something from you."

"That's not surprising," she mumbled. "What do you want?"

Oh God, what was he going to ask for now? She was already naked and in a bath with him. Now that he knew

Earth women gave blow jobs, he'd probably ask for that. Especially if women here did not.

"I'd like to take you up on your offer."

"Offer?"

"To lick my scars." He gave her a predatory grin that made her core clench.

This was obviously some kind of test. The way he stared at her smugly as if he was about to catch her bluffing stopped her from flat-out refusing.

Did Jade want to lick the handsome damaged man? Hell to the yeah. Did she think she should? Probably not.

If she got close enough to him and touched him, she might not be able to stop herself from doing more. An old children's book she'd loved flashed in her mind. *If you give a girl a chiseled pec, she'll ask for a bulging bicep.*

What other choice did she have? She needed to see Asivva. She had so many questions, and whenever she talked to Theo she just got flustered or angry.

"Okay," she said finally.

Theo cleared his throat and shifted in his seat. "Okay?"

"Yes. Okay," Jade said firmly. "I was embarrassed you heard me say that, but I wasn't lying about wanting to do it. I'll lick one scar only, and you'll keep your hands at your sides. Agreed?" Rules that were more for her than him.

He grunted but lowered his hands into the water at his sides.

Jade finished off her bottle and slowly made her way over to him. She made sure to stay below the surface of the water and accumulate bubbles along the way.

Damn. The closer she got, the more she noticed how delicious he was. His damp, raven hair was disheveled. His tanned skin was slick from the water, and the muscles of his arms and chest gleamed.

Which scar to choose? A jagged one along the top of his shoulder and a curved design over his heart drew her eye first. Then, she looked at his throat, remembering when he'd licked her there.

Jade decided to repay the favor. A long, dark line began at his nape, curled around his neck, and then ended in a point near his collar bone.

Once she neared him, she had to position herself between his legs in order to be close enough to reach his neck. She found his gaze riveted to her barely concealed breasts.

She snapped in front of his eyes to get his attention. "Remember, no touching."

He frowned at her.

She leaned forward and gently placed her hands on his chest to steady herself. His muscles jumped under her touch, and he stifled a groan.

As she drew nearer to his tattoo, she could feel his heartbeat pick up speed. He was excited, and she decided she wanted to make this good for him.

She licked her way up his neck, starting near his Adam's apple. Reaching the area where *her* sensitive spot was located, she started slowly kissing. When she used her teeth to give him a soft bite, he hissed in a breath.

Damn, he smelled good. His skin was warm and smooth.

When Jade moved up to a spot just under his ear, Theo's chest started to vibrate, and a rumbling sound came from him.

Pulling away from him, she laughed. "Are you purring?" Jade had never heard a sound like that come from a human. He was like a very large cat, and she thrilled at the fact that she'd caused him to produce that contented sound.

"What?" he said, dazed. In an instant, he changed. His eyes cleared and he grew rigid. "Back away from me," he growled.

"I thought you lik—"

"Back away!"

Jade jumped and hastily backed away. Looking down, she understood.

The bubbles had vanished, and her breasts were in full view.

23

Shit! He'd scared her again. The look on her face as she ducked into the water and covered her breasts with her arm said as much.

He inwardly shook himself. Why did he care if he scared her? *That's what you were trying to do!*

Still, he felt guilty. He hadn't meant to frighten her, but he was too aroused. When she'd stood in front of him, he'd first seen her magnificent smile and then her naked body. The sight had nearly caused him to break his word and grab her.

His words had sounded harsher than he'd meant them to be because he was barely holding onto his control.

Without saying a word, he exited the tub. *Running away.*

Theo had never run away from anything! Wars. Assassins. The occasional overly confident male. Threats were to be faced head on.

This small female had rattled him so much with her easy conversation and soft body that he was now retreating from his own bathing room!

Plucking a towel from the wall, he turned to see she hadn't moved.

He opened and closed his mouth a few times before finally saying, "I'll see you in the morning."

Before slamming the door shut, he stopped and added, "Don't try to run from me again. My Traxian blood will force me to chase you. It's instinct. I don't know how much control I'll have next time."

How had that encounter gone so poorly? Theo thought as he stomped through the house to his room.

Every time he thought he had the upper hand with her, she somehow managed to come out on top. He'd met his match, he concluded, dropping down into a chair in front of his fireplace.

He'd learned a great deal about her during the bath. She'd suffered greatly in her life. The look in her eyes when she'd talked about her family's death had convinced him she was being truthful. At least about that.

Pride welled in his chest at how strong she was, but he quickly stifled the emotion. *You cannot be prideful over something that isn't yours*, he told himself.

His still rock-hard cock twitched. *She was yours for a moment.*

He fisted his shaft, recalling her hot tongue on his ear. He needed release now.

Pumping his fist, he recalled her pert breasts. They were fuller than Clecanian females' normally were. They'd bounced when she'd pulled back from him. He came hard when he imagined taking one of her small pink nipples in his mouth.

Theo cleaned himself up and threw on some soft sleeping pants. They felt like sandpaper against his unrelenting erection, and he groaned. It was going to be a long night.

He retrieved the mott he'd left by his bed and returned to the fire to brood over Jade. Was she still in the bath? Still naked?

Theo punched the arm of his chair. *Enough! She's not for you!*

She should've been disgusted. Asking her to lick his scars had seemed like an excellent way to expose her lies. He'd expected a grimace at least, and a halfhearted swipe of her tongue at most. The way she'd lavished his neck had felt like heaven.

That reminded him, he'd have to make sure to repair the bench of the bathing pool soon. When she'd lightly bitten him, it'd taken all of his strength not to pull her onto his lap. The marble had suffered that strength.

Never in his life had he been touched with that kind of tenderness. Actually, no one had touched his markings after they'd blackened at all. When he was a child, he'd loved being touched. He remembered always asking to be held or hugged. Her closeness in the bath and the simple touch of her hands on his chest had drugged him with relaxation.

Losing himself, he'd unconsciously purred, something he hadn't done in ages.

Could what she said be true? What if for a moment he let himself believe her story? Believe that she'd truly chosen him and that she liked his scars.

Before meeting her, he hadn't recognized how lonely he was. If she was indeed the one female in the entire universe who wanted *him,* then she was a blessing. If he accepted her, he might know peace for a while.

Blanching, he thought back to how he'd treated her. Bellowing at her and trying to find ways to torture her. He'd likely ruined any chance he may have had.

Never being picked by a female had almost seemed like a relief to Theo over the years. He knew all too well that his aggressive and possessive nature wasn't compatible with three-month-long marriages.

His mother's people, the Traxian, were barbaric and vicious, but they also mated for life. That was one of the reasons his mother had chosen to stay with his father, even though the practice was highly unusual.

Theo could get by using the females who sought him out for sex rather than marriage. Jade was different, though. He found that he enjoyed talking to her, even when they were fighting. She had a sharp mind and a quick wit.

The few times he'd attempted to make her happy had caused him more contentment than any sexual encounter he'd ever had. Pride had spread through him when she'd complimented the food he'd chosen for her tonight.

He also enjoyed seeing her in his house. When he'd watched her walking around the living room earlier today softly talking to Cebo, she'd looked comfortable. Like she'd wandered his home a thousand times.

Allowing himself to accept her as his wife would break him in the long run. She wasn't his mate and at the first opportunity, she would leave him.

If his enemies had sent her here to make him miserable, they'd succeeded.

He knew what he needed to do. No more trying to expose Jade as a liar. No more trying to outsmart her so she gave herself up. For his own sake, he needed to stay as far away from her as possible.

***

After Theo had stormed out of the bathing room, she'd been confused and more than a little ticked off that he'd yelled at her again. She sat back in the tub and cursed at a sharp, stabbing pain on the back of her thigh.

Investigating, she found that the marble of the underwater seat had been cracked in a few places, leaving jagged edges behind. Right where Theo's hands had been.

Her eyes widened as she realized he must've done that with his bare hands. Because of her.

To keep his word not to touch me, she thought, a flutter in her stomach.

He must've left for the same reason.

"Do I care?" Jade said to no one.

"Yes," she decided. The more time Jade spent with Theo, the more conflicted she felt.

Grabbing a towel and Theo's abandoned shirt. Jade walked to her room. She looked at his door when she neared and muttered, "Should've picked dumb and pretty. Always pick dumb and pretty, Jade."

When she entered the room, Cebo jumped down from her bed and greeted her excitedly.

"Oh, good. You're here," Jade said to Cebo. "I need your help figuring out what to do with your daddy."

Cebo sat in front of her and tilted his head to one side.

She began to pace back and forth in front of the animal. Sometimes running through problems out loud helped to clear her mind. "He acts all tough and angry with me because he thinks I'm some kind of spy or something, but when he forgets that he's supposed to hate me, he's actually pretty sweet."

Cebo plopped down, his eyes following her pacing.

"He hasn't hurt me or forced himself on me. He's been a little rough and grabby sometimes, but let's not kid ourselves, Cebo." Jade leaned down and spoke out of the corner of her mouth, "I like my men to be a little rough.

"He has you, and he has this wonderful house." She gestured around her. "The two people I've met who seem nice say he's great."

Jade walked over to the fireplace, where a fire was burning brightly. She turned and looked at Cebo, momentarily distracted. "Are these always on? Is there some secret fireplace fairy I don't see keeping the fires going?"

Cebo huffed but stood and padded toward her.

"Anyway," she said, telling herself she'd contemplate the magic fires later. "All of his bad behavior stems from that one belief that I wouldn't have chosen him on my own."

Sitting in a plush chair, she gazed into the fire. "What if I could convince him otherwise?"

If Jade let go of her pride and decided to stop fighting her attraction to Theo, then eventually he'd see that it wasn't an act. The physical responses she'd have during sex, for example, would be proof enough.

Cebo laid his head on her lap, and she absently stroked his ears. "If I can make him like me enough, maybe he'd let me stay for a whole year."

An idea struck her. *Maybe he'd even be able to help me get home.*

If his job was to work undercover, then maybe he knew some folks who were underhanded enough to break the law and bring her home.

Jade had made up her mind. She needed to get as close to Theo as possible.

24

How am I supposed to get close to him if he's never here?

Jade had awoken in a warm bed with morning sunlight gently streaming in through her glass wall. She felt relaxed and excited now that she'd decided to make the big guy like her.

The night before, she'd lulled herself to sleep by thinking of different things she could do, most of them sexual in nature, to get on Theo's good side.

Ready to get started, she cleaned herself up in the bathroom, threw on his shirt, and headed down to the kitchen, quietly singing, "Hi ho, hi ho, it's off to work I go."

When she arrived in the kitchen, however, Theo was nowhere to be seen. Plates of delicious-smelling food were on the table, but there was no brooding man waiting to eat with her.

She searched the whole house and couldn't find him anywhere.

Must be out. Deciding not to be annoyed that he'd left without any explanation, she began to eat.

The food was as delicious as always. She noticed there were fewer plates than usual today, but they all contained the foods she'd enjoyed the most.

Her mouth full of a delicious tangy bean she'd decided was more fruit than actual bean, she smiled. Was he keeping track of which foods she liked the most and then making only those?

Her stomach gave a small flutter, and she wondered if she was setting herself up for failure. Her plan required her to seduce him and then eventually leave him. Would she be able to keep her feelings for him from growing stronger?

She'd only been here three days and already she felt warmth spread through her whenever she thought of Theo. If these sweet gestures kept up, she doubted she'd have much say in how she felt about him at the end of their marriage.

After she finished eating, Jade spent the next hour and a half cursing at different machines in the kitchen while trying to figure out how to clean a dish.

The square appliance she'd assumed was the dishwasher sprayed a large stream of water at her as soon as she opened its door.

Nothing in the kitchen was normal. Even the refrigerated foods were located throughout the kitchen in different refrigerated areas rather than one large area.

Since the evil super soaker appliance was the only one that had water, she guessed it was, in fact, a dishwasher. After being sprayed three more times, she gave up on trying to use the dishwasher and arranged the dirty dishes as neatly as she could on the counter.

When she was just about done mopping the floor—with a towel, since the mop also eluded her—she heard a knock at the door.

Cebo, who'd been wholly unhelpful through this ordeal, attempted to dash toward the door, but slipped on the sleek floor and ended up sprawled in the middle of the kitchen.

Chuckling, Jade walked to the door but didn't open it. It would not be the smartest idea to open the door to an unknown guest, wearing only a soaking wet T-shirt.

"It's Asivva," a woman's voice called through the thick door. "Jade, are you there?"

Quickly, or as quickly as she could manage, considering it weighed about a thousand pounds, Jade opened the door. Asivva's warm smile faltered when she took in Jade's appearance and faded completely when Cebo once again tried to run to the door but instead slipped and slid into an entry table.

"Is everything okay here?" she asked, starting to chuckle at Cebo's continued clumsy attempts to get to her.

"Yeah," Jade said blowing a piece of hair out of her face. "One of the appliances in the kitchen and I had a disagreement." Jade sidestepped, letting Asivva through. "I'm so happy to see you. Please come in!"

Jade was about to close the door after Asivva, but three more women wheeling racks of clothes and boxes followed her.

Asivva turned to Jade and said, "Theo called and told me you wanted to visit with me. I figured I'd bring you the clothes you ordered." She eyed Jade up and down. "It's a good thing I did."

Jade glanced down at Theo's shirt. "He has very comfortable shirts, but some real clothes would be nice."

Asivva directed the women to Jade's bedroom before taking a seat on the living room couch. A bitter twinge of jealousy sliced through Jade. *How does she know where everything is?*

Cebo finally managed to hobble over to Asivva, and she stroked his head before he collapsed at her feet, exhausted.

Trying at nonchalance, Jade asked, "So you've been here before?"

"Yes, all the time," Asivva said, patting the couch next to her in invitation.

"Why?" Jade snapped, no longer able to keep a cool tone. Why would this gorgeous woman come to Theo's home *"all the time?"*

Jade glanced over her shoulder. What would he do if he came home right now? It wouldn't be hard to choose between a drop-dead gorgeous model and Jade who, at present, looked like a drowned cat.

Asivva stared at Jade with a confused expression for a moment then said, "Did Theo tell you how he knows me?"

"He said women sometimes come by to have sex with him."

Asivva grinned. "After the ceremony, I was very concerned that you two wouldn't get along."

Jade scowled as Asivva started laughing.

Through giggles, she managed, "I'm so happy to see my *brother* has found someone who's so possessive of him."

"Brother?" *Theo had said his sister lived close by.*

Jade's face heated as embarrassment hit her. She'd never been the jealous type before. This guy was doing a number on her. She sat down and hastily began, "I'm sorry. I didn't mean—"

Asivva held up her hand and said, "It's already forgotten." She peered at Jade's shirt again. "Why don't we see if we can go and find you something…different to wear?"

Jade followed Asivva down the hall. When they arrived at her room, Asivva stretched out on the bed. "I'd love to know how things are going between you and Theo."

Jade had to stop herself from laughing out loud. The scene was all so…normal. Her friend had come over to her house to dish about boys and try on clothes. *Pillow fight anyone?*

"You have to understand, Asivva, I don't belong here. Your brother and I are getting along okay, but I need to figure out how to get back home." Jade hoped she would be understanding about this.

Asivva nibbled her lip and considered what Jade said. "Why?"

"Why what?" Jade said, confused.

"Why do you want to return to Earth so badly? I haven't heard you speak about it much."

Jade faltered. Why did she want to return? Her life back home was tedious and lonely. She'd originally rebelled against living on an alien planet out of fear and principle, but Asivva had a point. There wasn't much back home for her.

A figure moving behind her drew her eye. The three women who'd brought the racks in were almost done putting the clothes away in the closet. She kept catching them shooting curious glances at her.

"Ignore them," Asivva said. "They are just gossips."

Her tone was admonishing, but one of the women glanced over to Asivva with a playful smile on her face.

Asivva smiled back. "They know you chose Theo, and they had the same reaction many others did."

"Maybe I should wait until they leave before telling you about him." Stalling so as not to answer Asivva's surprising question about her life on Earth, Jade stepped into her closet and tried to decide what she should wear.

Everything she remembered picking was here, and it was all perfectly tailored to her. *A girl could get used to this.*

Looking around her closet, she noticed there were also many things she hadn't picked.

"I took the liberty of getting some additional pieces for you," Asivva said from behind her. "You were quite frugal with your purchases."

Jade had purchased enough clothing to last far longer than the three months she was supposed to be in this house. She'd felt quite bad doing it too. Spending someone else's money knowing she was going to eventually take all her purchases and leave felt wrong.

She'd picked out a ton of clothing and some shoes, but she wasn't greedy. She'd made sure to steer clear of the jewelry and accessories section.

Scanning the now-full shelves and drawers of the closet, Jade realized Asivva had purchased those things for her. She'd also done a much better job of it than Jade would have. She had great taste.

"This is too much," Jade said, even as she admired a delicate gold necklace with a glittering blue gem.

Forcing herself away, she shot a sidelong glance toward Asivva. "This must have cost a fortune, and I can't possibly wear all of it. Can we return it?"

"You hadn't purchased enough," Asivva said while rifling through some dresses. "Theo is very wealthy."

"I purchased enough for a whole year. This…this is…" Jade shook her head and gestured around the closet.

"This is just the start. On *our* planet," Asivva began, tilting her head at Jade, "a wife is supposed to be given these things. The style and quantity of items you purchased would've insulted Theo. It's known that he's extremely wealthy and if word got out that he'd only purchased those few items for you, he would've been viewed poorly." Furrowing her eyebrows, she wondered aloud. "I'm worried this may not be enough."

"That is so stu—" Jade stopped at the harsh look Asivva shot her. She knew Asivva didn't like it when Jade judged their customs, but this was ridiculous. "What about men who aren't rich? They just don't get to have wives? Or do their wives spend so much that they end up broke?"

"When you choose your husband, you choose what you'll spend. Wives will spend less if they're married to males who make less. Because you're married to Theo, you should be spending a great deal of money indeed," Asivva finished, holding out a royal blue flowing dress to Jade.

"What if I don't want to buy more things? I don't need anything else, and it's wasteful."

Asivva sighed and lowered the dress. "That's something you'll have to discuss with Theo. I'm merely trying to help." She pushed the dress into Jade's arms.

As she walked to the door to wish the other women goodbye, Jade thought about what she said. *Theo can't possibly want me to go crazy and spend all his money. What's the point of that?*

Jade changed into the dress and followed Asivva, who she found once again lying on her bed. "You should remember to take into account that this is an alien planet. The way we think about money is likely very different than it is on Earth."

Asivva had a point there. "Okay," Jade said slowly. "So, what would happen if he ran out of money? How would he pay for this house and food and medical care?"

Asivva squinted her eyes, looking confused by the question. "It's too bad there isn't more information about Earth customs on file. It would be easier for me to understand you. On Earth, do you have to pay for your food and medical care? Do you only borrow your home, not own it?"

Jade understood what Asivva meant. There were obviously very big differences between their cultures, but neither of them knew exactly what those differences were. "Yes, we buy our own food, and some places on Earth require people to pay for their medical care. You own your house, but most people can't pay for it all at one time. Many are paying off their house for thirty years or more. Some just rent a house because they can't afford to buy one."

"In the words of you, 'That's stupid.'" Asivva sneered. "Every being on this planet is entitled to medical care and food. They don't cost money. If you don't have enough money to buy a house, then you live with other males in housing that's provided until you make enough money. You'd never purchase something you didn't have the money for."

Asivva's response gave Jade more questions than answers. "So, the quality of food doesn't matter? Really good rare things and very common poor-tasting things are free? What about school and retirement?"

"It seems like this could go on forever." Asivva shook her head. "Let me try and explain what money is used for. Maybe that'll help.

"In our culture, the money you earn throughout your life represents your drive and hard work. That money is used to provide additional comforts to yourself and your family. If you decided to not make any money, you'd still live very comfortably and be taken care of until you died, but you wouldn't be eligible to have a wife because you didn't express a great enough drive to do so. You could still have a romantic relationship with whomever you wished, and children if you were so blessed.

"Food, shelter, and medical care are all rights each being living on Clecania is entitled to. A female and a family, however, is a blessing, and you must work hard and contribute to society to show that you deserve such a blessing. Basic needs are provided for by our government. Additional comforts such as a house, designer clothing and specialty foods are all things you can pay for."

A world like that would be wonderful. "What about the people who inherit money and houses?"

Again, with a confused look, Asivva said, "There is no inheritance. Whatever money or property is left when you die is given to the government. All children begin with the same opportunities."

Asivva leaned forward, interest showing in her eyes. "On Earth, do you inherit your parent's money? How do you make sure wealthy individuals don't just go on being wealthy without doing any hard work?"

"Well..." Jade couldn't think of an answer. Wasn't that one of the biggest problems on Earth? Financial inequality? If all the things needed to survive were free and you weren't able to pass on the money you made when you died, would people be as ruthless as they were? Greed would still be present, but the next generation would have to start from scratch and earn their money.

Throwing her hands up, Jade said, "You win. What you're saying makes sense. I'm sorry. Eventually I'll learn not to assume something is wrong before understanding it."

Asivva leaned back, looking smug. "The goal of the males on this planet is to make enough money to attract a wife. If he gets a wife, then he'll want to make sure to spend any money he's made on her. Ensuring her every desire is met and she's happy. It proves to her that he's capable of doing the same for a child."

Jade tried to keep any judgement from her voice when she said, "Does that feel unfair to men? Do women work and earn money too, or do they just use their husband's money?"

Sadness flashed over Asivva's face. "Our world is in distress. Females are the key to ensuring we don't go extinct. A female can work if she wants, but she'd be looked down on for it if she didn't also get married. In order to continue our species, we marry and have children. Then we move on and leave them behind in order to marry again and have more children.

"A Clecanian female gives up her children and any male she loves for our survival. Material possessions provided by our husbands can't fill the hole that's left, but it can help."

Jade realized this culture she'd been thrown into *seemed* on the surface to have archaic views of a woman's place in life, but as she learned more, she found this world was dominated by women. Everything they did was designed to keep their species from going extinct, not to force women into unhappy marriages.

The women on this planet were more honorable than any she'd ever met. They chose the good of their people over their own happiness. Jade felt tears welling in her eyes. Strength. She'd always admired strength, especially in women.

"I'm so sorry, Asivva," she whispered. "Do you have children?"

Asivva smiled sadly. "Yes, two. They live with their fathers."

"Can you go see them?"

"I could, but I fear that would hurt more. You may think the females here are callous, and we are. We must be so. If I were to go and see my children, I don't know that I'd be able to leave. If every female did that, we'd end up extinct. What kind of world would I be leaving for my boys?"

Asivva had been staring off into the distance but turned her attention to Jade. "Husbandry school, clothes, jewels, even a separate bedroom," she gestured around, "are all meant to ease our suffering and keep us from becoming too attached while also giving males the opportunity to prove they've worked hard enough to raise a child alone."

Jade wiped a stray tear that had fallen down her cheek. Asivva was always so patient and kind. To know the pain she had inside made Jade's heart hurt.

Originally, she'd thought the women of this world heartless. They'd shunned Theo because of his appearance and seemed to only care about material possessions or what their husband could do for them, but she now understood they had to be that way. With everything they'd given up—

the comfort of a permanent home, a partner to love, and children to raise—they'd earned the right to be as callous, vain, and as downright bitchy as they wanted to be.

Distancing yourself from everybody so you couldn't be hurt was exactly what Jade had been doing since her aunt had passed away. Being cold was a good way to protect yourself, but it was also very lonely.

Taking a deep breath, Asivva said, "Do you now understand that your lack of spending will reflect poorly on Theo? It's a slap in his face and tells him you don't appreciate all the hard work he's done to provide for you and your happiness. You'd be telling others you don't think he's fit to have a child. His chances of finding another bride after you, which were almost nonexistent to begin with, will vanish completely."

Jade nodded and walked to a chair near the fireplace. On her way, she caught a glimpse of herself in the mirror. "Oh, man," she said, eyeing herself. "You guys really know how to make a dress." The blue material was so soft, it felt like water against her skin. The cut of the simple dress clung to her curves in all the right places and flowed in others.

"Yes, we do. I knew that color would look wonderful on you." Smiling mischievously, she added, "It's Theo's favorite color."

Jade threw a smirk over her shoulder. *Sneaky sister-in-law.*

Asivva joined her by the fireplace, and they sat together. Jade felt a strange swell of emotion as she stared at the woman. She enjoyed speaking with someone like this. Jade hadn't had a friend in so long. All her effort had been aimed at not feeling too much for Theo, but she now realized she hadn't guarded herself with Asivva, and she was beginning to care about her.

It was difficult to admit, but she had more emotional ties to people on this planet than she did back home. Did she really want to return to her solitary existence after being reminded of what it was like to be close to someone?

"So," Asivva asked again, "how are things going with you and Theo?"

Where to begin? "Well… he thinks I'm a spy. Here to lull him into a false sense of security and then steal his secrets or kill him or some such nonsense."

"Hmm," Asivva said thoughtfully. "And are you?"

Jade swung her shocked face toward her. Seeing the playful look in her eyes, Jade laughed. "Ha-ha. Very funny."

"My brother has always been a little intense. He seems to be in denial." Brows drawing together, she asked, "Does he treat you poorly?"

"He tries to. I think he wants me to be upset so I'll reveal myself as a traitor and beg to leave." Jade smiled, thinking about Theo's failed attempts. "Without realizing it, he keeps accidentally doing things I like."

"Like what?"

"Like Cebo." Jade gestured to the bed where Cebo had settled himself. "I'm assuming women here don't like animals much and wouldn't want them in the house. I love animals, and I wouldn't want my pet to stay anywhere but by my side."

"Wives prefer to keep their distance from pets to make sure we don't get too attached to them," Asivva said matter-of-factly. "And how did you react to Cebo? He is a very strange animal."

"Not to me! I think he's related to a very common type of pet on Earth." Jade's face broke into a full grin. "You should've seen Theo's face. He was so sure I'd be mad."

"What else has he done to try and make you angry?" Asivva said with pursed lips.

"Well, he keeps saying sexual things to me too. He thinks I'll be disgusted and show it but, as you know, I find him attractive." Jade rolled her eyes in exasperation. "He also forced me to take a bath with him, but if that's the custom here, then I guess I had to do it anyway."

"The custom?" Asivva interrupted.

"Yeah, after two days, the husband and wife have to…take a…." Jade stared at Asivva's barely contained laughter. "There is no bath custom, is there?"

"I'm afraid not, no." Asivva laughed out loud now.

"Well, how am I supposed to know that! Damn alien." Jade threw her hands up. "Are there any things I should be aware of? I'd like to be able to call him on his bullshit next time."

"What is a bull?" Asivva asked curiously, then shook her head. "Never mind, it doesn't matter. The only thing you're expected to do is go to The Gathering with him so others can see you together. It's thrown at the end of the first month of marriage." She chuckled. "Anything else he tells you is probably a lie."

Standing, she said, "I have to get back home now. Botho, my husband, will be making dinner soon. Here." Asivva handed Jade a black device. "This is a communication device. If you'd like to talk to me or Zikas, you can use this."

Anticipating Jade's next question, she showed her how to use the device and which buttons to push to call her or Zikas.

When she reached the door, she turned and asked, "Do you think you could be happy here? With my brother?"

Jade answered honestly. "If he stops treating me like an unwelcomed guest, I might. I'm not sure if he'll be able to convince himself I picked him because I like him, though."

Asivva nodded. "I'll help you in any way I can."

A devious thought entered Jade's mind. "I think I know a way for you to help me, but it'll require lying."

Asivva smiled. "What's the plan?"

25

Theo had spent his day trying to learn more about human females. His contacts had been helpful but didn't know much more than he had learned on his own. Of the new information he did learn, very little was useful.

There were whispers among some of his seedier contacts that a job offer concerning humans had been circulating a few years ago. Once they knew more, they'd relay that information to Theo for a small fortune.

Making a quick trip to an underground trading outpost a few cities away in the Sparno desert, Theo had been able to find the trader who'd sold Cebo to him all those years ago. The trader had confirmed that Cebo had been bred from a line of domesticated beasts from a Class Four planet, but he hadn't known which one.

Theo had also enlisted the help of his close friend, Rhaego. Like himself, Rhaego was a mercenary hired through their government. Unlike Theo, Rhaego was a tall, horned Tuvasta male who Theo suspected took unpaid side jobs to aid the people of his home city.

Rhaego was an honorable male and had easily agreed to help Theo learn the truth. His imposing friend would stay near the informant who'd told him about the job offer concerning humans and make sure they didn't become distracted from their task of learning more.

Standing slightly taller than Theo with a bulkier frame and razor-sharp horns, Theo suspected they'd work extra hard to learn the truth just to get Rhaego to leave.

On his ride home, Theo found his thoughts returning to Jade. Try as he might to keep his mind on other things, the image of her naked before him in the bath kept slamming into the forefront of his consciousness.

It wasn't only her nudity that caused this image to be so visceral to him, although her glistening naked breasts were on his mind often. It was her manner in that moment. Jade had smiled brightly while looking at him. She'd seemed relaxed and happy while touching him.

Then I ruined it. Theo sighed, leaning his head back against his seat.

The rest of his trip home was spent inwardly berating himself for thinking about Jade and then consequently thinking about Jade.

When Theo arrived home, he ran into Asivva leaving.

"Hello, brother," she said, smiling.

Theo gave a quick nod in response. "Were all of her things delivered? Does she like them?"

Instead of answering, Asivva replied, "From what she's told me about your behavior, I'm surprised you care if she liked them."

Theo frowned but said nothing. *I shouldn't care if she likes them!* he scolded himself.

"She's an exceptional female, Theo. The more I talk to her, the more I feel sure she was created solely for you. I hope you realize that before it's too late. All of this nonsense about her being here to spy on you is... Oh, what was that new word she taught me?" She closed her eyes in concentration. "Oh, yes! Bullshit."

"I've seen it happen to males before, Asivva," he argued. "I've even set some males up to be seduced by females under my employ! Only last year I hired a Deali pleasure worker to seduce and drug a male I was monitoring. It's not improbable that someone would do the same to me." Once the male was incapacitated, Theo had been able to retrieve a biometric scan of his hand that he'd used to break into his home. He had planted surveillance devices throughout and continued to monitor him to this day.

Theo knew better than most that throughout the universe, many males had a tendency to vastly underestimate females.

Asivva pursed her lips but didn't press the issue. "Do you mind if I take your transport home?" Before he could answer her, she'd climbed in and waved a goodbye.

As the transport began to float away, he thought, *What the hell is a bull?*

***

Jade had picked out a few pieces of jewelry to go with her dress but decided to stay barefoot. After living in a T-shirt for a few days, even wearing a simple dress around the house felt extravagant.

She heard Cebo bark excitedly from where he lounged on her bed and then run out of the room.

He's home! Her stomach gave a small flutter. She frowned. Her excitement at his return was troubling.

You can like the alien. You can crush on the alien. You can enjoy some casual sex with the alien. You cannot fall for the alien!

She studied her appearance in the mirror again before leaving the room. Not sure what he preferred, she'd opted for minimal makeup and loose hair.

When she reached the living room, she found him leaning down to lovingly pet Cebo. His dark hair fell across his eye as he tilted his head up to look at her.

He stilled, and his gaze roamed over her slowly. Jade had the irritating urge to twirl for him but refrained.

Cebo let out a whine and nudged Theo's hand.

"Where did you go?" Jade asked.

"Out," was all he said.

Jade had to clamp her mouth shut to keep her retort in. *Don't let him get under your skin.* She went to sit on a couch near where he stood. "Did you have a nice time while you were *out?*"

He shrugged but didn't answer.

Work with me here!

"Asivva came over today," Jade tried. "Why didn't you tell me she was your sister?"

"It didn't seem important." Without glancing at her, he moved to the kitchen.

Jade let out a frustrated breath and then followed him. "You could've said something when I asked to see her."

"Yes. I could have." Theo stopped suddenly and examined the ground, lifting his foot comically, as though he'd never seen water. "Why is the floor wet?"

"I tried and failed to clean the dishes from this morning."

He blinked at her. "Why would you try to clean the dishes?"

"To help out." When her answer didn't seem to satisfy him, she added, "You cooked, so I figured I should clean."

Again, he scrutinized her. "I don't understand you, female."

Jade rested her elbows on the counter and propped her head in her hands. "I get that a lot."

"I thought…" He stopped and looked like he was deciding whether to continue.

"That's good. Otherwise you'd just be a handsome sack of meat," Jade said, trying to lighten his mood.

The corner of his mouth rose slightly.

"I thought you'd be angry after last night." He wearily added, "I don't understand your mood today."

"Something you should know about me is that my mood can turn on a dime." At his confused expression, she amended, "Right, no dimes here. I just mean my mood is quick to change. After you left the bath last night, I went from feeling frustrated, to angry, to lonely."

When he just continued to stare at her, she continued. "Ignoring the *way* I ended up in the tub," she said with an admonishing look that made him shift his weight side to side, "I had a nice time. I enjoyed talking to you." She shot him a coy smile. "I also enjoyed licking you."

His eyes darkened at that, and he scrubbed a hand over his jaw.

"I decided I'm done fighting with you. As time passes and I don't betray or kill you, you'll understand I'm not a spy. So instead of arguing with you about it and driving myself crazy, I'm just going to try and enjoy myself."

She felt an amused thrill go through her at the flash of panic that crossed over his face.

"And how, exactly, do you intend to enjoy yourself?"

She grinned. "Let's just say I'm not opposed to our weekly bath time anymore."

Theo swallowed then turned to grab a mott from a low refrigerated compartment.

"Except for next week, that is," Jade said.

"Next week?" Theo asked after taking a long pull from his bottle.

"Yeah. Asivva explained the custom to me." Jade grinned innocently. "Instead of a couples' bath, I get to choose what we do. She called it females' choice."

26

He was going to throttle Asivva the next time he saw her. "She said you probably just forgot to mention it." Jade reached for the bottle of mott, and Theo absently handed it to her. "I wanted to make sure there weren't any other traditions I didn't know about. She said those were the only ones."

He couldn't deny it now or Jade would figure out that the bathing ritual was a lie. He didn't think she would, but if she got upset and reported him, he could be in serious trouble.

He had to call Asivva and find out what else she'd told Jade.

Jade studied the bottle of mott. "Do women here typically drink alcohol?"

Realizing he'd given her *his* bottle on command without thinking, he said, "Yes, but not usually this kind." He snatched the bottle out of her hand. "It's very strong."

She rolled her eyes at him.

How was he going to make it through the next three months? She'd implied she would welcome his advances. It was almost impossible for him to keep his hands off her as it was.

She looked beautiful in her new dress. The silken material clung to her curves, and the neckline dipped low and exposed the tops of her generous creamy breasts.

Her only flaw was that she now smelled different. He'd realized with frustration that she smelled different than before because she was no longer wearing his shirt. His scent wasn't mingling with her own anymore. When she'd greeted him, it'd taken no small amount of effort to keep from running over to rub himself on her, marking her with his scent.

"I need your help with something," she said slowly. "But it's a little embarrassing."

"I am here to serve, wife," he said darkly.

She smiled at him. The sight was almost as beautiful as the unguarded smile she'd given him in the bath yesterday when he'd purred.

"After you left last night, I cut myself on a broken tile in the tub."

Shit, that was his fault. He'd cracked it to keep from touching her.

"It's in a very uncomfortable and difficult to reach spot. Do you have one of those magic healing sticks around?"

She had been hurt this whole time? "Why didn't you say anything?" he barked.

She jerked, surprised by his sudden anger. Rather than cowering, she said, "Don't you yell at me!" In a raised voice, she continued, "Last night you stormed out of the room and it was clear you wanted to be left alone! This morning you left without a word or a way to get a hold of you. I told you about it at the earliest opportunity. It's not my fault you've made yourself scarce."

Theo flushed. She was right. He had tried to keep his distance from her. "Come with me," he grated out. He led her to his bedroom but paused before going in. "You wait here."

She cocked one hip and crossed her arms impatiently but didn't move to enter his room.

Theo wasn't embarrassed about his room, but he didn't want even a hint of her scent in here or he'd never be able to sleep again.

He crossed to his bathroom to retrieve the home healing device and when he returned, she was standing in the middle of the room, examining it.

Impossible female! "Don't you ever listen?"

"I don't see what all the fuss is about," she said, ignoring his question. "This is a great room. I wouldn't have pegged you for a soft-and-fluffy type of guy though," she said, running her hands over one of his fur pillows.

"I like to be comfortable," he said defensively.

Jade leaned down to pet the fur rug, perfectly displaying her heart-shaped ass.

He felt himself growing hard. *Those curves of hers aren't fair. How am I supposed to resist?* His hand itched to touch her and he found himself taking a step forward despite his inner protests. "As I told you before," he said, clenching his fists, "I enjoy soft things."

She turned her head and smiled when she caught him ogling her. He quickly glanced away.

"No need to be shy," she said, sauntering over to him. "That's where my cut is."

"What?" Theo said, transfixed by her swaying hips.

"I cut the back of my upper thigh when I tried to sit on the bench. I can't reach or see that area easily."

As her words sank in, his shaft shot hard. *How high is the cut?* Would he get a glimpse of her stunning ass if he helped her?

He started to back away from her. "Maybe I should get Asivva to come and assist you."

"Don't be silly." She continued stalking toward him with a mischievous smirk on her face. "You're my husband. It'll only take a second to heal."

Her smile told Theo that she understood how she was affecting him. His anger began to rise.

Was she trying to get him to let down his guard because she was in his room? His office was next door, but there would be no way for her to access any valuable information.

"You're pushing too far." He scowled. "If your plan is to distract me so you can rifle through my things, it won't work."

Instead of getting as far from him as possible, like she should have, she bit her bottom lip and continued forward until only a foot separated them. "I don't want to look through your things. We can move to my room if you prefer."

Why wasn't she scared of him? Most females wouldn't even walk near him in the markets. This one had seen him in a rage just yesterday ago and yet he scented no fear on her.

She *should* be afraid of him right now. Every instinct he had was telling him to drag her to the bed, pin her arms above her head, and sink his shaft deep within her core until she screamed his name.

Her gaze roamed down his body. When it reached the evidence of his arousal, her eyes widened and her breaths quickened.

Goddess help him, he could scent that she was becoming aroused.

Jade's face shot back up to his when he began to growl low in his throat. His erection throbbed painfully.

Last night when he'd captured her on the beach, he'd barely stopped himself from taking her. The only thing that had stayed him was her whimper of fear.

Theo didn't think he had the strength to stop himself again, especially if she needed release as well. He wanted to give her what she needed. She may be slightly different than Clecanian females anatomically, but he was sure he could learn how to please her.

Theo wasn't known for being a gentle lover. His mother's ancestors were a dominating, brutal people, more predator than evolved civilized beings. The urge to chase, capture and possess a female were all urges that flowed through his

Traxian blood. No Clecanian female had ever called to that side of him the way this stunning human was.

She seemed to admire his power and brutality. Wasn't aghast by his appearance like others were. She may even enjoy his aggression in bed. Come to crave it. A shiver ran down his spine at the thought.

But...*she's so small. So delicate.* If he lost control with her, he may inadvertently hurt her.

Mine to protect. He didn't know where that thought had come from, but he immediately pushed it down. She wasn't his. Never would be.

Something in him warned that if they had sex now, he'd never be the same. She'd leave him and he'd stay behind with a hole no other female would ever be able to fill. His possessive instincts might even force him to try and steal her away, which would earn him a death sentence.

"You need to leave," he bit out. "Or you'll regret it."

"What about my leg?" she asked quietly.

He held the device out to her, even as he worried that the merest brush of her hand might send him over the edge.

She glanced at the device then looked up at him with a half grin. In an innocent voice, she asked, "Shall I lift my dress?"

27

With a snarl, Theo's hand shot out and locked around her throat, the healing device forgotten on the floor. His muscles were taut, and his immense chest rose and fell rapidly.

She'd pushed him too far. His dark stare bore into her. But then…his eyes changed. The soft green flashed to black and then back again. Had she imagined it?

He turned them both, guiding her with the massive hand at her throat and forcing her to back up until her shoulders hit a bedpost.

When her brain caught up to her present circumstances, she began clawing at his hands and struggling to break free. He bared his teeth and squeezed. He didn't apply enough pressure to hurt her or cut off her air. His hold was just firm enough to tell her she wasn't going anywhere until he decided to let go.

She stopped scratching at him. *Just let him calm down. He isn't hurting you.*

When she rested her hands on his forearm, she noticed his quick intake of breath. Keeping his hand in place, he stepped so close to her that she had to crane her neck to look at him.

He towered over her and, finally, Jade started to question her choice to seduce him, even as her treacherous core flooded with heat. He was so much stronger than her. She knew he could snap her neck like a twig in an instant if he wanted to. The logical side of her told her she should get far away from him.

Despite her fears, she couldn't deny that she was very turned on. Her panties were soaked, and her breasts ached for his touch.

"Let me go," she said, though her words lacked certainty. Did she really want him to?

He cocked his head down at her then moved his mouth over her neck, fanning her skin with his hot breath and grazing her throat with his lips. A soft moan escaped her at the contact.

Slowly he slid his free hand down her back and rumbled against her skin, "You need to come, little wife."

She let out an involuntary whimper and arched her back to him in answer. He looked wild and powerful and was unmistakably aroused…by her. His hand was large enough to encompass her whole neck. She felt so small in comparison, and it thrilled her.

He squeezed her ass hard and nipped at her ear. "You must be aching now. Your scent is driving me mad."

She shivered. "Scent?"

He moved to peer down at her with a predatory grin. "Your arousal."

Jade's eyes widened in surprise. "You...you can smell...smell when I..."

"I can," he whispered hoarsely.

She flushed with embarrassment. Placing her hands on his chest, she tried to push him away, but she may as well have been attempting to move a brick wall. He didn't so much as sway.

In a flash, the hand from her throat vanished, slipped under her dress and ripped her panties off her. "These mask the scent." Tossing away the offending underwear, he inhaled deeply. "Now let's 'lift that dress,'" he said, using her own words from earlier.

Jade started to tremble as his hot fingers explored her wet folds. When his slick thumb brushed over her clitoris, she released a strangled cry, fisting his shirt.

His hand stilled, and she wanted to whine with frustration. "Look at me," he growled.

Opening her eyes, she tried to focus on his. He was studying her face carefully.

He gave another quick swipe of his thumb over her clit, which caused her to buck in his hand.

Victoria Aveline

A deep, humorless chuckle emanated from his chest. "So that's what that is for. When I reviewed the section on human female anatomy in your file, I'll admit I was curious."

His smile vanished then and his thumb continued to stroke her. "So responsive. So wet."

Jade's eyes rolled back in her head as a throaty moan escaped her. When had she spread her legs farther apart?

"It won't take much for you to come, will it, wife?" His other hand slid up her body to palm her breast.

"Yes! Please, Theo!" Her cry must've shattered his control, because his movements became more aggressive. Faster. She was so close now. "Don't stop, please!" She panted, grinding her hips in time with his touch.

"Let me see you come for me, little wife," he rumbled.

He slipped a large finger into her sex, and her body exploded with her orgasm. Waves of pleasure cascaded over her as she screamed, "Yes! Theo, yes! I'm coming!"

"I can feel you. So tight," he bit out. His deft hands continued to work her flesh until her screams had diminished into soft, panted cries.

As the haze from the best goddamned orgasm she'd ever had lifted, she gazed up at him and a slow, sated smile spread over her lips.

He began to purr again. "Beautiful," he said as he stared down at her, brows drawn.

She felt a rush of affection come over her at his whispered compliment. "Tit for tat, big boy."

At his confused expression, she let her hand roam down his body until she palmed his rock-hard erection.

His shaft jerked in response, and he hissed in a breath.

Just then, a loud pinging sounded somewhere within the house. He groaned and cursed.

"You could ignore it?" she offered as she started to rub his length through his pants. His purring grew louder, making his whole body vibrate.

Distantly she wondered how it'd feel if he was able to vibrate like that during sex. *Who needs a rabbit when your boyfriend comes equipped with a huge vibrating dick?*

The pinging sounded again, more insistently this time. A snarl ripped from him, and he grabbed her wrist to stop her movements. "I need to see to this."

Seemingly with great effort, he backed away from her but continued to gaze at her as he did so.

Then he did something so unexpected that she found herself growing wet all over again. While looking her dead in the eyes, he raised the hand he'd used to bring her to orgasm and licked her juices from his finger and thumb.

"Stay here!" he demanded.

Her breath had caught in her throat until he'd left the room.

***

He was going to pummel whichever being decided it was a good time to come to his home. He ran a hand over his straining erection, willing it to subside. He could still feel her hot palm on him like a brand.

Taking a deep breath, he stomped to the front door and wrenched it open. Theo must appear furious at this moment, but standing before him, Xoris, a prominent member of the Tremantian council, looked unaffected.

"Good evening, Theo," he said coolly.

"Why are you here?" he said with a little more force than he should've.

Xoris had once been a powerful star commander but had become a trusted official of Tremanta after a gruesome battle with an insurgent group of Traxians. He'd never cared for Theo because of his ties to Traxia, and the dislike was mutual.

Xoris peered around Theo's large frame. "Are you going to invite me in?"

Impatiently, Theo stepped aside to allow Xoris to pass.

"I have news to share concerning Jade's kidnapping. Is she eating dinner?" Xoris said, glancing around the house.

Theo crossed his arms over his chest. "She's indisposed. I'll relay the news to her."

Facing him, Xoris tsked. "I hope you're not treating her poorly. Failing to meet your wife's needs could result in her being removed from your home, you know."

A muscle ticked in Theo's jaw, but he said nothing.

"Very well." Xoris gave a small, arrogant smile. "After reviewing the data taken from Jade's translator, we've learned it was only programed with Clecanian and English, an Earth language. No others."

Theo's brows drew together. Any translator on the market would've been automatically programed to translate all known languages from any class 1, 2, or 3 planet. There would be no reason for only two to be programed unless…

"It seems whoever took her from Earth did it with the primary goal of bringing her here," Xoris continued. "You're an intelligent male and as I'm sure you can deduce, there would only be two reasons to take a risk like that."

Theo nodded. "Because there's a Clecanian traitor among us who sought to steal a female for themselves."

"Possibly, but in order to pull that off they'd need to be able to bypass our atmospheric detection systems." Xoris puzzled. "There was no trace of her ship coming into Clecanian orbit or landing on the surface. Thirty loyal soldiers, at least, would've been involved to cover it up, and I can't imagine them doing it just so some selfish male could hide an alien female."

Theo's gut clenched. "She could also have been sent here as a spy. Other species have fooled our systems before. It's possible they have again."

"Traxians," Xoris sneered. "Traxians fooled our systems before."

Theo narrowed his eyes. "I take it you believe they're behind this?"

"Maybe, maybe not." His calm political mask back in place, Xoris continued, "I find it difficult to believe that a small, fragile human, who supposedly knew nothing of alien life before last week, was able to survive on her own for days in the wilderness. Many grown Clecanians wouldn't be able to manage that."

Xoris eyed Theo. "Has she given you any reason to suspect foul play?"

Of course, Theo had suspected her from the beginning, but he'd rather find the truth himself than hand her over to Xoris. If the rumors were true, Xoris wasn't against using pain to get information and, despite his concerns about Jade, he could admit to himself that he'd never put her in harm's way.

"She hasn't done anything that's a cause for concern," he lied.

Xoris didn't seem satisfied with his response, but he inclined his head sharply. "Keep an eye out. We don't—" His eyes grew wide and his nostrils flared.

Jade. Theo could smell her intoxicating scent as well. Why had he believed she'd stay when she disobeyed him at every opportunity?

They both turned to see Jade rounding the corner. She was flushed, and the unmistakable scent of her previous arousal wafted through the room. "Oh, hello again," she said sweetly to Xoris.

Xoris' glare became heated as he looked at Jade, who seemed to be unaware of the effect she was having.

Theo wanted to rip out the male's throat with his teeth. "Leave now, Jade!" he boomed.

A hurt look crossed her face for a moment but then became furious. "You have no right to talk to me like that!"

Xoris moved to step toward Jade, but Theo leapt in front of him. "She's mine, Xoris."

Choosing Theo

For a brief moment, Xoris seemed like he was going to challenge Theo. Then he shook himself. "Make her understand her error. Other males may not be as in control of themselves as I am."

After Xoris had swiftly exited the house, Theo rounded on Jade.

"What the hell was that about?" she exclaimed.

"I told you to stay in the room!"

Jade rolled her eyes and lifted up three fingers. "One," she counted off, "I don't take orders from you. Two, you *also* told me you didn't want to leave me in your room because you were worried I'd sneak around. I didn't want you to think I did, so I chose not to stay in there by myself. And three, the last time we had a visitor it was Asivva and I wanted to say hi to her. I didn't know it'd be the asshole from the meeting."

"You know nothing, Jade!" Theo said, storming away to the kitchen. "Use your head!"

Raising her eyebrows, she very slowly said, "What in the *Game of Thrones* did you just say to me?"

Game of Thrones? Taking a breath, he glared at her. "I told you I can smell your arousal. That's true of most Clecanians. It's a heady aphrodisiac, one most males can't resist."

Jade's face paled at that.

Through gritted teeth, he continued, "Not only did you leave my room still covered in the scent of your orgasm, but you also aren't wearing any underwear to mask that scent. I almost had to beat Xoris to make him leave."

232

She sighed deeply. "I'm sorry. I didn't know it was that intense or that anyone would care."

Theo tried to will himself to calm. Other male's reactions to her weren't her fault. It was the responsibility of the male to control his urges even if confronted with a female who seemed willing and ready.

Theo's rage burned in him not only because she vexed him so but because Xoris had looked at her with lust in his eyes. He was angrier about his reaction to Xoris than he was with her.

Theo had called her "mine"...again. If the big male hadn't backed down, he knew in his heart he would've beaten him senseless. Why did he feel so possessive of this female? Was it really just his Traxian blood? He'd never had a wife before, so there was no way to be sure whether this possessiveness was instinctual or unique to her.

"It won't happen again," he said without feeling.

"Okay," she agreed easily. Her stomach gave a rumble then, and he stifled a curse.

I can't even take care of her properly! She can't be mine.

"I'll make you some dinner." He inhaled, closing his eyes briefly. "Go clean yourself up."

Before she could argue, he'd walked to the kitchen to start preparing dinner, and after a moment she left.

***

Jade grumbled all the way to her bedroom, through the adjoining bathroom, and into her cleansing area. It'd been dumb to follow Theo out, she realized that now, but at the time she'd just wanted to be near him again.

She'd missed his firm touch and the warmth his big body radiated. As soon as he'd left, she'd felt cold and lonely. So, like an overzealous puppy, she'd gone chasing after him.

Dammit, they had made progress! Who knew where it could've gone if they hadn't been interrupted by that snarky ass. Now they were back to square one. He was furious and he couldn't get far enough away from her.

Why is that? What did Xoris say to him? Now intensely curious, she finished washing, found a jumpsuit made of soft, stretchy material similar to a fluffy cashmere and headed down to ask Theo why Xoris had been there.

She found him chopping a purple vegetable that she recalled liking. He handled the knife like an expert, chopping with fast even strokes. A vein ticked in his large bicep as he worked. She wanted to fan herself. *What a man.*

His shoulders tensed as she approached.

"Can I help?" she asked cautiously.

"Yes," he said without looking up at her. "You can help by going away until I finish."

Clearly, he was still upset.

"Fine," she grumbled. "Where is Cebo?"

He used the knife to point through the glass leading to the beach.

Her spirits lifted slightly when she saw Cebo had his face scrunched against the glass, licking fervently.

Cebo whined with excitement and circled her legs when she neared the glass and allowed him entry. "Are you cold? Let's go sit by the fire while your dad sulks." She said the last quietly, but the sound of a scraping knife told her Theo heard her just fine.

She threw an annoyed look over her shoulder then padded to the living room with Cebo. She took the opportunity to sit on the floor in front of the fire and finger-comb her tangled hair. When she was done, she leaned back on one arm, basking in the warmth of the fire. Small glowing orbs floated above her, helpfully providing her with light.

"How do these work?" she asked curiously, twirling a warm globe in her palm.

"They provide light and heat to anything in need," Theo said, rummaging around the kitchen.

Jade clicked her tongue. "Thank you, Captain Obvious. I meant, how are they able to provide heat and light? On Earth, lights run on electricity that's hardwired through the house." She examined the delicate bubble more closely.

She turned to see him glancing between her and a floating light near his head. "The exterior of the house traps the sun's rays and uses the energy in different parts of the house. When the orbs have used up their energy, they return to their charging stations."

"Many people on Earth use solar power too, but we're nowhere near this advanced yet. Is that why the outside of your house glows like that? And how do they float?" Jade had a million questions now that Theo finally seemed willing to answer her.

"Yes, that's why the house glows, and I don't really know how they float, just that they do."

Cebo laid his head in her lap, and she stroked his long ears. From her position, she could see Theo in the kitchen. "How do you not know how it floats? It's incredible!" Jade said, pushing the orb away from her.

"They're normal here," Theo said with a shrug. "They've always been present, so I never thought to question how they worked. I think it has something to do with magnets." He concentrated on his cooking once more, adding defensively, "Do you know how every piece of technology on your planet works?"

"I suppose not," she mumbled, trying to think of how exactly a TV worked.

Jade watched Theo in silence. He was so handsome she could sigh. His wild shoulder-length black hair was tied back at his nape with some unruly strands falling into his face. He wore it this way whenever she'd seen him working or exercising. His face with its high cheekbones, strong chiseled jaw and full lips was a mask of concentration.

Suddenly, a laugh ripped from her chest. He looked up, a question lingering in his beautiful green eyes.

No man should be this hot!

"Sorry," she said, waving him on while still giggling. "I was just thinking about how I'm sitting in front of a fire in the most beautiful house I've ever seen with a dog's head on my lap, coming off the best orgasm I've had in who knows how long, and watching the sexiest man I've ever seen making me what I assume will be some more of the greatest food I've ever had." She laughed incredulously. "It's too bad you don't like me very much, because I could get used to this."

Theo stared at her for long moments, an unreadable expression crossing over his face, then grunted and continued with his work.

Just when she thought he'd continue to ignore her he said, "Did you hear what Xoris told me?"

Jade laid down in front of the fireplace fully and stretched like a cat in the sun. "I walked in, and all hell broke loose. All I heard was immature male grunting and growling."

"He expressed the same concerns I've been expressing."

Jade rose to her elbows to study Theo. "He thinks I'm a spy too?"

Theo's cold look told her what she already knew.

"I really need to meet some more Clecanian females. Apparently, the women you two are used to are way more badass than most women I know." She flopped back down and threw her hands up in the air in front of her. "I'm done trying to convince you of anything. Believe what you want." Under her breath, she muttered, "Way to ruin a girl's good mood."

Jade felt a cold stab of sadness at Theo's news. After the events of today, she'd begun weighing the pros and cons of attempting to return to Earth. She felt more alive on this planet than she had on Earth in many years.

Yes, Earth was safe and familiar, but on Clecania there were so many new things to be excited about and to experience. Her life wouldn't consist of work then sleep day in and day out anymore.

The last few weeks had been filled with terror, despair, anger, sadness, passion, and wonder. For the first time in a long time, Jade felt like she was living in color.

Theo was slowly but surely settling himself under her skin, but his continued suspicions made her feel like he wouldn't want to continue to be married to her after the three-month mark, and for some inexplicable reason, that hurt.

"Dinner is ready," Theo said, setting a plate at the table.

"I'm not hungry anymore," Jade said petulantly.

She watched him walk to the door. "Eat it when you are. I have to go out for a bit."

Rolling to her stomach, she called, "You're leaving again?"

"Yes. I won't be back until late. I'm sure you can entertain yourself." And then he was gone.

Jade sat up and stared into the fire, trying to rein in her disappointment. She gave Cebo a half grin and said, "Well, at least we know he has blue balls right now. Serves him right."

28

"Please come in," Asivva said sarcastically as Theo stormed through her door without an invitation.

"What did you tell Jade?" he demanded.

She walked over to an overstuffed chair and sat instead of answering him.

Stalking over to her, he repeated, "What did you tell her?"

"It's very nice to see you too, brother. Thank you for visiting."

He threw his head back and let out a bark of frustration then slowly exhaled a breath. "Hello, dear beautiful sister. It's so lovely to see you. Is your husband home? How is month four of your marriage? Also…What. The. Fuck. Did. You. Tell. Jade?"

Her mouth spread into a grin. "Tell her about what? We talked about many things."

"About marriage and what you're required to do in a marriage."

"Oh, do you mean did I reveal the lie you told her that could get you into serious trouble?" she said, arching an elegant brow at him.

Through gritted teeth, he said, "I was thinking more about something she has called 'females' choice.'"

"Oh, *that*." Asivva smiled sweetly. "I thought it only fair that she has her own night where she does what she wants, since you apparently forced her naked into a bathtub."

Theo opened and closed his mouth, not sure how to argue with that. "Well, what did you tell her it was? I want to know what I'm in for."

Leaning back, she said, "Nothing big. I just told her that on that one night, she could tell you to do whatever she wants and you have to do it."

"What?" Theo clutched at his hair, imagining what she might ask of him.

"Judging from the last time I saw you two together, she may request that you stay in your room and leave her alone. I wouldn't blame her."

He sank into the chair adjacent to Asivva.

"You look weary, brother," she said, concern showing on her face.

"You don't understand, Asivva. I can't control my reactions around her." He hung his head. "I almost attacked Xoris when he stopped by today because he looked at her lustfully."

"Truly?" Asivva said with interest in her eyes. "I've never seen you lose control over a female before. Your temper, yes, but not control."

"Exactly. She does something to me I can't explain. I don't know how I'm going to get through the rest of the marriage."

Asivva rested her hand on his shoulder. "Maybe you should let go, Theo. Allow yourself to be happy for a few months."

He snorted. "And how will that end?"

"Well, right now your plan is to ignore her and get through these few months without much interaction, correct?"

"If I could discover any ulterior motives, that'd be better, but yes, that's the plan," Theo muttered.

"The way I see it, that offers you a very painful and frustrating three months, at the end of which she leaves." Asivva paused. "If you truly believe there's no way for her to breach your security and get information on your clients, then it'll end the same either way, I think.

"If she's a spy, you'll enjoy her for a few months, she'll get nowhere in gaining information, and then she'll leave." Asivva continued, "If she isn't a spy, you'll enjoy her for a few months and then she'll leave. In my mind, both of those options give you some peace. Even if it's temporary." She lifted his face to meet hers. "It's better than the misery you're in now. You may know happiness for a time."

What Asivva said made sense. Any way he looked at it, she'd be leaving him in three months. He could spend that time being miserable or spend it near her. Every day that passed made him want her more and more.

He had been mesmerized by the sight of her laying by the fire. Her red hair had curled into shining waves, and the firelight had danced across her pale soft skin. She'd told him she was happy and content just then. If he'd lain down with her, would she have stroked his hair the way she did Cebo's?

He shook Asivva's hand away and rose to leave, suddenly itching to see her again. "I'll think about it."

Asivva frowned at him but said nothing as he left.

***

Longing. Theo couldn't remember the last time he'd felt longing as strongly as now. When he'd returned home, he found Jade in one of his shirts, sleeping curled up on the couch. She was so peaceful. Even Cebo didn't give Theo his normal greeting. It seemed like the beast was keeping quiet for her. The whole scene looked…right. He liked his home to be full of soft, comfortable, beautiful things. She fit here.

"Alright, little wife. Let's put you in bed." Gently he lifted her from the couch, but she didn't rouse.

His heart clenched when she snuggled into the crook of his neck.

When he reached her bed, he hesitated. He was enjoying holding her and wished he didn't have to let go. When goosebumps spread over her bare legs, he finally tucked her under the covers.

Before leaving, he brushed the back of his knuckles down her cheek and whispered, "My life before, as I knew it, ended when I met you. Have a care for my life now."

29

Jade had no idea what had caused such a drastic change in Theo, but she wasn't complaining. The last few days had been downright pleasant.

The morning after he'd stormed off, she'd come down to breakfast, ready for another disappointing conversation in which she'd be friendly and he'd ignore her. While he'd been by no means happy, he had talked to her.

She'd asked endless questions about Clecania and how it looked in different parts of the world. She'd asked about his childhood and his parents. He'd told her about his four brothers and how they were rarely able to see each other.

Over the day, they'd continued talking and learning more about one another. She'd tried her damnedest to explain the allure of movies and television, but he hadn't seemed to comprehend their importance.

One topic she never went near was his job. Curiosity burned in her, but she didn't want to set him off or make him suspicious of her again. In general, Jade was very careful not to do or say anything that'd get him worked up. To her chagrin, that meant steering clear of sexy talk.

Yesterday he'd walked with her all through the woods, pointing out various plants and trees and discussing their possible uses.

In the evenings he was even allowing her to watch him cook so she could learn how to do it herself. He was still perplexed as to why she'd want to cook for herself, but he allowed it anyway.

Their time together was very nice, but there was still one problem. He continued holding back. While he didn't blow up or get angry anymore, he also didn't laugh or smile much. It was as if his passion were replaced with a lukewarm reluctance.

She could tell he still wanted her. Every so often she would catch him stealing hungry glances at her. At one point, when they'd been walking in the woods, she'd tripped and almost fallen on her face. He'd caught her easily and held her against him for a breath too long before he'd hastily righted her and let her go.

Still she hadn't pushed it. Made sure that whenever she felt aroused, she quickly left so he wouldn't scent her.

Tonight was going to be different though. It was females' choice. The made-up ceremony Asivva and her concocted ensured she could do what she wanted and he couldn't leave. Yes, tonight she'd break that calm demeanor he'd been sporting recently.

Did she want him to touch her again? Absolutely. But it was more than that. This man she'd been hanging out with the last few days was nice, but it wasn't really him. She struggled to admit it, but she missed him. Missed his ferocity, his sexuality, the way he pinned her with his dark stare. Jade wanted him to let go of that control he wore like a weight around his neck.

She had a plan. All she needed now was the guts to go through with it.

***

He looked nervous. Jade watched Theo cook as she'd done the past few days, but today, instead of the calm, focused expression he normally wore, a tight, anxious mien covered his face.

He kept sneaking glances at her, and she felt flush with success at her outfit choice. A sheer, gauzy material was covered in emerald green embroidery and lined with a flesh-toned fabric, giving the illusion that Jade was naked under the embroidery. When he'd first seen her in the tight dress, he'd had to clear his throat before speaking.

Dress? Check. Hot alien? Check. Cebo? Check.

Before heading down to dinner, she'd locked Cebo in her room so he couldn't distract them.

When he was done cooking, he guided her to the dinner table, mott in hand.

Each meal he made was somehow better than the last. The fact that he continued to examine her food habits in order to cook more of the foods she liked made Jade melt. It also made her even more certain that she was making the right decision.

She'd decided that she wanted to stay on Clecania indefinitely. She'd also decided, despite her fear of rejection, that she'd make herself emotionally open to a real relationship with Theo. Putting herself out there was terrifying, but she'd realized during her time here that terrifying could also be good.

For all his bark, Theo didn't have much bite. Not toward her, anyway. As she chewed a deep magenta vegetable similar to broccoli, she gazed longingly at Theo. Jade had come to learn that he was just a big softy with a hardened outer shell.

Theo glanced at her and then returned his gaze promptly to his plate.

"Do you like my dress?" Jade said with a smirk, not bothering to disguise her blatant compliment fishing.

Theo gave her an exasperated look. "I believe you already know how I feel about it."

Jade tilted her head at him. "A girl always likes to have verbal confirmation that her efforts weren't in vain."

The corner of his mouth lifted at that. "I received the highest grade possible in the culinary arts and yet I burned our food three times while cooking this evening. Is that enough confirmation for you?"

Setting her silverware down, she gave a mock shrug of disappointment. "I suppose it'll do."

Jade had finished her meal rather quickly tonight. Now she sat back and sipped the pink fizzy drink, which she'd dubbed prosecco 2.0. Theo, on the other hand, was eating much more slowly than normal.

Stalling, big man? she thought, downing her drink and pouring another.

Watching him eat like this made her notice that he didn't look like he enjoyed the food he'd spent so long making. Now that she thought about it, she couldn't remember him ever savoring any food. A pang of guilt ran through her to think that he might've been eating his version of liver and onions the past few days in order to keep her happy.

"So, what food do you like, Theo?"

He glanced down at his plate and gave a half shrug. "I like this food fine."

"I think you make these things because I like them, but it doesn't seem like you do." Jade leaned forward onto the table. "What's your favorite food?"

He gawked at her like she was asking, "What's your favorite season of *American Idol?*" Obviously, he'd never been asked this before.

"If I weren't here, and you wanted to make something special for yourself, what would you make?"

He chewed thoughtfully, and then answered. "A *resh* steak. I enjoy eating meat."

Of course he does. You don't get muscles like that without some protein in your diet.

"Can we have steak tomorrow?" she questioned.

He peered up at her suspiciously. "You don't like it. I've tried a few different types of meat, steak on the first night, and you always eat around it."

"That's okay. We don't always have to eat what I like. I can give it another try."

He gave her a perplexed look but then nodded. "As you wish."

Finally finished with his food, he sat back and took a long pull of his bottle.

She did the same from her glass. "I haven't said it enough before, but thank you for all the cooking and clothes and everything. I really appreciate the effort you've gone to."

The corner of his mouth turned down and he shifted in his seat as though uncomfortable with the compliment. "It's no trouble."

Alcohol, give me courage.

"Let's go sit on the couch," she said, grabbing her glass and the bottle of prosecco 2.0. Jade moved to the living room and sat with one leg tucked underneath her. After long moments, she heard Theo follow. He sat stiffly on the opposite side of the couch.

"You look nervous," she said, trying to keep the smile from her voice.

Jade felt powerful, knowing she could make a man as gorgeous and strong as Theo this nervous.

As though the words were pulled from him, he asked, "What do you want to do tonight?"

Feeling playful, she asked, "What do you think I want to do tonight?"

He stared fixedly at the fire and squirmed in his seat. "I cannot begin to fathom the torture you'll put me through."

Jade let out a laugh. "I sure hope it won't be too torturous." She reached over to trace an exposed scar on his forearm and grinned when goosebumps broke out over his smooth skin. "I want to teach you how to kiss."

He shot a sidelong glance at her then downed his mott. "Very well," he ground out, voice gone deep.

He made a move to stand, but she stopped him. "No, you can stay there. I'll come to you."

Jade started to crawl over to him on the couch. His eyes were now riveted to her. When she was right next to him, she slowly pulled her dress up to her thighs and then straddled him.

He seemed frozen in place. One arm was stretched long over the back of the couch. The other rested on the arm. Was he going to try not to touch her again? She could tell he was turned on. His chest rose and fell quickly, his eyes glued to her breasts, and when she settled herself in his lap, she felt his hard shaft jerk in response.

He was so large that sitting on his lap barely brought them face to face. She still had to tilt her head up to look into his warm green eyes. "You can put your hands on me if you want."

He gave a long exhale, set his empty mott bottle on a low end table, and then placed his hands gently on the still-covered areas of her upper thighs.

Damn his control. We're going to break that tonight baby.

She ran her hands up his chest and onto his shoulders, causing him to shudder. "Just follow my lead," she said, leaning in. "And don't bite me." Smiling, she amended, "Don't bite me…hard."

When she pressed her mouth to his, his hands tightened on her thighs but he didn't kiss her back. She continued to run her mouth over his, coaxing him to respond. Finally, when she gently bit his bottom lip, his quick intake of breath gave her an opening. Deepening the kiss, she touched his tongue with hers.

Theo gave a pained groan and slipped his tongue against hers in return. He began to kiss her back. Slowly at first but more feverishly as his confidence grew.

Soon, he'd taken the lead with a skill that made her moan and absently rock her hips against him. One of his hands snaked up to fist her hair while the other wrapped around her waist, crushing her to him.

Her nipples were tight, and even the soft material of her dress chafed. She pulled back, intending to remove her dress and his shirt so she could feel his skin against hers, but with a growl he wrenched her mouth back up to his and continued skillfully kissing her.

When he moved to nip at her jaw, she panted, "Theo, my dress. Take off my dress."

He stilled under her. She leaned back to look at him. "This can't happen," he bit out between clenched teeth.

Jade wanted to scream in frustration.

His large hands moved to clutch her waist, but he didn't let go of her.

Fucking overly controlled man! She could tell he was on the verge of losing it. His grip was firm as if he couldn't decide whether to set her away or keep her in place. Despite his words, his hips rolled. Why was he holding back?

She ran her hands up his strong arms, enjoying the feeling of his muscles jumping at the contact, and asked, "Why can't we do this? I can tell you liked kissing very much." She ground against his erection to emphasize her point.

In one swoop he lifted her and deposited her on the couch. He then sprang to his feet and backed away.

She'd known this was going to happen. It'd all been part of her plan, but it still stung that he was able to resist her when she could barely keep her hands off him.

"Why? Tell me why?" she shouted.

His eyes shifted to her mouth, and he licked his lips hungrily. "I'm not in control with you, Jade."

"That's what I want!" she said, throwing her hands up. "I want to see the real you."

"If I can't control myself, then I can't be sure I won't hurt you," he said, shaking his head.

He'd moved a safe distance away from her, but she could tell it was taking everything he had not to return. His hands clenched and unclenched as if wanting to touch her, and his eyes roamed greedily over her body.

"I believe you won't," she said stubbornly. "I'm not afraid of you."

He let out a strangled growl. "Don't you think I want to! All I can think about every day is pushing you down and sinking into your warm, wet cunt!"

He looked crazed as he shoved his hand through his hair.

"You asked about what food I like?" He barked a laugh. "No food has any taste. The only thing that makes my mouth water is the thought of devouring your sweet juices while you writhe and claw at me. I can still smell your arousal in my bed and I have to relieve myself ten times a night just to keep from storming into your room to taste you!"

He looked at her, defeated and pained. "Everything I want to do with you is rough and brutal and mindless and happens whether you want it or not. I would hurt you. I wouldn't be able to stop myself, and I wouldn't be able to live with my guilt if I hurt you."

Jade felt like she was on fire. Every single confession had cranked up her arousal until she felt hollow and aching with need. He didn't understand that she wanted him just as he was. Phase one of her plan had been a bust.

Time to nut up or shut up, Jade. Phase two, commence.

"Theo, I want all of that." One foot at a time, she backed up toward the glass door leading outside.

He watched her with brows drawn.

"I know you're never going to be that way with me though." She felt the glass wall nearing behind her.

His shoulders seemed to relax.

"Not unless I force you to lose control, that is." The cool night air rushed in as the glass parted.

Understanding lit his eyes, and he held up his hand. "Jade, do not do this."

A wicked smile curved her lips. "Catch me if you can, big guy." Then she darted.

30

She ran as fast as she could, head down, legs pumping. Instead of running down the beach as she had last time, she decided to run toward the forest. She'd have an easier time losing him in there.

She heard an ear-splitting roar sound from in the house and she grinned, knowing his control had finally snapped. Ahead of her there was a grassy field, the border of the forest on the other side.

She glanced behind her and spotted Theo at the edge of the beach, standing, watching her with eyes that had turned black. *I definitely didn't imagine that, then.* Every muscle was bulging, and he had an eerily calm expression on his face.

Fear and anticipation clenched her gut as she realized he was toying with her. Letting her get farther away before hunting her down. She'd just unleashed a predator. Was she ready for this?

Too late to turn back now.

She ran faster toward the forest, scanning the trees for a low branch. He might be big and fast, but she doubted he was a good climber too.

Almost to the forest, she concentrated on listening to movement behind her, but still she didn't hear him chasing her. She glanced back again to see if he was still standing there, but he was gone. Her eyes searched all around but didn't spot him anywhere.

Finally, she reached the tree line. *No low branches, dammit!* Her heart pounded furiously with both fear and anticipation. She charged headlong into the woods. The light from the moons was much dimmer within the forest, and the dense foliage muffled all external sound.

A twig snapped to her right and she spun, heart racing, but saw nothing.

He was here; she could sense him watching her. She felt like a stalked animal. A shiver ran down her spine. She liked it.

Picking up a fallen branch, she squinted in the dim light, waiting to swing at anything that approached her. Another rustle to her right had her running left. Jade dodged trees as she ran, navigating away from any sounds she heard.

Soon, she spotted a clearing illuminated by soft moonlight. It was so perfect here in the eerie forest. She realized he must've herded her here. Spooking her so she ran in the right direction.

Suddenly, hot breath on her shoulder made her scream and swing the branch behind her like a bat. Theo caught it in one hand mere inches from his face and wrenched it from her grip.

His eyes were still black, hair wild. At some point during his pursuit, he'd removed his clothing, and his glistening body drew her gaze. As she laid eyes on his cock, she had to remind herself to breathe. He was even larger than she'd remembered.

He prowled toward her, and she stumbled as she tried to back away. She fell onto her ass hard and landed in the clearing. A low, dangerous growl arose from him as she continued to back away.

"Mine." Theo's voice was ragged and deeper than she'd ever heard it before.

Only a few inches separated them now. He loomed over her, his gaze raking over her body and she took her opportunity to kick him in the shin, roll over and dash away. Her kick had little effect, though. Before she'd even made it off her knees, she felt two strong hands lock around her ankles, dragging her back.

As she lay face down in the grass, he crouched over her, pinning her hands above her head in one of his large hands. Then with one swift yank, he tore her dress free, leaving her in just her underwear.

He ran a shaking hand down her back until he reached her ass. With a second yank, he tore her underwear from her. Releasing her hands, he sat back on his haunches, admiring her.

When she tried to rise to her elbows, he gave both sides of her ass a hard spank and then kneaded them firmly. She gasped and fell back. His large hands explored her, rubbing and scratching until she was panting with need. Her whole body jerked, and she cried out at the sensation of a long finger being slipped into her sex from behind.

He removed his large digit from her core and she whimpered at the loss. He flipped her over onto her back and spread her legs wide. She lay still while his dark gaze roamed over her naked body. As he surveyed her, he started to purr loudly.

Guess he likes what he sees. The feeling was mutual.

Before she had time to mentally prepare, his hot, vibrating mouth was on her breast. He sucked and tongued her nipple, sending jolts of pleasure to her stomach.

She could feel his huge erection prodding her entrance, but he didn't push into her. He was trying to prepare her, she dimly realized. Affection bloomed in her chest for him. From the looks of him, he was out of his mind with lust, yet he was taking the time to make sure she was ready for him.

Slowly, he began licking and kissing his way down her shaking body until his head was between her legs, his large biceps under her knees. For a moment he just stared at her flesh. Jade grew uncomfortable under the scrutiny and tried to shimmy free. Gripping her hips, he held her in place.

Jade moaned and her eyes rolled back when his hot tongue made a pass over her slit. A deep purr sounded, and then he set upon her hungrily with his strong vibrating tongue. Jade cried out and ran her hands through his hair.

Still purring, he swiped his tongue over her clit, causing her to buck into his mouth.

"Yes, Theo! That feels so good!"

Theo growled in response, and his warm tongue flicked her clitoris again and again. The tension inside her was building to a frenzy. Her head thrashed and her hands fisted in his hair.

He slid one finger into her core, pumping in time with his licks.

"Yes! Yes! Theo!" Her back arched violently and her whole body came apart with her climax. Theo grabbed the tops of her thighs, pulling her down against his greedy tongue.

Her body was still reeling from the aftershocks of her orgasm when he flipped her so she was flat on her stomach. He looped one arm under her hips, lifting her until she was on her hands and knees before him. He nudged her knees farther apart with his own and with his free hand he palmed her breasts.

The touch of his hard shaft grazing her overly sensitive clit made her jump forward in surprise. Like lightning, a large hand wrapped around her throat and the arm around her waist tightened, holding her firmly in place.

She felt the crown of his cock breaching her entrance. Inch by inch he pushed into her, filling her almost to the point of pain, until he was seated fully. His hand released her throat but lingered, ready to clutch her again if she moved away. His body settled over hers, his hot breath at her ear. Licking and nipping her neck and back, he used his hand to tease her nipples until she grew wet again.

When she covered one of his hands with her own, wanting to touch him, he started to purr again. She cried out as the vibration shot through her whole body like electricity. The sheer size of him ensured that he was pressed tightly against every nerve ending inside her core.

Theo's whole body was shaking now. His shaft throbbing inside her. She pressed back against him more to let him know she was ready.

"Do you hurt?" he grated against her ear in a deep, guttural voice.

She turned her head to press a soft kiss to his lips and rolled her hips on him. "No, Theo. It feels sooo good. Keep going."

He groaned and nuzzled her neck as though relieved before pulling out and slamming back into her. She cried out with pleasure. He began pumping into her more quickly, building her pleasure.

The force of his bucks were pushing her forward and no matter how hard she fought to stay on her hands, she found herself collapsing to the ground. His big hands circled her upper arms and pulled her up, causing her upper body to hover off the ground as he rammed into her.

The tension in her was building rapidly. His deep moans, mixed with the vibration coming from his cock, were going to send her over the edge soon.

As though sensing this, Theo grated, "Come for me, wife."

Her second orgasm rolled over her, causing her body to tremble and jerk. When she cried out his name, his thrusts became erratic and rough, escalating her orgasm to heights she hadn't known were possible. He suddenly pressed her back to his front, hugging her to him while ramming into her, bellowing to the sky as he came. She could feel the hot jet of his semen coating the walls of her sex, and it made her shiver.

He leaned them back while still inside her so that she knelt between his legs. Languidly he kissed and rubbed every inch of her sweat-coated body he could reach.

They stayed that way for long minutes until their breathing became normal again. Jade's eyelids grew heavy as he petted and massaged her. Being wrapped up in his big body like this after experiencing two of the best orgasms of her life had her feeling relaxed and boneless.

She closed her eyes and turned her head to rest her cheek on his big chest. She smiled when she heard him softly purring once more.

***

As gently as he could, Theo extracted himself from Jade and lifted her sleeping body into his arms. Half asleep, she raised her hand to his chest and gave a contented sigh.

The long walk back to the house gave him time to reflect on what had just happened. Shame washed over him as he recalled how he'd chased her down and taken her like an animal in the dirt.

Earlier that night, she'd driven him into a lather with her kiss. Theo didn't know how Clecanians had gone without kissing for this long. After experiencing it, he couldn't imagine not taking her soft mouth with his hourly.

Already on the verge of ripping off her clothes, he'd tried to stop himself. Distance himself from her. But then she'd run.

The few minutes that he'd prevented himself from tearing after her had required every ounce of control he'd possessed, but eventually, the beast in him had prevailed, jumped to the fore even. All reason and logic had fled as he'd stalked her through the forest. He'd lurked in the shadows, like the predator he was, watching the pretty skin on her cheeks pinken with exertion. Scenting her arousal and fear.

The way she'd reacted to him had been so intoxicating. She'd fought, forcing him to make her submit to him, but she'd also soothed him when he'd feared she was in pain.

He looked down at her resting without fear in his arms. Bits of leaves were scattered throughout her wild red hair. Her nipples were light pink and swollen from his ministrations.

There would be no female in the universe more perfect for him than this one. For as long as he could remember, even before he'd been scarred, he'd been taught to hide his Traxian tendencies. His temper and animalistic aggression were all Traxian qualities and were therefore unwelcome by the pure Lignas females of Tremanta.

Jade seemed to crave that side of him. Tonight, for the first time in his life, he'd felt truly free and accepted. If only mates still existed. If she were his true mate, they'd never be parted. Laws of matehood outweighed all others.

Sadness and shame washed over him once more. He didn't deserve her as a mate. Hadn't treated her as such thus far. Only a few days ago, she'd told him she wanted to enjoy herself while she was here. That meant she was still intent on leaving him after the three-month marriage ended.

When he reached her room, he shooed a sprawled sleeping Cebo from the bed then laid her gently under the covers. Retrieving a cloth covered in cleansing foam from the bathroom, he set about cleaning the dirt and his seed from her.

She let out a small hiss when he pressed the cloth to her sex.

"Sorry," he said, quickly moving away. Maybe she'd see this as an invasion.

Rising to her elbows, she looked at him sleepily. "That's okay. Just a little sore." A sexy smile curved her lips. "You aren't exactly small." Yawning, she cuddled down into her blankets. "I'll just clean up tomorrow. I don't know about you, but I'm exhausted."

"Sleep well, Jade." Theo lingered at her bedside, not wanting to leave.

"You're not staying?" A hurt expression crossed her face.

She wanted him to stay? To share her bed in sleep? He remembered that his parents had done that, but they'd been unusual. Clecanian women tended to prefer separate sleeping quarters.

Theo had always longed to know how it felt to hold a female in his arms as he slept, but he'd resigned himself to the fact that he never would.

"I assumed you wanted me to leave. Sleeping together is…" He ran his hand over the back of his neck. "Well, it's just not done."

"You guys don't cuddle? Weird." She yawned. "Would you prefer to sleep in your room?"

Would I rather sleep alone in my room or in bed with a beautiful naked female?

Theo snorted, and Jade laughed sweetly. "Well then, come on in," she said, lifting the covers for him.

Still he didn't join her. "Are you sure you wouldn't like some space from me? After what I did to you…I thought you might not want to see me for a time."

Jade let out a frustrated breath and then sat up in the bed. The covers fell to her waist, uncovering her supple breasts, and he felt himself growing hard again.

She snapped in front of him and covered herself. "Theo, I'm not Clecanian. I enjoyed what we did in the woods. *A lot.* And in case you've forgotten, I'm the one who pushed you to do it in the first place. I knew what would happen. I even fought back to get you riled up. If I weren't super tired and sore, I'd jump your bones right here and now. I'd like to spoon with you if you want to."

The words she used didn't make much sense, but he gleaned her meaning, and pride swelled in his chest.

"Try and think about it this way," she began. "Forget about what normal Clecanians do, and just trust your instincts. I'll tell you if I don't want you to do something. Unless I specifically say no, then do whatever you want to do."

Whatever he wanted? Could he touch her and kiss her whenever he wanted? Hold her the way most females hated?

"What is 'to spoon?'" he asked, moving to lay beside her.

She smiled brightly at him and rolled to her side. "It's when we lay on our sides with my back to your front or vice versa."

Doing as she said, he lay on his side so he was facing her back. Pleasant, but he would've preferred to look at her face.

Jade glanced over her shoulder and chuckled. "I'm going to have to teach you everything, aren't I?"

She scooted back until her naked back was pressed to him, and his now-hard erection was pressed against her bottom. She guided his arms so one curled underneath her neck and the other wrapped around her stomach.

She wants to sleep like this? So close to me?

Testing his limits, he curled his body into hers and tightened his hold on her waist, pulling her more firmly against him.

"Are you comfortable?" she said softly.

Theo had never felt more comfortable in his entire life. He nuzzled her hair and neck, breathing in her scent. When he began to purr contentedly, she laughed.

"I'll take that as a yes. Do you always purr? Do all Clecanians do that? Do you just do it during sexy time?"

"So many questions, wife. I thought you were tired."

"Tired, but also curious."

"Many Clecanians do. Before you, I hadn't purred in a very long time." He wasn't sure how to answer her last question. "We purr when we feel…happiness without effort. When we are content."

When we feel whole, he said to himself.

"Mmm," Jade mumbled, half asleep.

Theo didn't know how long he laid there with her, listening to her sleep. Her slow, even breaths and her steady heartbeat lulled him, but he struggled to stay awake, to enjoy holding her this way.

He kissed her ear softly, and his chest clenched when she moaned and in sleep, turned her head toward his touch.

Was this how she'd be with him? Trusting and sweet? Would she choose to be close to him throughout the day and then give herself to him at night?

If he believed he'd be able to hold his sated female like this every night, then all the pain he'd been through in his life would've been worth it.

Theo now knew for certain that he'd never be able to let her go. There was no happy existence if she weren't with him. Maybe if he tried hard enough, he could convince her to extend their marriage, if only for a few more months.

***

When Theo awoke, he did so to a painful erection. At some point during the night, he'd rolled to his back. For a moment, panic overwhelmed him because he was no longer holding his soft female. He settled when the haze from sleep faded and he saw that Jade still slumbered peacefully on him.

Not a dream.

She laid with her head on his shoulder and her arm stretched across his stomach. Her leg was draped over his pelvis, trapping his shaft against her soft thigh. He stifled a groan when he felt her breasts against his rib cage and the heat of her sex at his hip.

She shifted in her sleep, and her leg rubbed against him, making him groan. He felt her body stiffen and knew he'd fucked up. She was awake and now she'd surely move away from him. His hold around her hip tightened in preparation.

She looked up at him groggily, and he held his breath, waiting to see her reaction.

Astonishingly, her body softened and she gave him a sleepy smile before stretching up and planting a soft kiss on his mouth. Settling her head back onto his shoulder, she began lightly touching his chest and stomach. "Good morning."

He managed to grate out, "Good morning."

"Are you okay?" she asked, concern showing in her eyes.

He grabbed her hand to stop her movements. His arousal was escalating with her soft touches. He should leave. Go relieve himself before he jumped on her again. He had no idea how long it would take a small human female to recover from sex and if he pounced on her before she was recovered, he could end up hurting her.

With most females, he'd keep a thought like that to himself, but she wasn't like most females. He recalled her advice about following his instincts, and he chose to answer her truthfully. So far, she hadn't scared easily. "Unless you want to be rolled over and mounted, you'd best stop touching me like that."

To his immense pleasure, her mouth curved into another sexy grin. The pressure on his cock eased when she removed her leg. Before he could exhale his sigh of relief, she gripped him in her soft palm. His head rolled back and he bucked into her hand.

"I'd like to clean off a little before we do that again, but it seems like you might need some immediate assistance."

He watched breathlessly as she rolled off him and knelt between his legs. She couldn't be doing what he hoped. It wasn't done here.

When she licked her lips, he almost came right then and there.

***

Jade gazed down at the powerful, virile man lying under her, and her nipples hardened. He was so handsome, so masculine. Slowly she began running her hands over his tightly corded muscles. Exploring him leisurely in a way she hadn't been able to before.

She thrilled at the way his strong body flexed under her touch, and the intense stare he was giving her let her know he was just as enthralled with her.

Despite her earlier claim, she would've been very happy indeed if he'd rolled her over, but she wanted to do something special for him. The look in his eyes when she'd admitted that Earth women gave blowjobs replayed in her mind.

His big body arched to meet her mouth as she kissed and licked down his abs, making it clear what her intentions were. When she hovered just over his glistening crown, she peered up at him. "Try to stay still, okay?"

He nodded hastily.

Jade took the crown into her mouth, swirling her tongue to lap up his precum. Theo's eyes rolled back and he bit out curses under his breath.

Emboldened, she used one free hand to cup and fondle his heavy sac. She used the other to firmly stroke the base of his shaft.

"Jade, that feels so fucking good." He shuddered.

She moaned around him and took him deeper into her mouth. She felt herself growing wet. Never in her life had she been this turned on while giving a blow job. The man before her was no typical man, though.

Sweat beaded his glorious chest, and his muscles bulged. *It must be killing him not to move.*

When she began to pump her mouth up and down on him, sucking wetly, his whole body shuddered violently and his hands reached out to touch her, but then he let out a curse and reached behind his head to grip the headboard instead.

"I can smell your arousal, wife," he growled in a broken voice. "You're going to make me come."

She pumped her mouth faster, taking him as deeply as she could. His large shaft was throbbing in her hand.

He stilled and then bellowed to the ceiling, the cords in his necks straining. His massive body quaked and she heard wood splinter as she swallowed his hot orgasm.

He looked down at her with adoration in his eyes and gave a desperate groan as she languidly licked the length of his gorgeous cock.

He pulled her up his big body and kissed her passionately, making her melt against him.

"Most guys don't like to kiss after a girl goes down on them."

He grinned. "I'm not most guys." His hand moved to cup her sex, and she released a soft moan.

"Let's take a bath first. You aren't a small guy, and last night wasn't gentle." She saw the uncertainty flash in his eyes and quickly added, "It was amazing, and I want to do it many more times, but it'll take me a bit to recover from our first time."

He nodded, seeming mollified. "Then I'll take you to the bath. I'll bring some breakfast for us to have in the bath as well."

"Ooh. Breakfast in bath. I like it."

Half an hour later, Jade was in heaven. Baths had always been something Jade loved. She could sit in warm water until every inch of her was puckered and be as happy as a clam about it.

Now she was sitting in a hot bath the size of a small swimming pool, eating a sweet, flaky food that reminded her of a dry baklava, while a tattoo-covered Adonis massaged her shoulders.

It was an understatement to say that last night had worked out the way she'd wanted it. Not only had he given up control, but now he seemed all but giddy.

He'd sauntered into the bathroom buck naked with a tray of delicious-looking food. His hair had been mussed from sleep and sex, and the purely masculine grin he'd shot her had made her weak in the knees.

Nothing is sexier than a well-loved Theo, she mused to herself.

He was different now. Affectionate. He rarely went a minute without finding some way to touch her or kiss her, even if it was just to brush a hair off her face. When he began rubbing her shoulders and back, he'd had to grab her around the waist to keep her from sinking into the warm water.

"Another well-deserved grade in massage, Theo." She moaned, thoroughly content.

He pressed a hot open-mouthed kiss to her shoulder in response. "How long does it take for you to recover from sex?" he rumbled while kissing the nape of her neck.

"Hmm?" It took her a moment for her brain to catch up. "Oh, I'm not sure. I'm probably fine now."

"Now?" he said incredulously, turning her to look in her eyes.

Jade faced him and backed away, treading water. "Yeah, why are you surprised?"

He gave her a hungry look and started moving toward her, but she held up a hand, indicating he should stay put. He frowned but sat back down. "Clecanian females need twenty-four hours to recover."

Curious, Jade asked, "What exactly do you mean when you say 'recover?' Are they hurt or something?"

Theo looked confused. "No, their bodies just don't allow them to have sex for twenty-four hours. I believe it gives the seed a better chance to take root. What do *you* mean by 'recover?'"

"Their bodies don't allow it? How?" she asked, ignoring his question.

"Their entrance closes tightly and they won't produce any lubrication for twenty-four hours until their entrance relaxes again, sometimes longer. Sex would be very painful if attempted during that time."

"Wild," Jade said more to herself than Theo.

"Jade, how are you different?" Theo said sternly.

"None of that happens to me." She shrugged, then asked, "So, does that mean Clecanian women can only have sex one time per day?"

"They only need time to recover if they've had an orgasm during sex. Technically they could have sex more than once a day if they didn't reach climax, but it's unlikely any female would stay with someone who was unable to bring her to orgasm." Theo rushed through his explanation then asked, "Jade, are humans able to have sex more than once per day?"

Jade scoffed. "Once. Ten times. It doesn't matter."

Theo's gaze darkened hungrily, but then a flash of concern lit his features. "Then why do you need to recover?" His jaw clenched. "Did I hurt you?"

A pang of affection ran through Jade when she saw how worried he was. She moved to stand between his knees. Wrapping her arms around his neck, she tried to reassure him. "I'm not really hurt, just sore. The more we have sex, the more I'll get used to your size, and I won't be as sore as often."

He ran his hands down her waist and settled on her hips. Eyes riveted to the tops of her breasts, he groaned. "Be sure to let me know when you're feeling better."

"You will be the first to know." Jade giggled.

Theo shot her an unguarded smile. If her plan was truly working, then maybe he was beginning to like her despite his earlier doubts. His treatment of her this morning gave her hope that he might want her to stay with him.

"Theo, what's changed?" she asked, searching his eyes for an answer.

"What do you mean?"

"You're treating me so differently. Do you still think I'm a spy?"

She could almost see him working through the question himself. "I don't know whether you are a spy," he said haltingly. "I do know that I no longer care if you are."

Jade flushed with pleasure. If his admission was true, maybe she had a shot of convincing him to let her stay longer.

Reaching up, he twined his fingers through the hair at her nape. "You could betray me a hundred times over, and I fear I'd still fall at your feet."

Sincerity shone from his eyes. She felt as though her heart had skipped a beat.

One good lay, and you're ready to latch onto him forever.

She had fallen for him. Was in so deep now that she knew she'd never recover. How could she persuade him to keep her? His parents had stayed together. Maybe he'd want to too.

She could tell Theo liked her; his declaration just now told her he may like her a lot, but that didn't mean he wanted her to stay. The sex was amazing between them, no question about it, but he was an alien. She couldn't be sure she was reading his signals right. If she admitted her feelings to him, she risked him becoming closed off again.

Asivva. She would know. That Gathering thing was in less than a week. Jade knew Asivva was going to be there, and she could only hope her sister-in-law would have some kick-ass advice for her on how to win her brother over permanently.

She leaned in to give him a quick kiss, but he snagged her around the waist, deepening the kiss. The student had become the master in the kissing department. He knew just how to lick and tease her to make her mind go blank. Her nipples puckered when they brushed across his hot, wet skin, and she whimpered.

"Jade," he said as he nipped his way up her jaw line. "I can do what I please unless you tell me no?"

Jade must be pretty easy when it came to him, because she couldn't imagine saying no to anything at the moment. She could only nod mutely as his tongue circled the shell of her ear.

Voice gone hoarse, he said, "Good. I'm starving."

He lifted and twisted her in the air until she was perched on the edge of the pool. His meaning became clear when he draped her legs over his shoulders and all but devoured her sex with his gaze.

Her head fell back when he began exploring her wet folds with his fingers.

"When I saw you here for the first time, I almost finished right then." He pumped one large finger inside. Her back arched in response, and a moan tore from her throat. "So tight," he said in awe. "I felt you come around me last night. Your little core convulsed around my shaft with your orgasm. It felt like heaven.

"And when I put my mouth on you…" His thumb began circling her clit in maddeningly slow circles. "It was like nothing I've ever tasted."

Her hands lifted to fondle her breasts. The tension was building inside her, and she was already so close to coming. She could feel his hot breath on her clit now.

"I could devour your luscious cunt for every meal and die happy." His hot tongue lapped her sensitive bud, and he pumped a second finger inside her.

"Theo, I'm so close."

He latched onto her clit, and his purring started up again. "I love to hear you moan my name like that."

The vibration on her clit was too much. Jade's legs shook and her whole body tensed with her orgasm. "Theo! Yes!" she cried as she fisted his hair, rolling her hips into his mouth. He removed his fingers and replaced them with his hot tongue. He growled and clenched her thighs painfully as his tongue licked her, prolonging her orgasm.

Jade's whole body relaxed, melting into the cool tile.

Theo lifted her and slid her back into the water with him, holding her tightly.

"You're really good at that, you know," Jade said through panted breaths.

He grinned down at her wolfishly, and she once again marveled at how handsome he looked when he smiled. "The bud at your entrance," he began.

"My clitoris, or clit for short," Jade corrected.

"Your clit is so sensitive. It's very easy to make you come."

Jade barked out a laugh. "Tell that to Earth guys."

He scowled at that. "I don't want to hear about other males you've fucked."

"No, no," she soothed. "I just mean that on Earth there's a running joke that men can be idiots when it comes to this.

Some men don't know what to do with a clitoris unless told specifically."

"Then they don't deserve to bed a female," he said with a shadow of a scowl still on his face. "I've never pleasured a human female before, but your reactions told me more than enough to discover how you like to be touched."

Clever alien.

A loud whine sounded from the bathroom door. Jade chuckled. "We should probably get out. I think Cebo is feeling neglected."

Theo grunted but nodded, lifting them both out of the tub. He wrapped her in a soft warm towel before getting his own.

She bit her lip as she surveyed him. His towel was slung low over his narrow hips, and rivulets of water ran down his chiseled physique. He caught her staring and glanced down at his body, turning to see what she was looking at.

"You have an amazing body," she purred.

He looked down at himself again, and the corner of his mouth lifted in an unsure smile.

She could tell he still thought of himself as ugly but enjoyed her compliments. Her heart tightened in her chest, and she decided she'd need to make sure to compliment him daily to undo the decades of damage.

31

Happiness had overwhelmed Theo for the last few days. He never knew it could be like this between a male and a female. Even his parents hadn't been this way. She let him touch her whenever he wanted, and she touched him as well.

When he sat on the couch, she'd cuddle next to him. When he passed her in the hall, she'd press a soft kiss to his mouth. She was more of a companion than a typical wife and he found that he never grew tired of her. He only ever wanted to be near her. In the mornings they'd talk and joke about one thing or another while he taught her about Clecanian history.

She had a wonderful sense of humor, and he'd discovered that he did as well. Before her, he'd never felt light; now he joked easily and his heart warmed every time she laughed. Jade was so free and unguarded. She laughed and smiled without restraint, and she welcomed all of his sexual advances with a lust equal to his own.

One morning he'd awoken to her heavenly tongue lapping at his semi-hard shaft. Late last night he'd boldly returned the favor. She'd come to consciousness on the verge of an orgasm.

Instead of being angry and ending their marriage as a Clecanian female would've done, she'd sweetly moaned his name, tugged him up her body, and wrapped her legs around his waist until he'd buried himself inside her. He'd found that he enjoyed having sex with her in this way, face to face. It was new for him but highly arousing.

The second time they'd had sex had been one of the most erotic experiences of his life. She'd straddled him on the couch in front of the fire and slowly lowered herself onto his aching shaft. He had two new experiences that night that had changed him irreversibly. Theo had never had sex face to face before, and he'd also never had a female ride on top of him as Jade had.

Seeing the pleasure on her face as she'd ground her sex against him had driven him wild. Her heavy breasts and soft pink nipples were within easy reach, and he could grip her ass while she'd rocked against him.

He'd kept himself from coming, wanting it to last for as long as possible. Finally, after they'd both been slick with sweat and she'd come, moaning in his ear, three times, he'd climaxed while taking her mouth with his.

There was another reason he enjoyed facing her during sex. From this new position, he could see her eyes. She really looked at him. Her eyes roamed over him with delight, and for the first time in his life he felt attractive.

Normally, he took Clecanian females from behind because it was the most effective position for a Clecanian female orgasm. Those females usually looked at him as little as possible and he assumed they closed their eyes tightly, imagining another male.

Jade couldn't seem to look at him enough. She would run her hands, and mouth, all over his body, over his scars. He could even scent her becoming aroused from just looking at his naked body. It thrilled him to know she was as attracted to him as he was to her and that his scars meant nothing to her. They were sexy to her.

It still amazed him that she accepted him completely. Their slow, erotic lovemaking was second only to their furious aggressive fucking.

Since she had no need for a recovery period, he'd enjoyed letting his "beast," as she called it, out of its cage whenever it overtook him. When that happened, he'd rip her clothes off and roughly fuck her wherever they were. She'd come screaming his name.

He still didn't understand why such a possessive feeling came over him. He'd become crazed in an instant.

Instead of pushing this feeling away, he'd begun to accept it as part of him just as she had. He knew for certain now that he'd never be able to let her go. He'd even begun thinking through a plan to steal her away if she decided to leave him in two months. There was no way he could live without her after experiencing what his life could be like.

She might be angry at first. He smiled. His Jade was a force to be reckoned with, after all, but he urged himself to believe that, in time, she'd come around and they'd settle back into this state of bliss.

At present, he reclined against her soft body, his head on her breast and her knees on either side of his hips. She played with his hair and hummed as he stared into the fire.

"What is the party tomorrow going to be like?" she asked quietly.

The one month Gathering. Theo had been dreading it. If there were any way he could get out of going to it, he would. "It's dull."

"What's it for exactly?"

"It's for nosy people without anything better to do, to come and gawk at the new couples. It gives them fodder for gossip. Which couples are getting along, which ones hate each other, which female has the finest gown, and…"

"And what?" He could hear the smile in her voice. She thought his dislike of the event was humorous.

He didn't want to reveal the other reason a Clecanian might attend The Gathering, didn't want her to know that she'd be courted and gawked at all night, and that he'd be expected to sit back and allow it. His temper flared even now just thinking about it, and he ran his hand down her thighs to soothe himself.

His ire settled somewhat when he heard that her voice had grown throaty. "Tell me what I need to know so I don't walk in blind."

"Males will be trying to speak to you." His jaw clenched when he realized there'd be many more onlookers at this Gathering than others. They'd come in droves to see the beautiful human female who'd chosen the scarred monster. Males would probably think they'd have an easy time seducing her away from him.

Her hands stilled in his hair for a moment. "Why?"

"Because they'll want to convince you to choose them at the next ceremony."

Little do they know she won't be attending any other ceremonies, he thought darkly.

"We've only been together a month. Isn't that... I don't know...insensitive?"

"It's the way of things here," he said, feeling his skin crawl.

What if she enjoyed speaking to another male? He could picture her face when she finally understood how beneath her he was. She would see him side by side with males who had the charm and looks he'd always envied, and she'd find him lacking.

Seeming to notice his tension, she tilted his chin up and forced him to meet her eyes. "Hey there, big guy. Don't worry. I'm not the type of girl to shop for ground beef when I have steak at home."

Her words were strange again and the meaning didn't completely translate. He thought she was telling him that she wouldn't need to look for another male because she was happy with him. A purr rumbled in his chest.

He rolled, pulling her under him. She wrapped her arms around his neck and tugged him down for a kiss. He needed to make sure she was well loved tonight. So much so that she wouldn't have the energy to even glance at any other male.

***

Hours later he carried her exhausted body to their room. He'd started thinking of it as "theirs." "Their" room. "Their" bed. The only reason he ever visited his old lonely room was to retrieve clothing or check his messages from work.

He scolded himself—he hadn't checked on work in days. It wasn't unusual for a newly married male to be absent from work during their marriage, but the clients Theo dealt with tended to be a little more demanding than most.

Cebo settled in his vacant spot on the bed after he tucked Jade in.

Before heading to his office, he whispered to Cebo, "Don't get too comfortable. She's mine."

Pace quickening, he walked to his office and reviewed his communications log. It had only been a few minutes, yet he itched to return to her.

Scrolling through his messages, he saw the normal requests for various jobs. He denied them all. Theo intended to never work again. Leaving Jade for unknown lengths of time to go on dangerous missions for large sums of money he didn't need was now pointless to him.

It'd be suspicious if he announced his retirement now, when he had two months of marriage left, so instead he sent polite but firm explanations of his temporary absence. When he did finally take Jade away for good, he'd notify his contacts of his retirement.

His heart rate picked up when he came across a message concerning Jade. The contact he'd met with a few weeks ago had given Rhaego information about Jade's abductors. Rhaego hadn't waited for Theo's go ahead and had instead tracked down and detained the two Cae males who'd transported Jade. He was keeping them in a classified location near Tremanta and was awaiting further instructions.

The last piece of information Rhaego divulged made his blood run cold.

There's treachery close to you. Contact me as soon as you get this.

That doesn't mean her, he told himself, but a twinge of uncertainty crept back into his mind. If he left now, he could make it to Rhaego and the imprisoned Cae within an hour.

He could finally discover what had brought her here. Either she was telling the truth and she truly chose him above all others, or she was a spy.

It no longer mattered to Theo how she'd come into his life, but he worried about how their relationship would change if he found out she in fact had been sent here by an enemy.

Tomorrow. He'd go and see Rhaego tomorrow night after they returned from The Gathering. He'd tell her how he felt, that he wanted her to stay with him and that he'd captured the two Cae. Then he'd interrogate them and learn the truth.

Theo desperately wanted Jade to decide to stay with him on her own. He didn't want to have to steal her away against her will. He knew she'd hate him, but for some reason his skin crawled and an emptiness clawed in his stomach every time he thought of her leaving.

If only his mother were alive. She'd be able to tell him why he was feeling this way and whether this extreme possessiveness came from his Traxian blood.

Could he go through with it? Taking her away to live like an outlaw? He doubted it.

He sent an encoded message to Rhaego arranging their meeting and returned to Jade, sleeping peacefully. Cebo groaned halfheartedly but jumped off the bed when Theo approached.

He pulled Jade against him and felt his heart ache when she snuggled closer to him, even in sleep.

If she wouldn't stay with him and he couldn't steal her, what would become of him? He whispered, into her hair, "Stay with me."

32

"Where is that damn dress?" Jade hissed, rifling through her closet.

Asivva had told her she'd selected a dress for The Gathering when she'd delivered all of these clothes a few weeks ago, but Jade couldn't remember where she'd put it.

It was no wonder Jade had trouble—her closet was stuffed full and she'd barely even looked through most of it, choosing instead to wear Theo's comfortable shirts.

"Ah-ha!" she said triumphantly, reaching into the back of a deep alcove.

A shiver ran down her back. Theo was going to love it. It was risqué in all the best ways. She wanted to make sure she looked her best tonight. All morning he'd been acting strange, and she assumed he was nervous about The Gathering. It seemed like it'd be a great opportunity to mingle and make some new friends, a.k.a, Theo's worst nightmare.

Her goal for the night was to dutifully ignore all other men except for him. She wanted to show him how smitten she was, and she wanted him to feel pride and not shame that they were there together.

After last night he deserved it. He'd been a man on a mission. They'd had sex three times and he'd kept making her come with his hands and mouth over and over until she'd finally had to tell him no.

He hadn't accepted any reciprocation either, knocking her hands away each time she reached for him. It was as if he'd wanted to prove to her that he could master her body. Could make it do whatever he wanted. He'd succeeded.

She'd show him her appreciation tonight. If all went well, Asivva would give her some good advice, she would convince him to let her stay, and they'd live happily ever after.

Where was he anyway? Earlier today he'd said he had to go take care of some business and then he'd left, promising to be back in time to get ready and ride with her to The Gathering.

She'd burned to ask where he was going, but his odd calculating behavior had kept her from doing so. He'd looked like he was working through something, and she'd wanted to give him space to do so.

"What do you think?" she said, holding up her dress to Cebo.

He lifted his head and cocked it to one side.

"This is gonna kill, I'm telling you."

Jade stood back and admired the dress again. The silky material was an inky black and glittered faintly. Asivva had told her it was unusual for females to wear black, but she'd chosen it for Jade anyway.

The obsidian color would look perfect next to Theo with his deeply tanned skin and black scars. Rather than wearing a brightly colored gown that'd appear incongruent next to Theo, she'd compliment him.

Remember to thank Asivva.

The cut of the dress was simple. The cowl neckline exposed just enough cleavage to be sexy without revealing too much. The back, however, rode low, exposing the majority of her back. She could just imagine Theo running his warm palm over her bare back.

Now what to do with her hair? She knew Theo liked it to be loose, but she thought an updo might work better with a backless dress.

"Over the shoulder it is," she said and started haphazardly pinning her hair in place.

"I approve," came a deep voice from the doorway.

Jade screamed, tumbling backward off the stool she sat on.

Theo laughed heartily, and she couldn't help but smile at the sound.

Clutching her heart, she chuckled. "That wasn't very nice."

She returned to sit on the stool. "I don't understand how someone who's your size can move so quietly."

He sauntered over to her, carrying a deep purple bag. "That's my job, remember? If my targets saw me coming, I'd be out of work."

Theo had always refused to talk about his job, and she'd learned not to ask questions. Why was he talking about it now? Did he finally trust her?

He crouched behind her, resting his chin on her shoulder and placing the small bag on her lap. "I have a present for you."

She grinned at his reflection in the mirror and began rifling through the bag. She opened a small box to find the most stunning pair of earrings she'd ever seen. "They're beautiful," she said, holding one up in front of her.

The earrings were made of large, glittering green jewels more vibrant than emeralds. They were long and would dangle just above her shoulders when in place. A second strand of smaller jewels curved upward and would wrap around the edge of her ear from her lobe to her cartilage.

There was no needle on the end of the earrings but rather a very small magnet. All of Jade's holes from piercings had healed in the magic tube weeks ago. Clecanians from Tremanta didn't believe in those types of body modifications, or so Zikas had told her.

"I'm glad you like them," he said, squeezing her arms.

"I *love* them. Is that what you went out to do today?" she asked, clipping one to her ear.

"Yes. I had to retrieve them from Asivva." She gave him a questioning look. "They were my mother's. A gift to her from my father. I never thought I'd have a wife to give them to, but Asivva convinced me to give them to her rather than sell them just in case."

Jade's eyes watered at the sweet gesture. He'd not only brought her a beautiful gift but a family heirloom. All her treasured belongings were still on Earth. He had no idea how much it meant to her to have a tie to a family now, even if she'd never met them.

Turning to look him in the eyes, her voice full of emotion, she said, "Thank you."

He studied her face for long moments before rising. "We need to leave soon; I'll go get changed."

Jade dabbed at her eyes and continued to fuss with her hair. "Okay, I'm moving."

He just keeps getting better, Jade thought as she finished getting ready and donned her dress.

As she hopped on one foot then the other, slipping on her sandals, she called out to him, "I'm ready!"

From just outside her doorway, he said, "There is no need to y—" His words died in his throat when he saw her.

She spread her arms. "You like?"

He gave her a predatory grin. "Your efforts weren't in vain," he joked.

"You haven't even seen the best part yet." She turned, watching him over her shoulder, and showed him the back of her dress.

His jaw slackened and he scrubbed a hand over his face.

Jade took in his formal attire. She didn't know why but she'd been expecting a suit or a tux. The clothes on Clecania had been so normal for the most part. His outfit now reminded her that he wasn't human.

His pants were black. The fabric like soft leather. His shirt was made out of the same silky material as her dress and flowed open at his chest. Hard charcoal plating covered the sides of his legs, arms and the tops of his shoulders. He wore a heavy cape, similar to those of Roman centurions, knotted at his shoulder. The outfit as a whole was sexy and dangerous and intensely alien.

"You look so handsome," she breathed.

"We should go before you turn around again," he said, grinning at her.

"Don't wait up, Cebo!" Jade patted the annoyed-looking hound on his head and hurried to join Theo. "How far away is it?"

Theo guided her outside to a waiting floating vehicle. "Not far," he said, gesturing for her to get in.

He sat opposite of her in the cab, reminding her of the first day they'd met. He'd been so angry and quiet then. Now he was angry and stoic. He sat stiffly and seemed to be lost in thought.

As the vehicle started moving, she crossed to sit next to him. Taking his hand, she asked, "Are you alright? Nervous?"

He glanced around, not meeting her eyes.

Maybe he is worried about me talking to other men.

"I probably won't even be able to speak to most of them, remember?" She tapped the ear in which her translator had been implanted.

Theo gave her a tight smile. "I'm sure most if not all of the Tremantians attending have had their translators updated specifically to speak with you." He glanced down at their joined hands and squeezed. "Others may not speak well of me tonight."

"What will they tell me?" She grazed her hand over his jaw. "That you're a brute?"

With a playful smile, she sat in his lap and kissed the corners of his mouth. "That you're going to chase me down in the woods like an animal?"

His purring started, and she could feel the corners of his mouth lift in a smile.

"Will they tell me all about your temper and how at any moment you might rip off my clothes and have your way with me?"

He sucked in a breath when she reached down to stroke his length.

Sliding down his body to kneel between his legs, she continued in a mocking tone, "Beware, Jade! He may even force you into a bathtub with him."

His hard cock sprang free when she released the odd fastening on his pants. She ran her tongue up his length then looked up into his eyes.

"Is there really anything they can say that will scare me away?" She sucked him in deeply, her cheeks hollowing. His head fell back, and he grated out curses under his breath.

It didn't take long before she felt him stiffen and begin to shudder, roaring to the ceiling.

Lovingly she lapped up his seed and then re-did the fastening on his pants. She sat next to him again and grasped his face in her hands. "Don't worry. I can think for myself." Raising an eyebrow, she added, "Haven't you learned that by now?"

He chuckled, his chest still heaving. "I may need another reminder tonight." Theo wrapped his arm around her shoulders and held her close, resting his chin on her head.

They rode in silence, enjoying each other's company until the vehicle gently floated to a stop. Jade frowned as she saw all the tension she'd just sucked out of Theo return in full force.

He exhaled, his shoulders slumping, then exited and held out a hand to help her.

The building before them was perfectly round. Climbing vines covered the high white walls. Jade gasped as she glimpsed the roof, which wasn't so much a roof as a dome built entirely out of shimmering stained glass. She couldn't tell from this vantage point, but she estimated the roof had to be the size of a football field.

Theo took her hand in his and tugged her toward the solitary door. "Let's get this over with."

When he ushered her through, she was temporarily blinded. Every inch of the walls and floor were plated in gold. Hundreds of people dressed to the nines were milling about. She shifted uncomfortably when she noticed that many of them were staring at her.

A small man began pushing his way through the crowd toward them, and she smiled when she recognized the man as Zikas.

"Zikas!" she exclaimed, releasing Theo and hugging the old man tightly.

Zikas blushed furiously, and Theo snatched Jade's hand back, scowling. "I need to announce you," Zikas said to Jade under his breath.

He turned to the onlookers and in a loud, booming voice Jade hadn't realized he was capable of producing, he said, "Husband and wife of one month…Theo and Jade!"

Polite applause filled the room, and she could feel her cheeks reddening. She sidled closer to Theo.

He gave her hand a reassuring squeeze and then let go. He leaned down to whisper in her ear. "Come back to me when you're finished."

Before she could argue, he'd moved into the sea of onlookers and she lost sight of him.

"Where did he go?" she asked Zikas, annoyed Theo hadn't bothered to mention they wouldn't be together during this party.

"To sit with the other husbands while you mingle," Zikas said nonchalantly. He started walking away and motioned for her to follow.

She tugged on his sleeve and said, "How long do I have to mingle for? When can I go stand with him again?"

"So, you're getting along? That's wonderful." He beamed at her. "You must talk to anyone who approaches you, and once no one else does, you may return to Theo."

Glancing around, Jade groaned. She could count at least ten men within a stone's throw who were watching her as if they were going to approach any minute.

"Will they be able to understand me?" she asked, hoping her foreign language might dissuade some of the men from attempting to speak with her.

"Most of the guests were informed they needed to update their translators with your language if they wanted to speak with you." Zikas motioned to a spot a few feet away and said, "I'll be right over there if you need me."

Jade glanced around, trying to locate Theo again, to no avail. There were too many people blocking her view.

Suddenly, a man stepped in front of her line of sight. She looked up into the handsome face of Fejo, the sexy pirate man she'd seen during the Viewing. His outfit tonight, with its extravagant embroidery, was just as ridiculous as it had been before.

"Hello," he said in a deep, rumbling voice.

"Hello, um, Fejo, right?" She reached out her hand, preparing to shake his. When he just stared at it bemusedly, she made a fist and then lowered it again.

"Yes, indeed. I'm Fejo and your name is Jade, correct?" He gave her a dazzling smile.

"Yep," was all she could manage.

"You look gorgeous tonight, though I'm sure you look beautiful most nights." When she only nodded, he continued, "I was quite put out to learn you'd chosen me but then neglected to test me."

Her eyes widened in surprise and she flushed. "You weren't supposed to know who chose you. It was supposed to be anonymous."

He shrugged and leaned down conspiratorially, "I have my sources."

"Well, when I passed your room you seemed pretty preoccupied, and I didn't want to interrupt." Narrowing her eyes at him, she asked, "Aren't you married, by the way? Shouldn't you be in the husband area with Theo right now?"

Fejo's eyes lit with amusement. "You're a fiery one. I'm very sorry indeed that you didn't choose me." He sighed, looking out at the crowded room. "Alas, every year I come for a bride, and every year I'm tested but ultimately never chosen. Very few females want to be wed to a male who travels for work, and even fewer want to travel with me while I work."

His attitude was relaxed, but she could tell that under all his swagger, he was disappointed.

"Maybe next time you could test me and tell me what I'm doing wrong." He waggled his dark eyebrows suggestively at her, and she had to suppress a giggle.

Fejo was definitely a charmer, but something told her his carefree roguish persona was just that, a persona. A mass of long, dark hair had been knotted roughly at his nape, and the shadows under his eyes told her he hadn't been sleeping very well. He spoke to her suggestively but there was no real feeling behind his words.

His intelligent eyes scanned the crowd over and over again. Finally, she asked, "Why are you here?"

For a moment, his gaze shot back to her and became inquisitive. He promptly let a roguish grin spread over his face and ogled her. "To meet gorgeous females such as yourself."

"Fine, don't tell me," she said, waving dismissively. "But don't pretend to be interested in me, either." Jade craned her neck, attempting to locate Theo, but the crowd before her was still too dense.

Fejo tilted his head and studied her. "You're very perceptive, Jade. Are most human females like you?"

"I'd like to think my bullshit detector is better than most."

"Bull? Shit?" He laughed heartily at that, earning sidelong glances from passersby. "Theo is a very lucky male."

Jade arched a brow. "So I've told him."

***

Fejo, she was speaking to Fejo. Theo ground his teeth.

The only thing that kept him from stalking over to her to interrupt was the fact that she didn't look all that interested in their conversation.

So help me Goddess, if he leans in to whisper to her one more time…

"Theo!" came a booming voice from his left.

Wrenching his gaze away from Jade, he found three males he'd never spoken to heading toward him. The leader of the three, the one who'd called his name, was Helas.

Helas was in charge of an ongoing research study meant to find compatible species for breeding. It made sense that he'd want to talk to Theo about Jade. The other two males who walked with Helas were unfamiliar to Theo.

Glancing back to Jade, he was relieved to see that Fejo had left. His relief was replaced with ire when he saw that two other males had taken Fejo's place.

Helas clapped Theo on the shoulder. "Theo, congratulations on your lovely wife. How has marriage been treating you so far?"

"Very well," he said, coolly eyeing the three males.

"Have you met Nedas and Yuvan?" Helas said, gesturing grandly. "Nedas has met your wife."

Theo's gaze, which had wandered to Jade, shot back to Nedas at the information. "Is that right?" he growled, eyeing the male in question.

Helas chuckled and elbowed Theo in the arm. "He was tasked with guarding her when she first arrived."

Yuvan snickered. Nedas scowled but said nothing.

Helas continued, unaffected. "She struck him in the face when she tried to escape. His eye was black for a week before he finally got around to healing it."

Theo smiled at that.

"Have you found her difficult to deal with?" Helas questioned curiously.

Theo turned and spotted her talking to yet more males. "She is…different, not difficult," he said absently.

"I'd love to have you both come in for a meeting. You know my research deals with inter-species pairings. The more data I could gather, the better."

"I'd prefer to keep my marriage private."

Helas' smile faded. He gave Theo a cruel smirk. "I understand. I'll just wait until her next marriage to gather my data."

Nedas snickered.

A muscle ticked in Theo's jaw as the males walked away. He crossed his arms over his chest and glared in Jade's direction. One of the males speaking with her reached out to touch her arm.

Theo seethed and began to stomp toward her, ready to rip off the male's offending fingers. Asivva stepped in front of him and with a warning look, she shooed him back.

"Hello, brother. I see you are having a good night," she said.

The male's hand was gone from Jade, and she strolled away from the group. She hadn't taken more than a few steps before her path was blocked yet again. How much longer was he meant to endure this torture?

"She looks very beautiful, Theo. You had to have known that many males would wish to talk to her."

"Knowing and having to watch it happen are two very different things." He shot Asivva a furious glare. "Couldn't you have picked out a less revealing dress for her?"

She chuckled, ratcheting his anger. "She could be wearing a sack, and they'd still all want to speak with her."

Theo crossed his arms again. She was right, of course. It didn't matter what she wore, Jade was gorgeous. He'd be waiting here all night.

"How's it going between you?" Asivva eyed him warily. "You seem quite possessive."

"I already told you this morning."

"You told me nothing this morning," she snapped. "You said 'great,' took the earrings, and ran off.

"They look wonderful on her, by the way," Asivva added.

Theo softened. They did look wonderful on her. "Her eyes grew teary when I told her where they were from."

"Theo, talk to me," Asivva urged. "I'm your sister. It may help. Besides, what else do you have to do? Torture yourself by mentally ripping apart every male who gets near her?"

Maybe she could help. Asivva would never approve of what he planned to do, but that didn't mean she couldn't give him advice as to how to broach the subject of extending their marriage with Jade.

"I want her to stay with me. I don't think I can live without her. I've never felt this way about any female. When it comes to her, I have no control over myself."

"Have you recognized her as a mate?" she asked thoughtfully.

Theo had considered this. If mates were still around, and he'd recognized Jade as his potential mate, then his intense feelings would make sense. There were old stories of males going insane when parted from their mates. But mates had disappeared and, in any case, Theo hadn't shown any of the normal signs, beside extreme jealousy.

"That would explain your sudden possessiveness," Asivva pressed.

He glanced at her impatiently. "Mates don't exist anymore, and no. My eyes haven't changed."

"Are you going to tell her you wish for her to stay with you?"

"Do you think I should?" he asked, staring longingly in Jade's direction.

"I can go speak with Jade if you like. I might be able to get an idea about how she feels toward you and how open she may be to an extension."

He watched yet another male reach out to touch her earrings, no doubt in an effort to graze her skin accidentally. Through gritted teeth, he said, "Go speak with her now, Asivva, before I drag that male away from her."

Without a word, she hurried off.

***

"How has Theo been treating you?" a tall, beautiful, turquoise-haired woman asked Jade.

She was getting really tired of that question. Jade had talked to at least twenty people already, and they all asked her that.

The men she'd met had all tried to sweet talk her and convince her she could find greater enjoyment with them in her next marriage. Although they were handsome and charming, she felt repelled.

On Earth, she would've let herself be flattered by these men, but Jade no longer wanted an easy good-looking man to shower her with compliments. She wanted her rough, poor-tempered, alien sexpot who rarely knew the right thing to say.

A few minutes ago, she'd retreated from the crowd into a portion of the large room filled with low comfortable couches. She'd hoped the Clecanians would pick up on her hint that she needed a break. No such luck. Not five minutes after she'd sat down and ordered herself a prosecco 2.0 from a very nice elderly man who couldn't have been more than three feet tall did the blue-haired woman come to join her.

Women, like the one she spoke to now, asked about Theo politely, but she could tell they wanted juicy gossip. She continued to disappoint them.

"He's been treating me like a queen," she said to the woman with a tight smile. What was her name again? Hessy? Hally?

"Hmm." The woman leaned back to recline on the couch. "And his scars don't bother you?"

Jade bristled and glared at her. "They don't look like scars to me. I like them."

"How interesting." She studied her nails casually. "Whenever I visited Theo, I always made sure not to focus on them."

A bolt of bitter jealousy shot through Jade. *Hussy. That's her name.*

"It's a good thing you don't have to visit him anymore, then. In fact, I'd recommend you refrain from looking at him at all."

Hussy sputtered.

Someone cleared their throat next to her, and Jade glanced over to find Asivva and the small waiter staring at them. Asivva was glancing between the two women with a worried expression. The small waiter looked amused. He nodded respectfully to her as he served her drink.

Hussy rose with her chin held high. "Good evening, Asivva. I'd steer clear of this human if I were you." She said the word "human" with disdain.

Jade flipped her the middle finger. Although the gesture must be unfamiliar to her, she appeared offended and skittered away. The small waiter snickered and followed Hussy.

"Well, you and Theo make quite the pair," Asivva said, seating herself across from Jade, who continued to stare daggers at Hussy across the room. "He's on one side of the room scaring off every male who tries to talk to him, and you're on this side scaring off the females."

"I'd been perfectly polite until she showed up, thank you very much," Jade said sourly. "What did he even see in her, anyway?" Was she beautiful and delicate and feminine? Sure. But she was also way too uppity. Was she really Theo's type?

Asivva pressed a hand to Jade's knee to draw her attention. "I can't be sure, but I think he saw an available sexual partner and nothing more."

Jade gave an annoyed grunt.

"I know for certain he likes you far more than he's ever liked any other female."

Jade fluffed her hair, slightly appeased. *Get your head in the game, girl! You wanted to talk to Asivva, remember?*

"I'm glad you're here, actually. I wanted to ask you something," Jade said, leaning forward.

Asivva nodded, indicating she should continue.

"Well, as it turns out, I do like Theo. A lot." Heat tinged Jade's cheeks, and Asivva gave her a knowing smile. "I was wondering how I would go about trying to stay with him instead of leaving in two months."

"How long would you want to stay?"

Jade shrugged sheepishly. "For as long as he'll have me, I suppose."

Asivva's grin widened, displaying her even white teeth. "I'm so happy to hear it."

Feeling vulnerable, Jade murmured, "Do you think he'll want me to stay?"

Without any hesitation, she said, "Yes. He absolutely would."

Jade's heart leapt and relief flooded her. Theo did like her. His behavior couldn't be chalked up to alien differences—he actually liked her and wanted her to stay with him. Suddenly she needed to be next to him.

"Asivva, do you think I'm done here now? I'd like to go find Theo. He was nervous about coming here."

"Yes, I think you've done your duty."

Jade rose to leave, but Asivva stopped her.

"Can I ask you a question before you leave?"

Impatiently, Jade said, "Of course. What is it?"

"Have you noticed Theo's eyes change color around you?"

"Yeah, it's pretty freaky, right?" She laughed, looking through the crowd, judging her best route. "How they go all black like that."

Jade noticed Asivva's thunderstruck expression but had no time to analyze it. She wanted to get to Theo, settle this once and for all. She weaved through the dense crowd. From behind her she heard Asivva call to Zikas.

Excitement coursed through her, thinking about what their life together might be like.

She broke through a group of statuesque women and spotted Theo. She grinned widely when she took in his glowering face. He looked so handsome and comically unhappy in the glittering ballroom.

His head shot in her direction as though sensing her. When he saw her, his shoulders relaxed and the corners of his mouth lifted.

Jade began to move toward him but was blocked by a large male figure. Xoris stood before her.

"Hello, Jade," he said, looking down at her with a frown. Xoris was an official of some kind. Recalling Zikas' words from earlier, she decided she'd better let him ask his inane questions.

Jade stepped to the side of Xoris so she could keep Theo in sight. Theo was fuming, his glare fixed on the back of Xoris' head. *If looks could kill.*

"How are you, Xoris?" she asked politely.

"I'm well," he said in an unusually raspy voice.

Curious to the change in his tone, Jade glanced at Xoris and noticed that he was surveying her body.

"You look very beautiful tonight." He said this more as a statement to himself than a compliment to her.

"Thank you," she said, slowly crossing her arms in front of her body. Something about his gaze made her skin crawl.

"I was quite surprised when I heard your choice of husband," he said, looking in her eyes again. "Theo is rather...jarring to most."

"Not to me," she countered.

As though she hadn't spoken, he continued, "It's his mixed blood, you see. His mother was Traxian. It causes him to be erratic."

Xoris looked like he had a very bitter taste in his mouth when he talked about Theo's "mixed blood." Was he racist? Or a bigot? Did he have something against Theo?

Stepping closer to her, his eyes grew heated. "I intend to court you, Jade. You deserve an honorable man. Not an animal." He ran his cold palm up her bare arm, and she recoiled.

She heard a low, dangerous growl from behind Xoris and knew who it belonged to.

"He isn't an animal. He's my husband, and I intend to stay with him for good." She began laughing. "Did you think you could lure me away from him?"

Xoris looked enraged by her laughter. He grabbed her painfully by the nape of her neck, bringing his mouth close to her ear. "He's Traxian filth, and soon you'll realize you'll be better off with me."

Xoris was wrenched free in an instant. She saw his body fly across the room. Theo stood in front of her, his eyes black and his fists clenched.

33

The whole room had gone silent. Everyone watched Theo now, their eyes wide. Some glanced down at his clutched hands; others were exchanging hushed whispers.

Xoris struggled to stand, his normally smoothed back hair disheveled. "You'll pay for that!"

Theo grabbed Jade by the arm and pulled her along as he made his way to the exit. He knew he held her too tightly, was probably hurting her, but he needed to get her out of here.

"Theo! Stop!" Asivva yelled from behind him.

Jade let out a sharp cry of pain when he increased his pace, all but dragging her with him.

Outraged yells started up behind him, but he couldn't distinguish them. His ears were ringing, and his only purpose was to remove his female from that male's presence.

Xoris had touched her! Clutched her to him! What had pushed him over the edge was her smiling, laughing face.

He loaded her into an available cruiser, set the controls to transport them at the fastest speed and then sat back, trying to regain some composure.

"Theo?" Jade whispered. She reached out to touch him. "Are you okay?"

He gnashed his teeth. "Do not touch me!"

She jumped back, and the scent of her fear washed over him. "What's wrong?" she asked shakily.

"Wrong?" he bellowed. "Wrong?"

She shrank back further into her seat. Away from him.

"You were smiling and laughing with Xoris! You let him touch you!"

Understanding lit her features. "Theo, no—"

"You did it within plain view of me! Don't lie!"

Her mouth snapped shut, but he saw her temper flare.

"You're mine, Jade! You won't talk to another male again."

"Excuse me?" she said in a deadly calm tone. "You cannot tell me who I can and cannot talk to."

He lunged forward and fell to his knees in front of her, boxing her in with his arms. Pinching her chin and forcing her gaze to remain on his, he said, "Oh, yes I can. You'll be staying with me, Jade, and I'll make sure you never so much as set your eyes on another male ever again. I'll lock you away if I have to."

She tried to break free, but he held her firmly. "That is absolutely not going to happen! Let go of me, Theo!" Her hands began clawing at his. When he didn't budge, she shot them out to scratch at his face.

He caught her hands and secured them in one of his own. She glared at him. "This isn't you."

His head felt like it was in a fog. Was she right?

Theo tried to shake his mind clear, but fury and lust roiled within him. He crushed her mouth to his in a punishing kiss. Instead of returning his kiss, she squirmed under him and bit him.

He drew back, licking away the trickle of blood oozing from his injured lip.

"No," she said sternly.

He leaned toward her and nuzzled her neck more gently this time. "I need to feel you, Jade," he rasped desperately.

Her breathing became labored, and he knew he was having an effect on her. "No," she repeated. "Not until you pull yourself out of this."

The vehicle came to a stop. Jade tugged at her hands in his grip. "I'm going to go up to my room now. Alone," she said slowly. "And you're going to go for a run or something and work off this mood."

He needed her right now. Needed to hear her feminine voice moan his name. He kissed a spot on her neck he knew was particularly sensitive.

He growled against her skin when he scented her arousal. Still, she tugged at her hands.

Breathlessly she said, "Theo, I said no."

Pulling back, he looked into her resolute eyes. She'd told him he could touch her unless she said no. She was saying no now. If he pushed her, took her against her will, even when she was aroused, would she ever forgive him? He sensed she wouldn't.

He released her hands and she scooted by him, leaving him alone.

Gripping his head in his hands, he willed himself to calm. Why did he feel like this? The rage was overwhelming.

Jade's mind was clearer than his at the moment. He decided to take her advice. He stripped down to his underclothes and began to run barefoot through the forest. Pumping his arms and legs as fast as he could.

He had no idea how far he'd run before his legs gave out under him.

***

What the hell had gotten into him? After leaving Theo, Jade retreated to her room, making sure not to run in case he lost control.

She'd never seen him like that before, and it scared her. He'd been livid. Overcome with rage. For a moment, she'd thought he was going to ignore her objections and take her right there in front of the house. She shivered. Jade knew he'd barely stopped himself from doing just that.

She could understand him being angry. Hell, she'd been pissed just talking to a woman who'd slept with him in the past, but his reaction was extreme.

Cebo sat alert at her feet. He could sense something was wrong. The hound hadn't settled since she'd come through the door.

He couldn't have meant the things he'd said. He wouldn't actually lock her away. Would he? Her heart broke, because she knew if he tried to do that, she'd have to leave him.

Something had happened to him tonight, but it was an isolated incident. She argued to herself that his reaction was made worse by his bad mood leading up to The Gathering and the inappropriate behavior of that asshole, Xoris.

She crossed to the window, peering out into the black night, searching for him. He'd set off running about an hour ago, and she had no idea when he would be back.

Jade was sure that when he finally did come back, his mind would be clear and he'd beg her forgiveness. But could she forgive that outburst? Logically, she knew his anger tonight was an extreme red flag, and she felt pathetic for wanting to stay with him anyway. The truth was she loved him.

She heard the front door open and close. Glancing to the bedroom door, Jade waited for Theo to enter with his head hung low.

Her body tensed when Cebo began to growl savagely. She took a few steps away. The door swung open, and standing before her with a cruel smile was Nedas, the burly guard who'd watched her those first few days.

Cebo snarled viciously at Nedas and lunged. Jade's scream caught in her throat as Nedas grabbed Cebo by the scruff and threw him hard against the wall.

She looked on in horror at Cebo's limp body. Nedas cackled and then lunged for her. She dodged him, shrieking and bolting for the door. Within seconds, his hand was over her mouth and his arm was wrapped around her arms and waist like a metal band. He lifted her and began carrying her out of the house.

She kicked and jerked in his arms, but he barely reacted, hefting her body easily.

Jade screamed into his hand and he squeezed her ribs hard, stealing the breath from her lungs. When she saw a dark floating vehicle just ahead, she began thrashing. If he got her in there and took her away, Theo would never find her.

Nedas shoved her roughly into the cab of the vehicle, and she let out a blood-curdling shriek just as the door closed.

He backhanded her across the face. "Shut up! The walls are soundproof, and I don't want to hear your screaming the whole way."

Her vision went black for a moment and she almost passed out. She struggled to sit upright in her seat. "Why are you doing this?"

Nedas sat back and watched her try and fail to remain vertical. "I'm under orders."

"From who? To do what?" The side of her face throbbed and she clutched it tightly.

"You'll find out soon enough."

Managing to peer at him with both eyes, she pleaded, "Just let me go. You don't have to do this."

He smiled deviously at her. "Are you going to ask me to let you go nicely this time?"

She could almost feel his slimy gaze roam over her. She scowled at him.

"That's what I thought." He chuckled. "It wouldn't change my mind even if you did. The boss says he'll give me a turn with you when he's finished anyway."

Jade spat, "You're disgusting."

Nedas' smile faded and, in a tone dripping with venom, he said, "If I were you, I'd be a little nicer to me. How you treat me now is directly related to how I'm going to treat you later." His grin returned. "You think I'm bad? I'm nothing compared to Xoris."

34

By the time Theo made his way back to the driveway of his house, he was wracked with guilt. All the anger he'd felt earlier was still present, but as he'd run himself to exhaustion, other details from the night had returned to him. When Xoris had reached for her initially, she'd pulled away.

Pacing in front of his door, Theo tried to figure out how he was going to apologize to Jade. His chest felt like it was going to rip apart, but he knew what he had to do.

He swore loudly when a vehicle almost barreled into him. Zikas and Asivva rushed out of the vehicle without noticing him and were on their way to his door when he yelled, "You need to be more careful with those things. You almost hit me!"

As they turned to look at him, their faces lit up and they shared excited glances with one another. "We need to speak with you immediately," Zikas said.

"Can it wait? I've had a rough night," Theo mumbled, glancing at Jade's illuminated window.

Better go and get this over with. Tonight, he'd gone too far. He'd threatened to lock her away, and in the moment, he'd meant it. Something was happening to him, and Jade didn't deserve to be a victim of his unexplainable mood swings. He had to leave her. He didn't know how he'd stay away, but somehow, he would.

"Asivva, look!" Zikas said pointing up at Theo. "They're changed even now."

Asivva stepped in front of him, blocking his way. "Theo, she's your mate!"

He groaned. "Not this again. Asivva I told you—"

"Your eyes are black, Theo! And I saw your mating marks appear and disappear from your hands when you attacked Xoris."

He glanced to Zikas, who was bouncing with joy. "The first mated pair in over a hundred years! Do you know what this means?"

It couldn't be true. Theo stormed past them into the house and stared at himself in the hall mirror. Sure enough, his eyes were pitch black. He peered down at his hands but no marks, save for his black scars, covered them.

"It all makes sense, Theo. I told Zikas and we rushed to the library to do some research on it, and all of your symptoms are consistent."

"What symptoms?"

Victoria Aveline

"Tell us again what happened when you first met her?" Zikas intoned.

"I was angry. I didn't understand why she picked me."

Zikas waved him away dismissively. "No, before that. At the Testing."

Theo thought back.

"I remember finding it odd," Zikas began. "Jade came out and told me you'd grabbed her and licked her."

Theo bristled recalling his unusual reaction to her scent.

"But it makes sense now," Asivva said, lifting an ancient tome. "This says that many mates identify one another through scent at first. Your reaction makes sense, and it's no wonder no one noticed your eyes changing. You were blindfolded. Jade wouldn't have understood the significance of it anyway."

Asivva continued quickly, "Your behavior has been so strange lately, and I've suspected for some time that she might be your mate. Tonight, I asked her whether your eyes had ever changed color, and she said they sometimes changed to black. She obviously didn't understand what that meant."

Theo stared at them speechless. Could she be his mate? He shook his head. "I may have recognized her as a possible mate, but that doesn't mean she's mine. No male would ever treat their mate the way I treated Jade tonight," he finished gloomily.

Asivva and Zikas' smiles widened. "Even that makes sense."

"What do you mean?"

"According to this, recognizing your true mate can be greatly affected by your mental state. You've spent the last few weeks questioning her motives. You've been in denial."

Zikas chimed in. "It has happened before. The longer one goes without accepting the bond, the more crazed they'll become. At this point, even smelling another male near Jade could push you to murder. Once your mating marks appear, you should start to have more control over yourself."

"Think about it, Theo," Asivva said softly, touching his arm. "You feel she's perfect for you, don't you? You kept unintentionally trying to make her happy. You've never hurt her no matter how angry you've been. You can't stand to be away from her for long periods of time."

Theo tried to digest everything they were saying. It was all true. It made sense. From the first day they'd met, he'd thought of her as his.

A spark of hope lit in his chest. He didn't have to be parted from her. He didn't have to steal her away. The only thing standing in Theo's way was Theo.

"Jade is my mate," he said under his breath, willing himself to believe his words. He pictured her beautiful, smiling face and with more conviction, repeated, "Jade is my mate."

Warmth spread through him at the declaration and when he looked down at his hands, he was unsurprised to see thin crystal-blue bands starting to circle his wrists and fingers.

Asivva and Zikas gasped, and a solitary tear fell down Asivva's cheek.

"I need to tell her. To explain," Theo said, glancing to her room.

Before waiting for a response, he dashed toward her room, but he was running so fast that he overshot her door.

From the kitchen, Zikas called, "Your body will be altered now. You should be quicker, stronger, better able to protect your mate. Be careful though, Theo. We have no idea how your Traxian half will affect your matehood."

Theo nodded and shook his head disbelieving his new position in life.

He crossed to her room but when he entered, his heart stopped. A chair was toppled, and Cebo was lying crumpled against a far wall. Rushing to him, he found the dog still breathing but whimpering in pain. Theo's blood turned to ice in his veins as he realized his mate had been taken.

He stood, a deadly calm overtaking him. Years of working as a hired mercenary had all led up to this. His mate had been stolen from him, and there was no male in the universe more equipped to retrieve her.

This was what he did for a living.

Gather intel. Locate the target. Complete the mission.

No, he thought savagely. *Gather intel. Locate the target. Slaughter anyone who stands in my way.*

He needed to meet with Rhaego. Now.

Jogging back toward the front door and stalking past Zikas and Asivva, he said, "Jade has been taken."

Speaking over their gasps, in a booming voice he added, "Asivva, I need you to go and heal Cebo. He's badly injured."

Theo knew they needed no more explanation at present. He jogged out of the door and jumped in the cruiser Asivva and Zikas had arrived in, setting his course to the safehouse Rhaego had established.

Gather. Locate. Slaughter. Gather. Locate. Slaughter, he silently chanted as the cruiser set off.

35

Jade had been confused and terrified while being dragged into the woods kicking and screaming. Were they planning to rape her here and then dispose of her body in the woods?

Her fear had transformed into dread when Nedas had opened a secret hatch in the ground and led her down into an underground facility.

Crazy horny dudes in the woods was bad. Crazy horny dudes with a secret underground lair was worse.

A spiral escalator led them down to a long white hallway. Jade's stomach roiled. The spotless all-white hallway was chilly and looked sterile. It reminded her of a hospital.

There were four doors lining each side of the hallway and one set of double doors on the end. Nedas moved toward the double doors, and Jade was too scared to lift a finger in protest.

The large doors swung open when they neared and Xoris grinned at her from within the room. Jade dug her heels in when she saw a large reclining chair bolted into the floor next to him. It looked like a dentist's chair except, to her horror, she noticed there were straps.

"Has she been fighting the whole time?" Xoris questioned in a bored tone.

"Nonstop." Nedas grunted. Lifting her bodily and slamming her down into the chair, he held her arms down and Xoris strapped her in.

"What is this place?" She glanced around, straining to see behind her.

"Good work, Nedas. You may go now. I'll call you back when I need you." Nedas nodded and left through a door somewhere behind her.

Xoris gestured around at the room. "This is where we'll save our species." He smiled happily and then turned to rummage through a few drawers out of sight.

Jade's voice shook when she asked, "What do you mean?"

"I see you're more than happy to talk to me now." He moved to stand in front of her, a thin cylindrical device in his hand.

The audacity of this motherfucker! Her rage washed her fear away. "I'd like to know what the fuck is happening before you kill me! Send me to my grave well informed!"

He chuckled and placed the base of the cylinder at her arm. "I'm not going to kill you, Jade. Just taking a sample." She felt a painful jab on her arm as he removed the device.

"I'm very sorry we had to go through all of this to get you here. If those damned Cae had done their jobs well, you would've never knocked me out. I would've taken you directly here and saved you from weeks of debasement at the hands of that Traxian."

"You kidnapped me?" she said wide-eyed, taking in his words.

"Yes and no," he said, moving to place her "sample" in a softly humming machine. "I gave the Cae certain parameters for what kind of female to take, but they chose you ultimately, not me."

Anger flared through her, but she tamped it down. Better to keep him talking to her than to make him angry.

He turned to her, clasping his hands behind his back. "As you know, our species has been going extinct for a long time now. *Some* Clecanians..." he scowled, "have taken to interbreeding with other species like Theo's Traxian whore mother."

Jade ground her teeth but again said nothing.

"A group of loyal Clecanians, who wanted to ensure the survival of *our* species, came together and formed this society." He said this with such pride. "We do what needs to be done to find a cure for our population."

"Even if it's against the law?" Jade tried to keep her voice even.

Xoris' face grew tight. "Our leaders are cowards who won't examine every possibility. Those laws have kept us from finding a real cure."

"I don't understand what you want with me. You hate other species and that's exactly what I am, another species." Jade tugged quietly, testing her restraints. They were secure.

Xoris looked at her triumphantly. "But are you? Haven't you ever wondered why we look so similar? How the features of an alien species could be so similar to yours? Do you think you're the first human we've examined?"

Jade's face paled.

"Facilities like this one were built decades ago by organization members all over our world." Xoris began pacing in front of her like a deranged history professor gearing up for a lecture. "You see, not all Clecanians migrated here. The way they teach it now makes it seem like we decided to leave our old world in a mass exodus, but really, overpopulation and finite resources had pushed droves of Clecanians to leave their home world in search of somewhere new for hundreds of thousands of years before we finally abandoned the planet."

"My clever forefathers set out to find those places where they'd settled. He posited that if our species survived and thrived on another planet, maybe they were the key to preventing our extinction. For centuries we've been bringing aliens with potential ties to Clecania here with no luck."

Jade felt her stomach turn. This was a jail. A testing facility for sick men to experiment on abducted species. How many captives were being held in places like this even now? How many places like this were there?

Xoris placed his hand on her chair arms, hunching over her. "About fifty years ago, one of our members spotted a human on a slave cargo ship. He knew she had to be a descendant of Clecania. Her features were too similar to ours. He brought her here and found enough likenesses in our DNA to confirm his theory."

Was he saying that humans were descendants of an old alien species? Jade glared into Xoris' eyes, unable to keep her anger in check. "Fifty years ago? What happened to her? How many women have you taken from Earth since then?"

His eyes twinkled maliciously. "Hundreds. As for the female, she died long ago."

"Why would you keep us here? If you already know we're an offshoot of your species, then why not tell the world what you've found?"

"We haven't found a cure yet. Human and Clecanian unions have yet to produce a viable pregnancy. If we exposed ourselves now, we'd be arrested as traitors, but if we expose ourselves after finding a cure, they'd have to thank us."

Xoris was the worst kind of evil. He thought what he was doing was right. In his mind, abducting humans and running tests on them until they died was somehow a moral imperative. If she ever wanted to see daylight again, she'd have to figure out a way to break out of here. Xoris would never let her go.

Assuming everything he'd said about this wackadoo organization was true, then she knew she'd never be found, either. They'd apparently operated in secrecy for centuries. In order to pull it off, there must be thousands of loyal organization members stationed everywhere.

What would happen to Theo? she thought miserably. He'd get back home, only to find her gone and Cebo dead. Would he think she'd left him?

She noticed Xoris' eyes had fixed onto her chest. She looked down and saw the chilly air had made her nipples hard. Their outline was visible through the thin material of her dress.

Maybe she could manipulate Xoris. He believed in this mission wholeheartedly, but she also knew he was attracted to her. He wasn't a stupid man, but he was arrogant. She'd have to earn his trust over time and wait until she found an opportunity to escape.

"I'm sorry," she said in a shy voice. "It's cold in here."

He glanced up at her and swallowed. "I'll get you a blanket."

He left but returned swiftly with a small blanket. His hand brushed over her breasts as he drew the blanket up to her chin.

She felt bile rise in her throat, but she sweetly thanked him anyway. He smiled down at her, seeming pleased by her gratitude. "What's going to happen to me? I just want to be prepared."

"I'm going to artificially inseminate you in the hopes that you and the donor are compatible."

"Who's the donor? Nedas?"

He looked taken aback. "Why would you say that?"

Turn them against each other. "He told me you were going to give me to him when you were done with me. Since you're a scientist, I assumed you wouldn't want to mix donors."

"True, I don't want you to have multiple donors. This sample is mine." He placed his hand on hers, and she had to bite the inside of her cheek to keep from flinching. "No one but me will touch you here."

Jade knew he meant for this information to calm her. He was oblivious to how repulsive she found him. She let out a sigh of feigned relief. "Oh, good."

Trying to keep the emotion from her voice, she asked, "What will you do about Theo?"

His hand shot back from her and he sneered. "Nothing. Why do you care?"

"Well, he's going to be furious when he finds me gone. He does have a very bad temper." She looked away from him as though embarrassed. "You're the last man to have shown interest in me. He was very angry about that. He may conclude that you took me."

Xoris relaxed and waved his hand at her. "Even if he does, he'd never be able to prove it or find this place. I'm a highly respected member of society. If he comes after me, he'll be thrown in jail."

***

Globs of greasy purple blood washed off Theo's hands as he reviewed what he'd learned.

"Xoris is behind this," Rhaego intoned from his side.

Theo looked over his shoulder at the two Cae, or rather, what was left of them. It hadn't taken them long to divulge all they knew to Theo. His torture had been vicious. So much so that even Rhaego had turned away.

When Theo had shown up to the safe house, Rhaego had explained that the two scaly Cae wanted to make a deal—give information about a traitor in Tremanta in exchange for their release. Theo had laughed maniacally at that and had explained, to the two terrified Cae, that their information would earn them a swift yet painful death rather than a long, painful death and nothing more.

Rhaego had watched as Theo had torn into the Cae abductors. His friend had understood his need for violence in that moment. Rhaego's people, the Tuvasta, held matehood as sacred even to this day, when mating marks hadn't been seen for so long. He'd initially marveled at Theo's mating marks and had comprehended the gravity of the situation instantly.

Studying the mating marks on his now-clean hands, he acknowledged that what he'd done to the Cae would be nothing compared to what he'd do to Xoris.

Before expiring, the Cae had told Theo that Xoris was the one who'd paid them to find and abduct Jade. To Theo's disappointment, they knew little else. Only that he intended to hold her somewhere in the woods away from prying eyes.

He needed to figure out his next move. She'd said that her pod had landed somewhere in the woods. He needed more information about where she'd run from.

"How is this possible? She's an alien," Rhaego asked, interrupting his thoughts.

Theo had been asking himself the same question on his ride here in an effort to remain calm and focused. "She's similar enough to us that we could have ancestors in common."

"Or maybe the Goddess has finally decided to bless us with matehood again," Rhaego mused, hope shining in his gray eyes. "We've treated our new world much better than the old one. We learned from our mistakes. Maybe this is our reward."

He gave his friend a tight smile. Rhaego was slightly larger than Theo, and his sharp horns and fangs made him look intimidating. His appearance could cause even the bravest of males to cower. In his own city, Rhaego was considered to be an attractive male; here in Tremanta, females tended to shrink away from him. He and Theo had bonded immediately.

What no one else knew about the male was that he was a hopeless romantic. Since they'd met as young males, Rhaego had always talked about finding a true mate. He returned to his home city to chase a bride every year.

"I need to find her, Rhaego," Theo said, letting his emotions wash over him for a moment. "I won't survive without her."

"I will help you in any way I can, old friend."

Regaining his composure, Theo used his communicator to call Zikas.

The old man answered quickly. "Have you found her?" he asked, the worry in his voice evident.

"I know who took her and I know she's being held somewhere in the Manta Forest. I need to know everything you can tell me about Jade's arrival here. I think she's been taken to a location near where she originally landed. If I can backtrack her journey to Tremanta, I might be able to find her."

"She was found near the Sauven-Tremanta intercity road," Zikas said swiftly. "On the east side of the forest."

"I know that when she was brought in to Meya, she'd been without food for two days," Asivva chimed in from the background.

"Yes!" Zikas agreed. "She said she'd been running through the wilderness but was too afraid to eat anything."

Jade was smaller than him and couldn't cover as much ground as a Clecanian could. She must've been scared, and there was no way to tell how much energy she'd had when she'd started running. He motioned for Rhaego to follow him to the cruiser he left waiting outside. He set a course for the old intercity road. "Anything else you can think of?"

There was a moment of silence. "Possibly," Asivva began. "She told Meya she'd seen the cruiser from above. She had to run down into the valley to hail it."

"That helps. Rhaego and I are headed there now. I'll call with any other questions."

"Wait, Theo!" Zikas interjected.

"What?"

"I'm not certain how true this is, but you may be able to sense her if you get close enough to her location."

"From her scent?" Theo asked.

"Your soul is bound to her. She's your mate. There are some stories that suggest mates can always find each other because they can instinctually sense where they are," Asivva explained.

"Since Jade is human and can't experience the mating bond, we can't be sure your sensing will work but, if you start to feel an urge to move in one direction or another, trust it," Zikas added hastily.

"Thank you both," he said before ending the call. He glanced at Rhaego, knowing his excellent hearing would've allowed him to hear his conversation easily.

Rhaego nodded eagerly. "Our people have stories about similar occurrences. You may be able to find her through instinct."

Theo hoped with everything in him that what they said was true.

36

Jade's stomach turned yet again. She had an idea about how she might get Xoris to remove her restraints, but she couldn't bring herself to follow through with it.

He'd informed her that he was preparing for the artificial insemination. If she could convince him that normal sex might yield better results, she might be able to get him to let her out of this chair. The constant accusation that she was a femme fatale spy must've gone to her head.

What if it doesn't work?

It'd be difficult but not impossible for him to have sex with her while she was still strapped to this chair. What if she gave him this idea but he kept her secured? She would've orchestrated her own rape for nothing, and in order to get another chance at freedom, she'd have to pretend that she liked it.

If she persuaded him to free her, though, she could surprise him and hopefully knock him out before anything could happen. Was it a risk she could take?

"Can I ask you something, Xoris?"

He glanced at her from over his shoulder then returned to his work. "Yes. What?"

"Have you always used artificial insemination on the human females?"

"Not always," he said absently.

"Interesting," she said, considering.

He finally scrutinized her, then faced her fully. "Why is that interesting?"

"Well, as you know, human women are different than Clecanians in a few ways, but if we're truly Clecanian descendants, there could be similarities in how we're able to get pregnant."

He cocked his head at her. "Such as?"

"I learned that Clecanian women have a recovery phase that helps with becoming pregnant. I also learned that in order to have this recovery phase, they need to have an orgasm. It makes sense. I heard that on Earth too. They say that if a woman orgasms during sex, it can increase the likelihood of pregnancy."

"What are you suggesting?" His voice had gone hoarse.

Xoris was attracted to her. There was no doubt. He also seemed to respond to her no-nonsense scientifically minded act. She needed to make him think this was the most logical course of action.

"That copulation may result in pregnancy more often than artificial insemination would. Since you're going to be using your own semen either way, it may be more likely to work if we have sex."

Xoris narrowed his eyes at her suspiciously. "And why would you allow this?"

Jade had expected this. She sighed and glanced to the ceiling. "There's no way for me to get out of here. I've accepted that. If I want to be free again, then my best bet is to help you solve this."

She took in his speculative expression. He was starting to buy it. "You said that when you're able to produce viable pregnancies in humans, you'll reveal your work to the world. If you do that, then you wouldn't need to keep me down here anymore. If I think about it logically, becoming pregnant is my best option to see the sky again."

She let her gaze roam up and down his body. "If we do it this way, I might even be able to enjoy myself a bit."

Xoris was working through her words. She knew she made sense. Knew that he'd push himself to believe her, because he wanted her anyway.

Jade decided to throw one more thing at him to really convince him they were making an arrangement. "I want one thing from you in return."

"What's that?"

"I only want this to happen with you. You have to promise you won't pass me around to Nedas."

Xoris grinned at her. In one fell swoop she'd boosted his ego and convinced him she was going to follow through. "You have my word," he said, ringing his hands together.

He walked over to her quickly and flung her blanket off. He reached for his belt, and she gasped.

"Here?" she breathed, trying to appear incredulous.

His hands stopped, and he glanced up at her.

She let herself appear embarrassed. "Can't we move to a bed or something? In order to have the best chance, I should probably be comfortable." She tried to peer over her shoulder. "Anyone could walk in."

A muscle ticked in Xoris' jaw as he thought about her request. She held her breath. His hands traveled up her thighs, and his eyes bore into hers.

This is a test. She had to pretend like she didn't hate his touch.

When his hands disappeared under her dress and settled on her hips, she closed her eyes, letting her head fall back.

Picture Theo. Picture Theo. She thought back to the night she'd ridden him on the couch.

Xoris' hand moved to cup her sex, and she imagined it was Theo's instead. She was able to make herself slightly aroused by recalling his mouth on her sex.

She knew the exact moment Xoris smelled her arousal. His hands were gone from her and he was pulling at her restraints, releasing her.

***

Theo looked around from the top of the hill he'd just climbed. Before him to the left was an open field illuminated by moonlight. In the distance he could see the trees of the forest. The terrain to his right was filled with rocky outcroppings and foliage.

"Which direction do you think she came from?" Rhaego said, finally appearing behind him. Zikas hadn't been wrong. Theo was much faster now.

His Jade was smart. The field may have seemed like an easier trek, but if she were running from someone, his instincts said she would've wanted to hide. If she came from the right, the boulders and bushes would've given her that option.

He pointed solemnly in that direction. "I'm going to run ahead. Can you follow my trail if you fall behind?"

Rhaego chuckled. "*When* I fall behind," he corrected. "You have a mate now. You're much too fast for me to keep up with."

Theo nodded and set off.

Locate the target.

Theo ran faster than he ever had, leaping over towering boulders with ease. He could see the edge of the forest ahead.

Suddenly he felt sick. He stopped, clutching at his stomach. He took another step but faltered when a sharp pain shot through him. He stepped back, and the pain eased somewhat.

Was this mating bond telling him he was headed the wrong way? He turned in place slowly, until the feeling in his gut disappeared. Tentatively he took a step in the new direction. No pain. He continued forward at a trot. Still no pain.

He grinned and dashed forward at full speed, changing course here and there when he felt ill.

He bellowed to the sky. He could find her! He was going to be able to get to his mate!

An evil thought crept in. *What if I'm too late? What if she can't forgive me for not getting to her in time?*

He pushed those thoughts away.

Locate the target. Locate the target. Locate the target.

37

When Jade was free from the chair, Xoris grabbed her arm, leading her through the back door. They entered a large open room with long tables. There were trays scattered here and there, and she realized this must be some kind of cafeteria.

How sick can you be? she thought as she surveyed the mundane-looking cafeteria. *Abduct, rape and impregnate women from all over the universe and then come eat lunch. Just sick.*

Nedas was seated at a table a few feet away, and he shot up when he saw them. "What are you doing with her?"

"That's none of your business," Xoris said to Nedas in a condescending tone.

Nedas bristled and approached them slowly. "You said I could have her after you were done. You've never taken one out this way before." He scowled at her, and Jade moved behind Xoris, pretending she trusted him to protect her.

Xoris released her arm, allowing it. His chest puffed up with pride.

Idiot, she thought. The two males continued to argue, and Jade took the opportunity to look around for anything she could use as a weapon. She found none.

"You will obey my orders, Nedas!" Xoris barked. In a calmer voice, he added, "If you do, then I'll make sure the next human brought here is all yours."

Nedas crossed his arms but said nothing more. Taking his silence as agreement, he grabbed Jade's arm once again and worked his way through the cafeteria.

A knife! On a table just in front of her, there lay a tray with an empty plate, fork, and knife.

How to get to it?

Jade heard a snarl from behind her. She turned to see Nedas running full speed at them. He barreled into Xoris just as he spun to face Nedas. Xoris hadn't let go of Jade when he was knocked down. She felt a sickening pop in her shoulder, and her vision blurred before he finally released her. Pain shot up her arm when she tried to move it, and she realized it was dislocated.

Jade scrambled back in horror, watching the two males fight. Nedas was on top of Xoris. Bashing his head into the white tile floor.

Jade came to her senses when she saw blood. She leapt forward, grabbing the knife, and then bolted back in the direction of the spiral escalator.

She reached the door that led to the exam room and glanced back. Fear stabbed at her when she saw Nedas running toward her, dark intent in his eyes.

She willed her feet to keep moving through the exam room and down the hallway. Pain lanced through her shoulder with every jarring step.

She sensed Nedas at her back even before he lunged for her. She screamed in pain when his heavy body landed on top of hers. He rolled her over, and she took the opportunity to sink her knife deep into his gut and twist.

Bellowing angrily, he clutched her injured shoulder. Jade shrieked in agony, releasing the knife.

Nedas tore the blade from his stomach and threw it over his shoulder. "Stupid human! You'll never leave here!"

She tried to use her good arm to gouge his eyes. He slammed his fist into the side of her face. She felt the bones in her cheek give way. Her head lolled, and her consciousness wavered. She fought to stay awake, to keep fighting, but she couldn't get her body to respond to her.

Her cheeks were hot with her tears. Jade absently noted that her temple felt warm and sticky.

An ear-splitting roar sounded all around her, and in the next moment the weight of Nedas was gone. She could hear vicious snarling and bloodcurdling shrieks of pain. One particularly awful shriek abruptly ended and was replaced with a muffled gurgling sound.

Jade needed to keep moving. She lifted her good arm and was able to drag herself a few more feet toward the stairway.

Through her bloody vision she saw a massive demon standing before her. She whimpered and collapsed at the sight.

Warm hands clutched at her face, and she yelped in pain. "Jade?"

Theo? Was that his voice? She tried to force her eyes to focus on the person crouching over her. Finally, his face came into view.

She started to sob, pain erupting through her torso with the action. "You found me." Her words came out garbled and broken.

His beautiful face was splattered with blood, and his eyes were black. When he gently smoothed her hair, his hand was shaking. "I will always find you, Jade."

Theo looked up to where the demon stood. "I need you to get her to safety. I have to make sure I find Xoris. He can't get away with this."

A booming voice replied, "I'll protect her with my life."

He peered down at her again. "Rhaego is going to take you somewhere safe now. I trust him."

The ground shook as the massive demon approached her. His hands were infinitely gentle as he lifted her, but the movement made her cry out in pain all the same. "I'm sorry, little human," he rasped.

"Theo," she called out weakly.

In an instant, he was by her side. "I'm here, beautiful."

"There are more prisoners here. Humans."

The demon's eyes widened, and he shared a tense look with Theo.

"Promise me you won't leave without finding all of them."

Theo's face was hard. Unreadable. Jade's vision faded to black, but just before she lost consciousness, she heard him whisper, "I promise."

38

Warmth and weightlessness washed over Jade as she came to. Her lids were heavy, but she forced her eyes to slide open.

She found herself lying in a small bed. The room was unfamiliar but not unpleasant.

"You're awake!"

She glanced over and saw Asivva sitting on a low couch. The demon who'd carried her out was also sitting there staring at her curiously. She smiled when she saw that Zikas was leaning on him, snoring.

He must be a big softy to let Zikas use him as a pillow.

Asivva hurried over to her. "How do you feel?"

Jade thought on it a moment and then giggled. "I feel high."

Asivva's brows drew together in confusion.

"High as a kite." Jade continued to giggle uncontrollably. "Did you guys give me drugs?"

"Oh, I forgot," she said and quickly reached over to a low machine behind Jade's head. "Yes, they did." The giddy feeling began to fade. Asivva looked at her apprehensively. "We healed your body, but we didn't know what your mental state would be when you woke up. After everything you went through, we thought you might wake up screaming or swinging."

Jade rubbed her temple trying to clear away her mental fog. "How long have I been out?"

"A few days," Asivva said, still watching her intently.

Jade sat up in the bed and looked around the room again, searching. Disappointment flowed through her. "Where's Theo?"

The demon answered in his booming voice, causing Zikas to jolt awake. "He stayed behind to aid the other captives as you requested."

She softened. He'd kept his promise. "I'm sorry. I forgot your name. Do you know what happened?"

Zikas leapt off the couch, running to her other side. She gave him a smile and then focused her attention on the demon.

"My name is Rhaego. I believe all prisoners have been located and he's handing off the investigation of the facility to enforcers from The Intergalactic Alliance."

"How many humans did they find?"

"A dozen female humans and about twenty other females of different species."

"Did they capture any of the assholes who kidnapped them?" Jade noticed Rhaego's fingers tighten on the arm of the couch.

In a growl, he said, "Some were captured, some escaped."

Asivva faced the two males. "Can you please excuse us? I'd like to speak with Jade privately."

Zikas gave her hand a squeeze. "I'm glad you're alright, Jade."

"I'll alert Theo that you're awake," Rhaego said with a bow.

"Rhaego," Jade said, stopping him in his tracks. "Thank you."

"It's nothing," he said with a quick incline of his head.

"No, I mean thank you for helping me. You're a good guy."

Rhaego opened and closed his mouth wordlessly. He gave a sharp nod before leaving.

When they were alone, Asivva chuckled.

"That guy is not good at receiving compliments."

Asivva gave a shrug. "I expect he hasn't been given many compliments in his life. The Tuvasta are a hard people, and in Tremanta he's treated with fear and wariness." Her stare became serious. "Jade, can you tell me what was done to you? We found evidence of physical assault but not sexual. Is there anything that happened that you want to tell me about?"

"No, I'm fine," she said, patting Asivva's hand reassuringly. "Theo got there in time. That asshole Nedas jumped Xoris and attacked me."

Asivva still looked fraught with worry.

"Now that I'm safe and everything is okay, I'm almost glad it happened."

Asivva's head snapped back like she'd been slapped.

"If it hadn't, then no one would've known what they were doing down there. All of those women would still be trapped. If a little pain means we've uncovered an underground organization of dickheads bent on kidnapping and impregnating women, then I think it was worth it."

"*Dickhead?*" Asivva parroted with a chuckle. "I agree that it's good the 'dickheads' were revealed." She touched Jade's arm. "It was more than a little pain, but I admire your bravery."

Asivva gave her a bitter smile. "I need to tell you some things, and I hope you take them well."

Jade tensed. *What the fuck now?*

"First, I want to explain that there was a reason for Theo's behavior at The Gathering."

Jade held up a hand. "We don't need to talk about that. He was just being a pissy possessive alien. I'm sure he's over it by now, and so am I."

"Indeed, he is." Asivva smiled. "So, you still wish to stay with him?"

"Yes." Jade sighed. "I haven't had the chance to tell him yet, but I've fallen in love with the pissy possessive alien."

"I'm so glad to hear that, because something extraordinary has happened," Asivva said, clutching Jade's hand in a tight grip. "His mating marks have appeared. You're his true mate."

"Mate?" Jade smirked. "I thought that was just a fairy tale you guys had."

Asivva shook her head silently. "They're real, but haven't been seen in years. The last mates died off a hundred years ago at least, but Theo has his marks. His eyes changing was the first sign, but you didn't know what it meant. His temper flare-ups and his uncontrollable possessiveness were all symptoms that got worse because he didn't recognize the bond right away."

Jade's smile slowly faded as she took in the significance of what Asivva was telling her. Hadn't Zikas said that true mates stayed together for life?

Jade knew she must have a goofy look on her face, but she didn't know how to take this news. "So, what does that mean? He doesn't want me, so he didn't accept me at first, but now he has to? Is he, like, trapped in a relationship with me now?"

Asivva laughed. "Not at all. He didn't accept you because he's an idiot, and his deep insecurities made him think he didn't deserve someone like you. Now that he's finally accepted you're his mate, he won't want to be apart from you for long stretches of time." She raised her delicate brows sardonically. "I'm surprised he's stayed away as long as he has, to be honest. Promise or not."

The corner of Jade's mouth lifted in a grin. "So, he's stuck on me?"

"Stuck?"

Jade clarified. "He wants to stay with me. He won't ever want to leave."

"Oh, yes. He's very stuck on you. Your happiness will be his only priority." Asivva's brows drew together. "Well, almost his only priority."

"What do you mean?"

Asivva shifted from side to side nervously. "When the doctor was healing you, they discovered that you're with child."

"No, I'm not," Jade said immediately. "I'm on birth control. I can't get pregnant. I got the shot—it's supposed to last for months."

"Well, either your birth control failed or it doesn't protect against Clecanians, because you are." She gave her a nervous smile.

"Xoris did tests on me. He would have said something."

Asivva shook her head. "I can't say for sure, but from what I know of Xoris, the idea that you might have slept with Theo probably never crossed his mind. He was extremely bigoted toward Traxians."

Jade thought back to the blood test Xoris had run. From the information he'd relayed to her, all the test showed was that she had traces of Clecanian DNA. Would he really have been so arrogant as to not test to see if she were already pregnant?

Pregnant? I'm pregnant. Jade didn't know how to feel about this. She hadn't even decided if she wanted kids or not. She rubbed her stomach absently. An image of a little tattooed boy popped into her mind, and she smiled.

Jade nodded slowly, still smiling. "I guess that's okay."

Asivva let out a breath she'd been holding, clearly relieved by Jade's response. "No one but me, you, and the doctor know," she said, smiling. "I wanted to allow you to tell Theo in your own time."

She and Theo had never talked about children. Their relationship discussions had always been limited to three months. Nervously Jade asked, "How do you think he'll feel about this?"

Asivva opened her mouth to speak but suddenly the door slammed open, making both women jump.

Speak of the devil.

Theo stood in the doorway. He looked out of breath. His hair was disheveled, and dark circles stood out against his overly pale skin and black eyes. His eyes flashed to Asivva, then, without warning, lifted her and set her outside of the room, ignoring her loud protests. He closed the door in her face and pushed the couch in front of the door as easily as if it were inflatable.

He turned to stare at Jade again, then self-consciously glanced down at his body. His shirt and pants were splattered with dried blood. Removing his shirt, he tossed it out of sight.

Jade didn't know what to say. So much had happened over the past day. Tears began streaming down her face. "I'm so sorry about Cebo."

"No, Jade." He rushed to her and knelt at her bedside, looking stricken. He reached his hand out to her but then pulled it back. "Cebo's okay. We were able to heal him."

Relief washed over her. Jade had felt so guilty about the goofy loyal hound being killed because of her.

"Jade…I… I'm sorry about what I said and how I acted. I can understand if you'd prefer we end our marriage now." He said each word as though it had to be extracted from him.

Jade smiled. If what Asivva said was true, Theo was standing before her offering to give up his own happiness. "Are you going to lock me up? Beat up any man I talk to?" she asked, already knowing she'd forgiven him.

Theo winced. "No. I regret what I said. The mating bond was causing me to act erratically."

He flexed his hands again and rested them on the edge of her bed, still not touching her. He looked so unsure.

She snagged his hand, examining the new bands on his wrists. The resulting purr was instantaneous. "Are these the new mating marks?" Two thick bands circled his wrists, and four smaller bands wrapped around each finger from base to fingertip.

He nodded tightly but said nothing for long moments. "Do—" he croaked before clearing his throat. "Do the marks offend you?"

Jade felt herself melting. He was worried she wouldn't accept him now.

She leaned down and pressed a soft kiss to his mouth. "I wish I had some," she said, smiling at his shocked expression.

The worry on his face faded, his eyes returning to a pale green. He crushed her to him in an instant. Theo kissed her desperately, running his hands along every inch of her body he could reach. She wrapped her hands around his neck and pulled him down until he was lying atop her, supporting his weight on his elbows.

He clutched her head in his hands and looked down at her. "I'm so sorry I didn't get to you sooner."

"I didn't think you would ever find me. How did you?"

Grinning widely, he said, "The marks. They led me to you. I'll always be able to find you." His eyes grew serious. "Jade, I want to be with you forever. No more marriages. You'll be mine and I'll be yours alone. You are my heart. Do you think you could be happy staying with me forever?"

Jade could feel him holding his breath. "Theo, I wanted to tell you after The Gathering. I love you."

His body sagged with relief and he leaned down to kiss her softly. "I love you too. More than you can know."

Jade pushed him back. "I can't agree to being yours alone though."

He tensed and opened his mouth to argue.

"I can't agree," Jade began, "because we'll both need to be there for someone else."

His perplexed eyes searched her face.

Jade raised her eyebrows and placed a hand on her stomach between them.

Theo glanced down at her hand and then did a double take, looking dumfounded. Like lightning, he sat back on his knees, removing his weight from her.

Rising to her elbows, she chuckled. "You can't hurt it by laying on me."

Still staring slack-jawed at her stomach, he whispered, "You're with child?" His voice broke. "My child?"

"Well, that's a little offensive," Jade said in an amused, admonishing tone. "Of course it's your child."

He blinked up at her before returning his gaze to her womb and smiled sheepishly. "I know that. I just…" He rested his large palm against her abdomen. "I never thought I'd be lucky enough to have a child."

Easing back down to kiss her, he murmured, "I have a mate and a child? How did I ever get so lucky?"

He began laughing heartily.

"What?"

"I've hated my scars for as long as I can remember, but I believe I have them to thank for drawing you to me."

"I guess you're right." Jade smiled at him. "Now take me home so I can finish licking them."

Epilogue

Five months later

"A re you sure we have to do this?" Jade whined, feeling, at present, more like a whale than a woman. Clecanian births were only six months long, which meant, at this stage of pregnancy, she felt very, very uncomfortable.

Theo tilted her chin up to his face for a soft, lingering kiss. "Yes, little wife. It's tradition."

"But I look like a house," she said petulantly, looking into their bedroom mirror.

Jade turned, narrowing her eyes at Theo suspiciously. "Is this a real tradition or a 'couples bath time' tradition?"

Theo threw his head back and laughed. "A very real and very ancient tradition, my love." He stood behind her as she studied her reflection. "You are as beautiful as ever." He placed his hands over her large belly. "Don't you want to know the sex of our child?"

She rolled her eyes. "Obviously I do, but I don't understand why it has to be revealed in front of your whole family."

She gazed at Theo in the mirror and covered his hands with her own. Jade's moods had been swinging out of control for the last few months, and yet he always looked overjoyed to be in her bitchy presence.

Jade leaned her head against his arm and sighed. "Okay. Remind me who I'm meeting again."

"Rhaego, Zikas, and Asivva, you already know." He gave her neck a quick kiss before continuing. "There will be a few government officials and distant relatives that Asivva trusts as well. The only other important people you need to know are my brothers. From youngest to oldest, their names are Izor, Maxu, Luka, and Auzed."

Jade twisted in Theo's arms and gave him a sarcastic shake of her head. "That's way too many alien names with odd consonants for me to remember."

Theo chuckled lightly. "Izor, the youngest, is training under my other brother Auzed to be a guard in The Pearl Temple. Auzed has been the head guard of The Pearl Temple for some time now."

"So, he's in charge of protecting all the ladies?" she asked, raising her eyebrows suggestively.

Theo gave a smirk and admitted, "I believe the easy access to single females is one of the reasons my two brothers joined the temple guard."

"Typical," she teased. "What do your other brothers do?"

"Maxu was a mercenary like me but retired long ago. Luka is more secretive about the specifics of his job. I believe he works in the medical research field under Helas."

"Did he know about the Insurgents?" she asked tensely, not wanting to offend Theo. Over the last few months, Theo, the Queen, and a trusted group of Theo's mercenary friends had been investigating the underground group Xoris had told Jade about.

"I can't imagine he does. He's a good man."

Jade nodded, mollified. "Okay then, let's go. Can't keep all our party guests waiting."

Theo took her hand and walked with her down the hallway to the open living area, where a group of people mingled. They all glanced up at Jade and Theo's approach and grew silent.

Three large, handsome men scattered throughout the room caught her eye. They must be Theo's brothers. The similarities were too numerous to be coincidental.

The largest of the three looked like a fair-haired twin of Theo. He was tall and very well built, but instead of Theo's dark hair and skin, he had light blond hair and pale skin.

Another one of Theo's brothers waved at them excitedly from across the room. From his lighthearted boyish manner, she could only guess the man must be Theo's youngest brother, Izor.

Theo leaned down and pointed at the excited young man. "Izor." He then pointed at the fair-haired brother near the kitchen. "Auzed." Finally, he pointed at the last dark-haired well-built man. "Maxu."

Jade had thought *Theo* seemed difficult to read when she'd first met him, but he had nothing on his brother Maxu. The tall, well-built man wore a mask of indifference. He looked neither happy nor unhappy to be where he was. His unreadable expression and perfect stillness gave him an air of danger and mystery that would've garnered the attention of many Earth women.

Theo led Jade forward until they were in full view of the crowd.

Jade noticed a few individuals begin to move toward them. Zikas politely meandered through the group of people, trying to get to Jade and Theo.

Izor, however, pushed clumsily through the group to the front. He looked embarrassed and apologized profusely to an older man he'd knocked over.

Theo leaned down with a wide grin to whisper, "We thought he was the runt of the group because he was so small for so long, then last year he sprouted up and started packing on tons of muscle. He isn't quite sure how to navigate his new body yet."

Jade giggled as she watched the large man stalk over to them, his cheeks bright red.

When he reached them, he gave an awkward bow to Jade and said in a rumbling voice that didn't quite match his personality, "Hello, sister. It's wonderful to meet you."

Jade smiled, already liking the Great Dane puppy-like man. "It's nice to meet you too, Izor."

He shot her a handsome, infectious smile and leaned toward her. "You can call me Izzo if you want."

She nodded at him, unable to keep herself from smiling, *He's going to be a heartbreaker if he ever learns how to control his body.*

Theo leaned toward Izzo and whispered, "Do you know where Luka is?"

Izzo's wide grin faltered at that. "We need to discuss that later. No one was able to contact him. He wasn't at his home, and his communicator isn't working." He shrugged at Jade and donned a reassuring smile. "He likes to go off by himself a lot. He probably just wanted some alone time and didn't realize you two had been mated." Jade nodded but noticed the worry clear in his pale blue eyes.

Zikas approached at last and beamed at them with tears in his eyes. He turned and in a loud, clear voice, said, "We're here to celebrate this mated pair and to reveal the sex of their first child."

All of the party attendees cheered politely with the exception of Izzo, who hooted and clapped.

Zikas shot him an annoyed glare and then handed him a small folded piece of paper.

Gesturing to Izzo, he continued, "The youngest member of the family will now reveal the child's sex."

Izzo's large fingers fumbled with the paper for a moment before finally unfolding it. He beamed and with his fist raised in the air, he roared, "It's a girl!"

Jade looked up at Theo and found him smiling down at her belly, a dreamy expression on his face. "Are you happy?" she whispered to him.

A loud purr erupted from his chest. He planted a soft kiss on her lips then stared deeply into her eyes. The rest of the party faded around them as she saw the emotion shining on his face. "You've given me so much. A mate, companionship, love, and now even a baby girl. I'm whole again because of you, Jade."

Sincerity shone in his eyes, causing emotion to well in her throat. They'd both lost so much in their lives, but they'd found each other. Theo was right. Jade felt whole again.

"I'm the happiest male on the planet. I love you now more deeply than I thought possible, and yet I can still feel my love for you and our child grow with each passing day."

Jade threw her arms around Theo and kissed him. She couldn't believe how lucky she was. All the pain and loneliness she'd experienced in her life seemed to fade to a distant memory. She now had a true family and a gorgeous alien husband who doted on her endlessly. All she'd had to do to earn her new life was get kidnapped, be forced into marriage, be repeatedly manhandled, get kidnapped again, and finally be beaten.

Was it worth it?

Jade studied Theo's handsome grinning face and felt her little girl kick in her womb.

Absolutely.

Their surroundings came back into focus when Izzo leaned over, curiosity and humor showing on his face. "What are you guys doing with your mouths?"

Looking around at the spectators she'd forgotten about, Jade now realized that most of them were gawking at their affectionate display.

Theo shot him a lopsided grin. "A human custom called kissing. I can only hope that one day you're lucky enough to experience it."

Izzo crossed his arms over his chest. "I sincerely doubt I'd enjoy it. It looks like you guys are trying to eat each other."

Theo leaned down and whispered in Jade's ear. "Eat? Mmm, maybe later."

Jade slapped Theo playfully on the shoulder and leaned up to kiss her big, scarred alien once more.

About the Author

Victoria Aveline is the USA Today bestselling author of The Clecanian Series. She lives with her husband, dogs, and about sixty thousand badass honey-making ladies. When not writing or fantasizing about future characters, she enjoys traveling, reading, and sipping overpriced cocktails.

www.victoriaaveline.com

Printed in Great Britain
by Amazon

46409516R00209